ABOUT THE AUTHOR

Kerri Turner is a historical fiction author who lives in Sydney, Australia, with her husband and miniature schnauzer. She trained from a young age to become a ballerina, but life had other ideas for her. After gaining an Associate Degree (Dance) and Diploma of Publishing (Editing, Proofreading and Publishing), she combined her love of ballet, history and books to discover a passion for writing which far outweighed anything she'd done before. She still dances, passing on the joy of ballet to those who never got the chance to experience it—or thought their dancing years were behind them—by teaching adults-only and over-55s classes.

She loves to share details about her writing process, and the books she is reading, and can be found doing so on Facebook, Twitter, Instagram, Goodreads, Pinterest and Litsy. For book updates and other material visit her website www.kerriturner.com.

The Last Days of the Romanov Dancers is her first novel. She intends to write many more.

The Last Days of the Romanov Dancers

KERRI TURNER

FICTION
HQ

First Published 2019
First Australian Paperback Edition 2019
ISBN 9781489256706

Published by
HQ Fiction
An imprint of Harlequin Enterprises (Australia) Pty Limited (ABN 47 001 180 918), a subsidiary of HarperCollins Publishers Australia Pty Limited (ABN 36 009 913 517)
Level 13, 201 Elizabeth St
SYDNEY NSW 2000
AUSTRALIA

® and TM (apart from those relating to FSC®) are trademarks of Harlequin Enterprises Limited or its corporate affiliates. Trademarks indicated with ® are registered in Australia, New Zealand and in other countries.

A catalogue record for this book is available from the National Library of Australia
www.librariesaustralia.nla.gov.au

Printed and bound in Australia by McPherson's Printing Group

I praise the dance.
Saint Augustine

To Ross,
My first reader, and first (and most ardent) believer

PROLOGUE

Winter 1917

Luka Zhirkov pulled out his rose-gold pocket watch: it was almost midnight. Two minutes until their arranged meeting time.

A footstep rang on the street. The gas streetlamps had been extinguished by vandals so he peered into dark shadows for a glimpse of her face. The person that looked back at him before disappearing underneath a dark hood was a disappointment. It had been that way all night: every footstep igniting a spark of wild hope; every face proving by a quick glance his way that it didn't belong to her.

Waiting had never been so hard. Luka was tense with impatience, his palms damp with sweat despite the frosty air. So much was at stake tonight. If all went to plan, it would be the culmination of so many things he had never realised he wanted until it was almost too late. A gunshot sounded nearby. Luka didn't jump. The violence that swamped the streets of Petrograd was no longer any surprise to him. He just hoped she would stay clear of those wielding weapons—policemen, Cossacks and revolutionaries alike. Freedom was being bought with guns and murder, and there was no way of telling any more who was the enemy.

Another glance at his watch—the same Buhré watch she had given him—showed it was five minutes past midnight. A new day had begun. Another day with more for them to fear. Luka's stomach turned as he tucked the timepiece away and peered down the street again. The heavy coat he wore was pulled high around his ears in an effort to hide his face as well as keep him warm, but it also impeded his view. It didn't matter; he could tell from the isolation that hung heavy in the frigid night air that he was alone.

He should have waited with her. He knew that now. He should have made himself deaf to her arguments until she had no choice but to leave with him. But he hadn't. Instead, he'd allowed himself to be swayed by her logic and had left her alone, agreeing to meet at midnight.

Now midnight was slowly turning to morning.

By one o'clock his dancer's muscles were starting to seize, unused to standing still in the cold for such a long stretch of time. He shifted his weight from foot to foot to relieve the tension, but there was only one thing on his mind.

Where was she?

'She will come,' he whispered, as if by saying the words out loud they would have to come true.

He repeated them over and over as the dark hours slowly ticked by. The icy air made the words stick to the walls of his throat, but somehow he forced them out. 'She will come; I know she will.'

She had to.

CHAPTER ONE

Autumn 1914

Valentina Yershova gritted her teeth beneath her painted smile. The Queen of the Dryads, with its controlled balances and sudden but soft springs into the air, was a difficult variation and one she was ill suited to. The other dancers who shared the stage were frozen in their positions, watching as the electric spotlight glared down on her movements. There was nowhere to hide. Every minute wobble as she struggled to balance on the tip of her pointe shoe for longer than she'd achieved in rehearsals would be noticed. Valentina felt the sharp eyes of the new corps girls taking in her every movement, learning from her while simultaneously hoping she would make the very public mistake she was pushing herself to the edge of. But she had to take the risk; she had to show the company that these lithe young bodies couldn't compete with her sheer determination.

She lowered her eyes briefly; a demure expression the audience expected. They would never know how her mind raced;

3

how from beneath her lashes she scanned the watching faces in the *bel étage*. Valentina was always aware, always calculating. She knew the name of every balletomane, the face of every imperial hanger-on. And she knew what audiences wanted. As she turned to the backdrop, she quickly wet her dry lips. Now was her moment. The variation ended in a show-stopping series of controlled Italian fouettés—a moment of energetic bravado the crowds adored. She felt the shift in the audience's energy, the held breath of anticipation. She had to deliver.

The music moved, and Valentina moved with it. After the first fouetté into an attitude, her smile became real. The first was her test; if she perfected it, the rest would follow. The audience began to clap even before she had finished. They were appreciative tonight.

As she curtseyed to accept their applause, she tried to look gracious rather than triumphant. Triumph was an expression best reserved for the likes of Mathilde Kschessinska, the prima ballerina assoluta. But she had noticed the two youngest Grand Duchesses were in the imperial box with the Tsarina, Empress of all Russia, and all three had risen to their feet. The Tsarina applauded with detached politeness, but the younger Romanovs with genuine enthusiasm.

Dimitri was waiting for her in her dressing room when she returned to its quiet confines. He kissed her on the cheek, and handed her an expensive-looking bouquet of yellow and orange tulips surrounded by sweetly fragranced mock-orange blossoms. 'A performance to bring even royalty to their feet,' he told her.

Valentina enjoyed the pompous exaggeration, but wondered if his kiss had been a little perfunctory. Her protector was usually at his most excitable after she'd danced, and the attendance and recognition of the imperial family should have made him ebullient.

'I should have been Kitri,' she said, handing the bouquet to her dresser to deal with, as she had done with the rest of the flowers already received. She sat down on a silk-lined chair and picked at the knots in her laces. Her feet were throbbing, a pain she'd been able to ignore when she was on stage. 'These aren't the roles I deserve, Dimitri.'

He grinned. 'Don't give me that face, my Valechka. I have news.'

Valentina's fingers stilled. The dresser attempted to release the wig from her head, but she shooed her away impatiently. 'What news?'

'*Les Millions d'Arlequin.*'

'You've heard the casting?'

'The Good Fairy.'

Valentina took a deep breath, but showed no emotion. She peeled the battered shoes off her feet—angry red and marked with lines, but thankfully not bleeding—and set them on the long bench before her. She had to get two more performances out of the pointe shoes before she was allowed a new pair, and the thought made her press her lips together. She wanted roles that would grant her new shoes every performance.

'A good role. Not principal, though,' she said.

'There's more.' Dimitri was bouncing on his toes, twitchy and smiling. He was waiting for her to ask, as though withholding information somehow made it more exciting.

Valentina didn't show her irritation. Instead she gave him what he wanted. 'Don't leave me waiting in curiosity. What else do you know?'

'The Tsarina has issued an imperial invitation. You're to be received at the Alexander Palace.'

The world stilled around Valentina. Even her breath caught in her chest. The two other dancers, who had hovered at the back of the shared dressing room, stopped pretending not to listen; they gaped at her with eyes hot with fury and envy. Dimitri just about bounced right out of his shoes.

'It's because of *Les Millions d'Arlequin*, isn't it?' Valentina breathed. The whole country knew the ballet was a particular favourite with the Tsarina, to whom the score was dedicated. 'She saw me tonight, and learned I would be dancing the Good Fairy.'

'Exactly.'

Now, Valentina couldn't help the expression of triumph that spread across her face. This would keep her a step ahead of the new corps girls, and cement her place in the ballet company. Being singled out by the Empress of Russia would make her unstoppable.

Valentina discreetly took in her surrounds. The Tsarina's formal reception room had seven large windows that let in the golden autumn sun. Lace curtains dappled the light to create intricate patterns on the parquetry floors and Savonnerie carpet; and were in turn framed by heavy cranberry curtains, which, at night, would block out the view of the Alexander Park stretching beyond. Above the collection of apple-green chairs that sat in the centre of the room—designed for decoration rather than comfort—hung a crystal chandelier with a ruby-red glass centre. Valentina longed to study the exquisite piece, for red glass was exceedingly rare. Even Mathilde Kschessinska didn't have any in her many abodes. The movement would be too obvious, though, so she contented herself with eyeing the paintings, tapestries and marble carvings that decorated every wall. There was a striking portrait of the Tsarina wearing a gown and tiara in the midst of a gloomy forest, and Valentina wondered how much it would cost to commission such a portrait of herself. It would look impressive in her entry foyer, and show those who entered that she had been in the Tsarina's personal rooms. She filed the idea away for later.

The Tsarina and Dimitri were talking animatedly in English about the war. Valentina had hoped the conversation would dwell on *Les Millions d'Arlequin*, but the war was all anyone seemed to talk of these days. The Tsarina was no exception. She spoke at length about the German declaration of war against Russia—carefully avoiding any mention of it being the country of her birth—and how the Tsar was determined that Russia would not bow to Germany's threats. The subject held little interest for Valentina; she had no one to lose to the fighting, and it was said Russia would emerge triumphant before long. Three months, at the most.

She shifted on her chair as a twinge of pain bit her littlest toe. The skin had split during her last performance, and her button-up boots were pinching the spot. She was trying to wriggle the offending toe away from the leather when a knock sounded at the door. Her lips twitched in relief and she turned to see who she had to thank for the reprieve from artillery rankings and munitions supplies.

The carved door opened to reveal the towering figure of Grigori Rasputin, advisor and close friend to the Romanov family. Valentina's smile faded. The monk strode towards them, his black robes billowing behind him as though he brought a dark shadow into the otherwise sunny room.

The Tsarina stood, her waist-length pearls clattering. Valentina bit her lip to stop from gasping at the sight of the Empress of Russia rising to greet one who was beneath her. The Tsarina tilted her dark head to receive words from lips pressed far too close to her ear. There were those who said the monk's hold over the Empress had to be sexual.

'Ah,' she said, a pleased look softening the lines on her face. 'Our other guest has arrived.'

Dimitri nodded as if he knew what the Empress was talking about, a twitch of a smile showing beneath his greying beard. Valentina gave him a quizzical look.

'Show him in,' the Tsarina ordered.

Rasputin nodded once and turned, but instead of leaving, he rested one oversized hand on a Wedgwood bust of Tsar Alexander I, as though blessing it. His head turned slowly, owl-like, until his dark-circled eyes were staring at Valentina. The back of her neck tightened. She had the impression that his long features were being pulled towards the floor, as though some demon were trying to draw him to hell, where many said he belonged. Even his dark hair, parted severely in the centre and knotted tight behind his head, contributed to the downward pull. Only his wild beard, flecked with food from his last meal, defied it. Valentina had heard the stories about Grigori Rasputin. Society women whispered that he was a drunken lecher with a penchant for seduction. He advised that to be cured of sin, one first had to be guilty of it—and offered both sin and redemption in one convenient package. The way his eyes stared at her from beneath his pronounced brow made Valentina feel as though he were making the same offer to her.

She couldn't be outrightly dismissive of Grigori Rasputin—it would damage her position with the Tsarina irrevocably—but she shifted her gaze away slightly, and hoped to hear his footsteps retreating. A moment later they did, weighted sounds that expressed ownership over the palace room, and she let out a long breath through her nostrils so the Tsarina wouldn't detect it. There was a heaviness in the air around the monk, an oppression so tangible she wondered how the imperial family didn't feel it.

Valentina forced herself to smile at the Empress. 'Might I ask who is joining us, Your Imperial Majesty?'

'Of course. We have the pleasure of Maxim Sergeivich Ilyn's company today. Perhaps you have heard of him? He is an art critic for the *Novoe Vremya* newspaper, and a personal favourite of Grigori Rasputin's.'

Valentina had heard of Maxim Sergeivich. The son of a famous painter, he had moved from Moscow to Petrograd a few years ago and quickly made a name for himself with his exacting standards and razor-sharp takedowns. He was reportedly rich, educated and very well connected.

'I know of him, Your Imperial Majesty. I hear his taste in art is immaculate. I'm sure we are lucky to have him join us today, especially if he comes recommended by Grigori Rasputin whose own tastes are unsurpassable.'

'You should thank Dimitri Mikhailovich,' the Tsarina said. 'Maxim Sergeivich has long admired your dancing, and when Dimitri Mikhailovich heard this he begged Grigori Rasputin's assistance in arranging a meeting.'

Valentina glanced in surprise at the man who had been her protector since she was eighteen, with whom she had shared not just a bed but all his thoughts and dreams. Or so she had thought. 'Well … thank you, Dimitri,' she said, unable to think what else to say. She stared at him, wordlessly asking why he hadn't confided in her this sudden expansion of his vast network of *svyasi*. Yet her protector was studiously avoiding her gaze.

The Tsarina was already greeting her new guest, who had walked in with such silent footsteps he could almost have been a dancer himself. Valentina turned to face them, noticing the Empress stayed seated this time.

'Maxim Sergeivich, welcome. I'd like to introduce Dimitri Mikhailovich, although I believe you've met before. And this is one of our imperial dancers, the ballerina Valentina Fedorovna Yershova.'

Valentina stretched out her hand to greet the dark-featured man standing before her. He was tall, slim but well built, and his starched collar and tailored jacket were of an expensive cut and cloth, giving him the aura of being accustomed to money that Valentina always found so alluring. When he took her hand she noticed that his was fine-boned, not fleshy like Dimitri's paws. But his grip had an undercurrent of strength, as though here was a man whose slender build shouldn't be mistaken for weakness.

When he smiled at her, his eyes ran down her body then up. It was a more subtle gesture than Rasputin's open stare, but its intent was the same. Valentina's innards shivered. It was suddenly clear to her why this man had been invited, and why she hadn't been told about it. She was being traded to him.

'It is an unparalleled pleasure to meet you, Mademoiselle Yershova,' Maxim said. He spoke in English, the Tsarina's preferred language. 'I've seen you dance at the Mariinsky many times.'

'Thank you. I hope it was an enjoyable experience for you.'

Valentina felt an ugly flush creeping up her neck, and swallowed twice, trying to force it down. Her lips curved into a polite smile, but her mind was unable to move past the realisation that this meeting had nothing to do with the Tsarina recognising her achievement in gaining the Good Fairy role. That had merely been an excuse created by Dimitri, Grigori Rasputin and this Maxim Ilyn. And the role itself had probably come to her because of Dimitri—he had used his influence to bring about this moment without Valentina becoming suspicious or alert. Her pride was wounded: for falling for the ruse, and even more so for having believed she had taken a step towards the promotion she so longed for.

She sat straighter, forcing herself to look Maxim Ilyn full in the face, grimly pleased that her hands, folded against the tissue-soft silk of her skirt, did not tremble. He had a thick moustache and heavy aristocratic eyebrows that twitched under her gaze.

The Empress Alexandra gestured for Maxim to take a seat near her. 'We were just speaking of the war,' she said, seeming unaware of the shift in the air around her.

It was no surprise; the Tsarina, unlike her husband, frowned upon such arrangements. The men would have gone out of their way to disguise the true nature of this meeting from her. Valentina gritted her teeth, then released them, not wanting her companions to see the tension in her jaw.

'I would be happy to join your conversation, but I'm afraid I don't have much of worth to contribute,' Maxim said. 'I'm a man of art, and know very little about fighting and political intrigue. However, I've no doubt you'll find me an excellent listener.'

The Tsarina gave one of her rare laughs. 'Then listen away, as we have plenty to discuss.'

Valentina didn't join in the renewed conversation. On the outside, she knew she was the picture of poise, her narrow shoulders straight and her pale features schooled; yet inside, her mind worked furiously. A fork had appeared in the path Mamma had so meticulously planned out for her. She should have seen it coming, but she'd become complacent and lazy with pride. Now she was left scrambling to decide what she should do.

Dimitri was leaving her; that much was inescapable. Without him, her life would be empty of the hard-won wealth and security she had come to rely on. Should she refuse to take this Maxim Ilyn as her new protector, Valentina would be self-reliant—navigating company politics and winning influence in an echelon she wasn't born to—for the first time in a life begun in dirt and poverty. Her stomach churned with her old companion, fear. She couldn't go back to that. Not after so long. She'd rather join the men fighting at the front and be run through with a bayonet.

Yet the other path … Valentina stared at Maxim Ilyn. She knew nothing about this man, except that he must be able to afford to maintain her current lifestyle, and was clearly interested in doing so. He was handsome—a fact that would make sharing his bed easier to tolerate. But was he generous with gifts? Did he know how to use his connections to manipulate the favours of the Romanovs and Valentina's ranking within the ballet company?

For the first time in a long while, Valentina wished Mamma was there to give her guidance. She would have sized up the situation in one sharp glance and told her exactly what to do.

And if Valentina had doubted or questioned her, she would have boxed her ears until she did as she was told. But without Mamma, the thoughts running through her head made no more sense than the disjointed notes of an orchestra tuning up.

'I hear the Ballets Russes have reformed,' Maxim said, breaking into her train of thought. He was looking at her with his head cocked to one side, his fingers neatly steepled together. 'Is that correct?'

'I believe so.' Valentina had little interest in the avant-garde company.

'Do you think their reformation is likely to affect the Imperial Russian Ballet?'

Valentina couldn't tell if the man was hunting for information or just making conversation. She wished she knew, so she could give the response he wanted. As it was, she'd have to settle for sharing her own opinion.

'I shouldn't think so. They haven't performed in Russia once since their founding and I don't see why they would start now. They seem to have established themselves as a touring company.'

'It seems rather an exhausting life for an artist. Not much appeal in always moving from city to city, never establishing a home or their place in society. Wouldn't you agree?'

So that was it. He was trying to gauge the likelihood of her being tempted to join the travelling company. It was understandable—no protector would want to invest money in a woman only to have her darting between foreign countries—but Valentina almost snorted out loud at the thought of doing so. She had invested all her effort, given her body and spent years clawing her way to the top of Petrograd society. She would never run away from that.

'I couldn't imagine giving up the security of the Imperial Russian Ballet to spend more time on trains than on a stage. And no reliable pension at the end of years of hard work? No, thank you. It's not for me.'

Maxim sat back, his hands folded across his stomach, and Valentina knew she had answered correctly. Perhaps she could give this man what he wanted after all. But did she want to?

She thought of the three women who had joined the company that year. Three younger bodies to add to her constantly evolving list of rivals, who could prove to be more talented than she was, and might come with their own protectors. This Maxim Ilyn had the ear of Rasputin; distasteful as the monk was, it was almost as good as having the ear of the Tsar himself. Better perhaps, with the Tsar distracted by the war. Yet it meant once again giving herself up to a man who would see her as a good to be traded when she was no longer valuable to him. And there was the risk that she would let her guard down and forget that every single day was a fight she mustn't lose, the way she had with Dimitri.

Unless … Valentina eyed Maxim Ilyn from under her eyelashes. His confident gaze rested on the Tsarina, only occasionally flickering to Valentina in an attempt to read her features. Perhaps this man could be of benefit to her not as a protector, but as a husband. It was not unheard of. Anna Pavlova had married Victor Dandré. It was rare, though, and wouldn't be easy to accomplish. Maxim Ilyn wasn't looking for a wife; he wanted the benefits of a woman without the limitations of permanent commitment. Still, Valentina knew men were notorious for not being able to help themselves when their hearts became involved. Was it too far a stretch from lust to love?

Mamma would approve of such a plan. Valentina felt that old sensation of her mother's eyes on her, and her skin tingled with the impression that here was a plan she must live up to. The thought made her shiver.

Maxim Ilyn noticed, and his moustache twitched with curiosity. Valentina slid him a coy smile and saw his eyes darken. She recognised desire swimming in them. That was what she traded in, and a spark of confidence lit within her. This would be the last time she was traded from one protector to another as though she were disposable.

CHAPTER TWO

Sunlight danced threateningly up and down the razor-sharp blade of the bayonet. It sliced through the air with an audible *swoosh*; the weapon flew a second and third time, and suddenly the sky was sprinkled with gold. The recruit holding the bayonet had split open a hay-filled dummy from navel to neck. The drilling officer bellowed his approval, and the line of men moved forward, past Luka and around the edges of the square to let another lot through.

Luka realised he had been holding his breath, and slowly exhaled. On the other side of the square was the Mariinsky Theatre, his new home. Its elegant green walls and white trim provided an incongruous background to the carefully practised violence taking place before it. Each represented such different worlds; just like Luka and his brother. They had stood together in the grounds of St Petersburg's Winter Palace—it had still been St Petersburg then, not the newly named Petrograd— when the Tsar made the proclamation of war. Luka had felt the ripple of fear skitter through his veins, and had clung to his brother's shoulder as the crowd of thousands spontaneously broke into prayer. Was it really only ten weeks ago? So much had changed during that time. Luka's long-held dreams had formed into a reality that afforded him exemption from conscription. And his brother had volunteered to fight.

Luka knew Pyotr wasn't among the practising troops. He'd already been sent to the Eastern Front. But he couldn't stop staring at those needle-fine bayonets, each with unwritten names waiting on their blades. Names of men whose existence would cease on a battlefield somewhere far away, with only the dying groans of others for company. The German weapons would be just the same. Did his brother have one waiting for him?

Luka shuddered and turned away. He couldn't be late for his first class.

He willed his feet to move fast, and being part of the well-trained body of a dancer, they obeyed. Within minutes, Luka was inside the Mariinsky Theatre—the home of the Imperial Russian Ballet. Only dancers from the associated Imperial Ballet School—a school which had been decreed by Empress Anna Ivanovna Romanovna—were accepted into the company. Being part of the Imperial Russian Ballet was to be part of a great heritage, connected to, and under the protection of, the Romanov family. Moscow had their Bolshoi Ballet, but they didn't have that.

Adjusting his grip on his leather bag, Luka walked to the dressing room. He hung his woollen coat on a hook, and slipped his hand into its pocket to caress the pair of gloves nestled there. They were tattered and ugly from years of being patched by his mother with mismatched scraps, and no longer fitted him, but the worn fabric gave him comfort. At the Imperial Ballet School he'd often touched them to remind him of his mother's belief in his dancing, and to bring himself luck.

The sudden death of Luka's mother when he was only eleven had removed the buffer that softened the relationship between father and son. Wanting Luka to leave the Imperial Ballet School and go to work with his brother instead, his father was not able to see his dance as anything more than a pointless frivolity indulged by a mother they'd both loved too much. That his dancing had now allowed Luka to join the ranks of those who would never need to worry about money, as well as providing him with a safe haven against conscription, had only caused resentment.

Pyotr did not share their father's anger. The older of the two brothers, he'd always taken a protective role towards Luka. That day at the Winter Palace, listening to the declaration of war, Pyotr had whispered to him, 'You will reach the stage of the Mariinsky, and that will protect you, just as the school did. I can fight for our country knowing you are safe.' Pyotr didn't understand the ballet any more than their father did, but he had seen the rewards the school had given his younger brother, and wanted him to belong to that life—happy and unharmed.

Luka saw that many of the men in the dressing room seemed to know one another; a product of having been with the company for years, he guessed, or dancing in the recent off-season charity benefit performance of *Don Quixote* that select members of the company had performed in front of the Tsarina and her daughters. They greeted one another with handshakes, trading stories of past performances and gossiping over which promotions they felt were undeserved. Luka slipped his feet into calfskin ballet slippers, which smelled faintly of birch bark oil from his bag, then padded in the direction of the studios with cotton-wool knees. The chatter was too much for his already over-stimulated mind. If he thought about this being his first ever day with the Imperial Russian Ballet, he would be sick. He needed to find a rehearsal room and exercise away his nerves, so that when the class began he wouldn't look out of place among those who had earned the title of Romanov dancer.

'*Excusez-moi*,' he ventured, touching the sleeve of a well-dressed man who was dawdling in the hallway. Luka assumed he was a dancer on his way to the dressing room to change into his practice uniform, which was why he spoke in French, the language of the ballet.

The man's lip lifted in an expression of distaste underneath his burnt-umber moustache.

Luka faltered. '*Pardon*. I was wondering … could you by any chance tell me which room the class of perfection is in?'

One dark eyebrow lifted. 'Do I look like the kind of person who works here?' Even before the disdain had finished dripping off his words, he was walking away.

'Never mind him.' Two other men, this time wearing practice uniforms identical to his own, joined Luka. The one who had spoken smiled, although the expression was cautious. 'We get all sorts around here. Imperial hangers-on who don't actually care for the ballet; balletomanes who'll drive you crazy with how much they do care; fathers who think they can improve their child's chances of getting into the company. Did you say you're looking for the class of perfection?'

Luka looked down to check the letter in his hand detailing his acceptance to the Imperial Russian Ballet, then nodded.

'But you're new, aren't you?' the second man asked. He sounded annoyed.

'Yes, it's my first day. I … is there something wrong?'

The two men shared a glance loaded with meaning.

'The class of perfection is by invitation only,' the first speaker said. 'There are people here who've spent years trying to get in.'

They stared at Luka with obvious displeasure. It reminded him of the expressions of those who lived among the factories, his neighbours and friends, when he'd gained acceptance to the Imperial Ballet School all those years ago. They'd viewed him as something of a traitor who hadn't known his place.

Luka tried to think of a reply. His mouth opened, but no sound came out. With a shrug, one of the men pointed out the room he wanted and then they both took their leave. Luka was sure he heard mutters of rivalry as they made their way to a different studio. It seemed his first day as a Romanov dancer had begun.

Ignoring the sensation of resentful eyes hot on his skin, Luka walked into the rehearsal room the men had indicated. The odour of stale sweat greeted him like an old acquaintance. He'd spent eight years training in a studio that smelled just the same: it was the aroma of hard work, and he felt his face settle into determined lines as he took a place at the barre.

The rest of the class filtered in slowly, hardly anyone speaking. Most had their eyes cast down, but it was impossible to miss the shrewd glances they threw at each other, sizing up their competition. Luka executed an entrechat quatre, then rested his hand gently on the barre. This was where he was at home, where he experienced magic. He didn't need the mysticism of monks like the famous Grigori Rasputin. Whenever he danced, everything around him disappeared, and his emotions reached heights that simply weren't possible in real life. Once a dancer had a taste of that, it became a drug they could not live without.

The ballet master arrived, and the dancers assembled themselves into fifth position. They began a lengthy plié exercise.

Luka forced himself not to look at the dancers around him; instead he focused on his own movements, pushing his knees out to the sides as he bent them, keeping his body in alignment, not too far forward, no bending at the waist. His arms swooped low, then through first position.

As he moved his feet into second position, the door to the rehearsal room opened and a small figure with dark hair and a piece of lace tied around her forehead walked in. Luka caught his breath. At the Imperial Ballet School, anyone late to class was dismissed for the day, left to wallow in their shame and the knowledge that their classmates would be getting ahead of them. But this was not the school, and the woman was no ordinary dancer. It was Mathilde Kschessinska: prima ballerina assoluta, and the crown jewel of the company.

With an apologetic wave and a grin at the ballet master, Mathilde took a place at the front of the barre, forcing the dancer who had been there to move elsewhere. She joined in the exercise, her small limbs moving in time with the tinkling piano music, sunlight glinting off the diamond earrings she wore.

Pliés turned into battements tendus, which were followed by battements glissés, until they had gone through a full barre. There was a brief break to get some water, and for the women to switch from their soft flat ballet slippers into their pointe shoes. And then centre work began.

It was here that Luka realised the class of perfection was something of a competition. As the exercises became more difficult, the dancers who were able to pulled ahead. None more so than Mathilde. When the ballet master asked for a double pirouette, she gave a triple. When told to balance, she held it at least a second longer than anyone else in the room.

Luka tried to emulate her. His allegro had new height, and he pushed himself so hard that by the time the class came to an end he'd sweated through his practice uniform and his strong muscles were quivering.

'There's still rehearsals to go after this,' one of the other men chided him.

Luka didn't respond.

Perhaps he should have paced himself—his first day would require more of him than the Imperial Ballet School ever had. But he had to prove himself; to show them all he belonged here. More than that, he wanted to cement the life his brother and mother had wanted for him. The life he wanted for himself. Luka would do anything it took to be allowed to dedicate his life to this exquisite, demanding art form he'd made his own.

They were in their second hour of rehearsing scenes from *Les Millions d'Arlequin*. It was a ballet that offered more excitement for male dancers than many others, but so far Luka had done nothing but wait. The ballet master, Nikolai Legat, had been rehearsing a pas de deux between the Good Fairy and Harlequin, and had not called the corps to the stage. The desire to step out onto the vast expanse made Luka's muscles quiver, his feet stroking out restless battements tendus on the ground.

Many of the dancers had brought along knitting or drank cups of tea to keep themselves occupied. A few had gathered at the back of the stage to practise variations. Luka joined this group at first, hoping to show any watching eyes how eager he was to learn and perform. But the limited space allowed only the most restricted movements, and it quickly became more frustrating than standing still had been. Eventually he gave up and joined the other corps members in the wings. Sitting on the floor, he pulled back on his toes to stretch out his calf muscles. The familiar pain that answered was satisfying, and he smiled.

Luka allowed his gaze to travel beyond the stage into the auditorium, Legat's counting in French fading into the background. Even in the daytime, with the crystal chandelier and azure velvet chairs shrouded with drab tawny holland to keep the dust off, the interior of the Mariinsky Theatre was breathtaking. He half closed his eyes, dreaming about the day those sixteen hundred chairs might be filled with people there to watch Luka Zhirkov dance the roles made famous by men before him: love-sworn Prince Siegfried, disillusioned Prince Charming, hapless Don Quixote. And perhaps, one day, a role created just for him.

He was brought out of his reverie by a particularly ferocious shout from Legat. '*Non!* Why do you dance her so sourly? This is a *ballet comique*, and the Good Fairy is light, precise. She offers her help to Harlequin so *le grand amour* will triumph. Do you think anyone will be laughing at such a pinched expression?' Legat waved his hand so close to Valentina Yershova's face that the soloist took a step back, grimacing.

'Perhaps they will laugh when I fall over from trying to keep up with this music,' Yershova snapped back. 'He's deliberately playing too fast because he dislikes me.'

Luka shuffled forward to peer into the orchestra pit. The pianist was staring belligerently at the stage, a smirk on his lips.

'You!' Legat pointed at Yershova's partner, making him jump. 'Do you find the music too fast?'

The man shrugged, not wanting to be drawn into the argument. Luka thought him wise; it was best not to get on the bad side of the pianist. The man had the power to make a dancer's life difficult.

'It appears our Good Fairy is the only one with a problem,' Legat said.

'Of course it's not difficult for him. In this moment all he has to do is stand there and lift me while I do all the dancing,' Yershova shouted, stamping her foot.

Luka heard those around him draw in their breath. He, too, was shocked. He had never imagined anyone would dare speak to the ballet master that way.

'Once I'm offstage, he will slow things down again,' Yershova continued. 'Just you see if he doesn't. If you can't hear he's playing too fast now, then you must be a ...' Her voice died in a tight strangle.

As Luka watched, he saw the physical effort that went into changing her angry features into a smile.

'I must be a what?' Legat asked.

His voice now held a note of amusement, and the muscles in the soloist's neck tensed as she widened her smile.

'A great ballet master who knows when his dancers are simply being temperamental,' Yershova finished smoothly.

Legat let out a bark of laughter. 'From the top then, shall we?'

Yershova walked to where the pas de deux would start, ignoring the sniggers that came from the wings. As she waited for her partner to join her, she pushed a stray hairpin back into her honey-coloured locks, her eyes fixed on the auditorium. Luka thought he saw a tremble in her hand.

The music began again; it was undeniably just a touch too quick, but Yershova's features stayed resolutely in a large, if somewhat stiff, smile.

Curious about what had changed the soloist's attitude, Luka craned his neck to see into the auditorium. Standing in the front rows of the shrouded chairs was a man; the same man Luka had asked for directions to the class of perfection. One finger stroked his thick moustache, and Luka thought he saw him lick his lips. His skin prickled with distaste, and he wondered why the man's appearance had affected Yershova.

'Careful! If you stare any harder your eyes might fall out of your head.'

The speaker was a woman seated cross-legged just behind Luka. Her long hair, darker than Luka's own ash-brown, was parted in the middle and tied neatly at the back of her head, and her almost-black eyes were carefully trained on her knitting. Luka recognised her as a fellow corps de ballet dancer, one of those who made up the bulk of the company. She was not in the class of perfection with him, but he had seen her on stage.

'I'm sorry,' he said, moving further back into the black curtains of the wings. 'I just wanted to see—'

'What made our refined soloist switch off her temper?' With a swift movement, she pushed the stitches down to expose the sharp ends of the needles.

'Is she always like that?' Luka asked.

Valentina Yershova was not in the class of perfection either, so he hadn't had much chance to see her up close. But he had watched her perform many times before and knew that she came from a background similar to his own, which made her position as a rising star both on stage and in society all the more impressive. Both she and Luka had been expected to toil away in factories for little money instead of gracing the stage of the most famous ballet company in the world. They were perhaps the only two in the entire company who would ever understand what it was like to rise so far above their family and birthplace.

'I'm Xenia Nicholaievna,' the woman continued, not answering Luka's question. She put her knitting in her lap and tilted her head, taking him in. 'And you, I believe, are Luka Vladimirovich Zhirkov.'

Luka's surprise must have shown on his face.

She laughed. 'If you thought the Imperial Ballet School was bad for gossip, you'll find it's nothing compared to the company.'

'I see.' Luka didn't know what else to say. He wasn't fond of the constant whispers that had lined the halls and studios of the school, and had hoped the company would be different—more focused on the art than the inconsequential. He glanced into the auditorium again. He couldn't see the man any more, but somehow knew he was still there.

'There's a man out there watching Valentina Yershova dance.'

Xenia Nicholaievna snorted and picked her knitting up once more, winding the loose wool around the needles. 'Unsurprising. Only a man could get that one to behave once she's made up her mind not to.'

'What do you mean? Nikolai Legat is a man.'

Xenia burst out laughing, earning her a glare from the ballet master himself. She winced apologetically, but a grin still danced on her angular features. 'My, we have quite the *malysh* here, don't we?' she teased.

'I'm not a baby. I just don't understand what you mean.'

'I wasn't talking about just any kind of man, Luka Vladimirovich. I was talking about protectors—you know, men who bestow money and gifts, and influence the rankings within the company in return for exclusive use of a dancer's body and bed. Like Victor Dandré did for Anna Pavlova, or Diaghilev for Nijinsky. You didn't think they became so famous based on talent alone, did you?'

Luka had thought exactly that. He saw Xenia's wide mouth curve up at the corners again, her dark eyes lit with amusement as she watched the expressions flitting across his face.

Thankfully, he was prevented from having to say anything further by a shout from the stage. Legat had finally called for the corps.

Luka took his place towards the back of the stage, rolling his shoulders. As Legat counted out the beat, he allowed himself a glance towards the wings where Valentina Yershova now stood. Her head was hanging low, her fingertips pressed to the bridge of her nose. He saw her take a deep breath, as if readying herself, then once again a change came over her. Her rosebud lips settled into a peaceable smile, her chin tilted at a challenging angle, and her delicate shoulders set to a square line. It was as though the curtain had lifted and Yershova was ready to put on a show.

CHAPTER THREE

Maxim was quick to begin exercising influence over the ballet. He mentioned Valentina to Grigori Rasputin when the monk asked him to assess some works of art, and through these whisperings got Valentina the role of Aurora, Goddess of the Dawn in the upcoming *Le Réveil de Flore*, when the company had earmarked her for the lesser role of Hebe, Goddess of Youth. There were also rumours that *La Perle*, which hadn't been performed in five years, was going to be restaged with Valentina as one of the two Black Pearls.

Maxim had also gained her another meeting with the imperial family; the Grand Duchesses this time, as a favour to their mother who was concerned the number of hours they were devoting to their volunteer work in the temporary hospitals for wounded soldiers might not be healthy. Valentina had accompanied the four young women on a walk through the Lower Park of the Peterhof Palace. The underground pipes had not yet frozen, and the Chessboard Cascade fountain had been turned on at the special request of the youngest Grand Duchess, Anastasia. She chattered almost non-stop during the walk—about the father she missed, their ill younger brother, her desire to once again go sailing, and stories of all who had succumbed to her pranks with the trick fountains.

When they reached the Monplaisir Garden, with its earthen paths divided into swirls and corners dotted with blue and white urns, Valentina had thought to make the girl laugh. She coaxed Maxim into sitting on a white bench set in the midst of a square of inlaid stones. The bench had a gilded smiling face peering out from the back of it, and Maxim was commenting on this when streams of water shot up in graceful arcs, wetting his shoulders. The Grand Duchess Anastasia had shrieked with laughter, and Valentina was gratified. This was a story the girl would likely tell her mother, and the Tsarina would look on Valentina with favour for giving her daughter a moment of enjoyment.

But Maxim's smile had dropped; and as the small party, flanked by the ever-attentive eyes of their escorting guards, moved on, he grabbed Valentina by the elbow and held her back. 'I do not expect a woman I am protecting to succumb to the kind of behaviour expected of children,' he'd hissed, a muscle pulsating in the side of his neck. But a moment later he kissed her on the cheek and nudged her forward.

Valentina knew the fickle nature of men and their whims. She'd learned that at an early age, after her father had left her and her mother to fend for themselves. It was best to submit to their desires with grace while things were working in her favour, and keep any complaints to herself, where they couldn't do any damage.

Now, Valentina sighed and turned away from the stage, where the corps was going through the *galop generale* that Legat had called sloppy and tired. She'd been watching them rehearse from the auditorium, and walked between the rows of chairs, careful not to let the material shrouding them touch her skirt. She was lost in thought as she came to the door, and didn't see the woman on the other side until she'd almost bumped into her.

'*Pardon*,' she said, taking a step back so the woman wouldn't tread on the hem of her dress. She looked up, a polite smile forming on her lips, then saw it was only a corps dancer. She was an older woman, already past the age of retirement in Valentina's opinion. She wouldn't have recognised her if the woman hadn't been with the company so long. Letting the smile slide off her face, Valentina gave a single nod in greeting.

The woman didn't return it. There was enough room for each of them to pass through the door at the same time, but neither woman moved. The older dancer raised one eyebrow pointedly.

Valentina knew she was waiting for her to move out of the way first. That was the way of the company: dancers who had been there a long time were to be treated with respect and deference, regardless of their rank. It meant that nobodies like this corps dancer could treat Valentina, a soloist, as if she were below her, instead of the other way around.

Valentina was already in a dark mood. She'd spotted the young thing she'd found out Dimitri had exchanged her for prancing about on stage as though she weren't just an insignificant corps dancer relegated near the waters. To be confronted now by the insolence of yet another corps dancer made Valentina grind her teeth. If she were married to a man as powerful as Maxim, this woman would be afraid to assert herself so.

The woman sighed loudly, twitching her cheap-looking coat, then craned her neck to look past Valentina towards the stage.

It was only a matter of moments before she drew attention to the stand-off, and they both knew Valentina could not win. Not only would she be reprimanded, perhaps even fined, there was every chance Maxim would find out about it. And his instructions to her about obeying the rules of polite society had been explicit.

Trying not to pull a face, Valentina stepped to the side and gestured towards the auditorium with a short flick of her wrist. 'You're welcome,' she muttered as the woman passed by.

As she adjusted her clothing, as though it had been ruffled by the mere proximity of the corps dancer, she wondered whether a man as connected as her new protector could change the career trajectory of a dancer for the worse as well as the better.

Perhaps it was time to test how much Maxim Ilyn was willing to do for the woman he'd bought.

Valentina pulled off her sable-lined gloves as her *dvornik*, Madame Ivkina, let her into her house. The bite of approaching winter was in the air, and the warmth from dancing had long since left her limbs. She waved the housekeeper away and dashed up the timber imperial staircase in her entry foyer—not as opulent as the white marble stairs in Mathilde's mansion, but not bad all the same. She would take off her hat when she was upstairs and the cold had faded from her skin.

As she made her way through her house, Valentina took pride in ignoring its finery—paid for by Dimitri, but furnished to her taste. Only poor people looked around them to admire beautiful things. It had taken her some time to realise that, but since then she had steadfastly refused to acknowledge the opulence of her own dwelling, only smiling humbly when visitors paid it a compliment.

She glanced at the wooden doors to her studio as she passed; but her legs were aching and she decided she was done with dancing for the day. Walking into her winter garden room instead, with its soothing vine-covered walls and shining wooden floor, she almost jumped. She had expected to be alone, but Maxim was standing there, fingertips stroking his moustache as he perused a painting that was leaning against the wall. Valentina bit down on her irritation. It wasn't the first time Maxim had had a painting delivered to her home, and she didn't like him treating the house as his own.

She reminded herself that was the thinking of a poor person, though, someone who thought that everything they had could be taken away by another. She forced herself to smile and kissed him on the cheek. At least now she could tell him of the older woman's insolence.

He picked up her hand and kissed the back of it, his eyes never leaving the painting.

'What is it?' she asked.

'*The Doss House.* By Vladimir Makovsky.' Maxim moved to the side to look at it from another angle.

The painting was a winter scene: in muted colours, with soft edges and blurred faces, it showed a crowd of poor people waiting to enter a charitable lodging house. Valentina's breath caught in her throat as she looked at it. These were her people, the ones she kept trying to escape. The child with her mother gazing at a crouched man could have been her, longing for both food and a masculine presence in her life. Valentina's mother wouldn't have rested a gentle hand on her daughter's back, though; she would have spoken sharply to her for pausing. But still, it could have been her. She felt tears sting the backs of her eyes, and a muscle worked in her jaw to keep them back.

'Look at the brushstrokes in the foreground,' Maxim murmured. 'And the way the buildings to the left are depicted. So real compared to the rest; almost like a photograph if it could capture colour.'

'It's very moving,' Valentina said. She was proud to hear no catch in her voice.

'Oh, I don't care much for the subject matter. Too melancholy. I prefer something nobler.'

He wasn't looking at Valentina as he spoke, which was probably a good thing as she was unable to keep her face expressionless. This was what she'd always wanted: to so completely erase her old life that no one would remember where she had come from. It seemed she had finally done it. Why then did she have this strange feeling? It was almost like loss, but that would be madness.

'It's certainly not my favourite either,' she said, turning her back on the painting.

Pulling out a hairpin that was digging into her scalp, she lifted the round mink *shapka* off her head and held it in her hands. The fur was so soft she could have used it for a pillow. On one side she had pinned an elaborate diamond brooch that Maxim had given her, and she ran her finger over the smooth, cold stones. The feel of them underneath her warm fingertip gave her confidence. This was the life she'd always wanted, the life she and Mamma had worked so hard for. There was nothing to grieve over in her previous life. She needed to keep looking forward and gain all that would otherwise not have been hers. Just as Mamma had taught her.

'Are you ready for tonight?' Maxim asked, still not looking at her.

'Tonight?'

'I thought I'd told you. I've tickets for the Imperial Opera. Chaliapin has come up from Moscow to give a rare performance with them. It's *Boris Godunov.*'

'I've just come from the Mariinsky.'

Maxim's eyes flickered to her. 'Are you saying you would have stayed had you known, and worn your daytime clothes to the opera?'

Valentina gave the softest laugh she could manage. 'Of course not. I'll bathe and dress, and make myself beautiful for you.'

'Not just for me. For every important man who will be there.'

As soon as Valentina saw Grigori Rasputin ensconced in the imperial box, she knew the real reason Maxim had arranged this outing. He would use any opportunity to ingratiate himself with the monk—which was why, once the performance had ended, Valentina found herself hovering in the background while Maxim sidled his way up to him. He wasn't the only one attempting to do so, but he won the upper hand when he pulled Valentina forward by the elbow and planted her in front of Rasputin, asking the monk if he remembered their previous meeting.

'Hard to forget,' Rasputin intoned, those fierce eyes boring into Valentina's. She wanted to take a step back, but the small crowd pressed in behind her, preventing it. 'You're an imperial ballerina, correct?'

Valentina was answering when he reached forward and pretended to pluck something from her dress perilously close to her breast. His fingers flapped, as though ridding themselves of the invisible lint or dust. Colour rushed into Valentina's cheeks, and even Maxim's eyebrows had risen. She glanced at him, remembering his instructions on how to behave in society.

She cleared her throat, pretending the touch hadn't happened, and said, 'Tell me, what did you think of—'

'No drink?' Rasputin interrupted. The words died in Valentina's mouth and she gave a half-shake of her head. 'Maxim Sergeivich, why don't you fetch the lady something to wet her lips?'

The small crowd rippled with interest. Maxim's face flushed an ugly purple, then quickly turned to white. His eyes narrowed, and he flicked Valentina an accusatory look as he turned to follow the monk's instructions.

She had tried her best, but somehow failed. Valentina knew she would pay later that night for Rasputin's interest in her and his public dismissal of Maxim.

'Ridiculous,' Maxim snarled. 'Utterly ridiculous.'

They were in Valentina's room, where she was trying to undress. Her maid had only got as far as undoing her fastenings before Maxim had stormed in.

'I'm sorry,' Valentina said for what must have been the hundredth time. She saw how the maid avoided her eyes as she stepped carefully out of her dress. The woman shook it out, then hung it up to brush down the skirt.

'Making me look a fool—like a servant!—in front of so many,' Maxim snapped. He kicked a nearby hatbox, not noticing how he made the maid jump—Valentina wasn't sure if he even realised she was there—then threw himself into a chair, his legs splayed. His hands clutched the seat beneath him as though they wanted to break it.

'No one could ever think you a fool,' Valentina soothed, watching him in the mirror as she stepped into her silk chiffon nightgown.

His body was shaking all over, but she knew he was embarrassed more than angry. The embarrassment was made worse by his inability to show any ill feeling towards the person who had caused his humiliation. The monk wouldn't have meant any deliberate offence by ordering Maxim around; he'd simply treated him the way he treated everyone. But therein lay the problem: Maxim wasn't everyone.

Valentina gently pushed the maid away from the pink ribbons she was tying in bows and stepped over to Maxim. Kneeling on the floor in front of him, she rested her hands on his cheeks. They felt feverish.

'You are right to be angry,' she said. 'But don't you see? This is evidence of how well you've established my reputation with him. His rude behaviour was merely an attempt to emulate you and your admired position for a moment.'

Her words were intended to be a salve, but Valentina saw Maxim's nostrils flare, felt his jaw tighten under her palms. She quickly sat back on her heels, snatching her hands away. His breathing had become so loud she thought any staff walking by the closed door would hear him.

'You dare to impugn Rasputin? The man who is responsible for furthering my career; and yours? My greatest ally in this city?' He leaped up and started pacing the length of the room. 'Damn it!' he yelled suddenly, whirling around and slamming one fist into Valentina's mirror. A crack spread across the glass.

Valentina jumped back in fright, her hands pressed to her chest. She could feel her heart pounding underneath her skin. Maxim let his hand drop, not bothering to check it for scratches or cuts. He didn't even shake it to rid it of the pain he must surely feel. It was as if he were completely unaware of what he'd done as he continued to pace.

A piece of glass fell from the mirror, bounced off the dressing table and landed on the floor. Valentina stood frozen, unsure of what to do. Maxim, still pacing, stepped on the piece of glass, crushing it underneath the heel of his boot. The sound made him stop, and his eyes, which had been distant, regained their focus.

He reached out, and Valentina thought he was going to caress her face. She was relieved; his temper was over. Instead, he grabbed her chin in a vice-like grip. His eyes met hers in a withering look, as though she'd displayed unbearable stupidity. She held her breath, expecting further violence, but a second later he released her and sauntered from the room.

Valentina touched her chin with trembling fingers, then tip-toed to the door and closed it quietly. Turning, she saw that her maid stood with her back pressed against the wall, her face white. Trying not to show how unsettled she was, Valentina gestured for the woman to help her finish preparing for bed. Before them, the brown underside of the mirror was exposed where Maxim had broken the glass. Valentina stared at it as if she'd never seen such a thing before. The tiny piece marring an otherwise perfect surface disturbed her. She would not allow superstition to get the better of her, though; the mirror was not a symbol of her relationship with Maxim, merely evidence of a fiery temperament not unusual to artistic types.

She turned away, pulled a purse towards her and yanked out a wad of paper notes. 'Here,' she said, holding it out to the maid.

The woman stared at her for a moment, then reached out her hand, just as Valentina knew she would. When her fingers closed around the money, Valentina didn't let go.

'If you tell anyone, any of the other staff, what happened, I will find out,' she said. 'You will not work in this house again. Nor any other of consequence.'

The woman nodded her understanding, and Valentina let go of the money.

It would not be the last time she paid for silence.

CHAPTER FOUR

The audience was so quiet, Luka was sure he could have heard if a single person so much as shifted their weight. He took a deep breath and placed his hands on the satin-clad waist of his partner; then the orchestra's music swelled, and they were dancing. Luka was buried behind two lines of men and women, but a spotlight was on him. No one else could see it, but he felt it surrounding his movements, the warmth of it showing everyone that one day they would know his name and recognise his dancing.

Bracing his legs, he lifted his partner in the air, and his heart lifted too. When he placed her back down, it was a gift to the audience, his movements reaching out to them, inviting them to become a part of his glorious world. It wasn't enough trying to draw the audience's eyes to him. Luka wanted to know they were seeing the passion that ran through him with every move-ment. He wanted to be like Nijinsky, the star of the Ballets Russes, whose very name conjured an artistry that bordered on genius. He wanted what every one of the hundred and eighty men and women around him also wanted.

In what must surely have been the blink of an eye, Luka was offstage again, trying to catch his breath in the darkened wings. His part was only that of a peasant in the corps de ballet, but he'd lost himself so thoroughly in the role that it was a shock to realise he was still Luka Zhirkov. Placing his hands on his knees, he took in one large mouthful of air and held it. He would be onstage again in just a few moments and his muscles tingled with the ecstasy and anticipation of it.

Straightening, he raised his arms above his head to lengthen his spine. A group of corps women were in the wing before him, preparing to go onto the stage. The first took a step out, the rest rising to demi-pointe ready to follow.

'Wait!' Luka gasped, lurching forward and catching Xenia Nicholaievna's arm.

She looked at him in panic. It was her cue to go on, but Luka's firm grip was preventing her from moving.

'Your socks!'

Xenia looked down and Luka saw her blanch underneath the heavy stage make-up. Over her pointe shoes were a pair of scarlet woollen socks, intended to keep her feet and ankles warm while not on stage. Luka let go of her; she bent to pull the socks off, then she was onstage, a step or two behind where she should be.

Butterflies jostled in Luka's stomach as he watched her catch up, but there was no time to dwell on the near disaster. The music was indicating the approach of his own re-entry to the stage, and he rushed to his wing, pushing past one or two men who glared at him for nearly being late.

The rest of the ballet went without error, showcasing the perfection the Romanov dancers had come to be known for and which audiences expected from them. In one scene, when

Luka was miming conversations with the other peasants and townspeople, he found himself near Xenia Nicholaievna. She took a few casual steps over so they were beside each other.

'Thank you,' she whispered, her face held in an exaggerated smile for the audience. 'You saved me a month's fine, I'm sure.'

'Perhaps in future you should wear pale socks. Just in case,' Luka whispered back.

He thought he saw a real smile hovering underneath her stage one.

The incident with the socks marked the beginning of a friendship between Luka and Xenia. She was able to show him a side of his home city he'd never been able to explore before, confined as he was by the rules of the ballet school or the poverty of his early life. On days when they weren't performing, she directed him through the crowded stalls of the Jewish markets, or alongside the Neva River which was beginning to ice over, never nearing the palaces others might have thought more noteworthy.

Luka enjoyed touring Petrograd with Xenia. She talked as they went, regaling him with stories of past performances or spats between company members. She made him laugh, and it was because of this that Luka didn't notice the singing couple at first. Gradually, though, he became aware of the noise and turned to see a man and a woman with their arms wrapped around each other. 'Oh, Maria, oh, Maria, how sweet is this world,' they cried, laughing as they tried to match the length of their steps.

Luka laughed too, then realised that Xenia was softly singing along. 'Friends of yours?' he asked in surprise.

'No. But I know where they've been.' She gestured to a slightly ajar door across the road from him, from which a splinter of light and cigarette smoke emerged.

The couple passed by with a wave, but as their voices faded Luka could still hear the song. It came from behind the door, muffled yet recognisable. Xenia beckoned for him to cross the road, and as he got closer he saw that above the door was a sign: 'The Wandering Dog'. The voices inside sounded irresistibly joyful.

Xenia pushed open the door and Luka followed her into a narrow hallway partitioned from a larger house. Even though it appeared to have the wiring for electric lights, it was dimly lit by gas lamps. Like many other places, the owners must have found it had become too expensive to run the electricity in recent months. Writing scrawled on the wall pointed towards some rickety wooden stairs leading down, and Xenia headed in that direction.

As they reached the last step, Luka realised The Wandering Dog was a club. What was formerly a cellar had been converted into a crowded area scattered with chairs, tables and crates. A few people were lounging on the floor, their feet stretched up against the walls or curled underneath them. A man with a guitar—who Luka later learned was the host of the club—stood in the centre of the room, playing the song the couple had been singing. Some of the patrons were listening to him, while others went on with their loud conversations, but whenever he reached the chorus they all stopped what they were doing and joined in the refrain: 'Oh, Maria, oh, Maria, how sweet is this world.'

Xenia wound her way through the crowd, shrugging off her seal fur coat, stopping when she found a couple of spare crates for them to sit on. Luka followed, feeling as though he were being watched by the numerous photographs and paintings that hung on the walls: Tartaglia, Pantalone, Smeraldina, Brighella and Carlo Gozzi, all smiling or grimacing at him. The air was heavy with the scent of smoke and spilled drink; and the patrons—bohemian-looking women, soldiers recovering from injury, men who were too old or too rich to go to the front—were crammed so tightly together that it was impossible to move without brushing up against someone. It should have been claustrophobic, but instead it was intimate and comforting. It was the kind of place Luka knew Pyotr would have loved, were he here to share it.

The host finished his song, and Luka clapped along with the rest. Having peeled her mittens off, Xenia procured two glasses of *sbiten* from somewhere, and handed one to Luka. There were a few minutes of indecipherable chatter, then a man with bandages just visible beneath his hat stood up from his seat and spoke loudly. He was reciting a poem. It was not one Luka recognised and he guessed the man had written it himself. As with the singer, not everyone bothered to listen. Those who did either nodded emphatically, or closed their eyes to take in the words. The soldier-poet finished, and there was another smattering of applause as he sat back down.

'Xenia, what is this place? And how did you find it?'

She laughed, lifting her *sbiten* high in a salute. 'It's my refuge when the world of the ballet gets too much for me.'

He stared at her, looking for traces of the joke in her face. He found none. 'How could it ever be too much? I want to live and breathe the Imperial Ballet. All I ever wanted was to get into the company, but now I'm there I find myself battling constant fear my contract won't get renewed at the end of the season.'

The idea that he might be allowed only a brief taste of all he had worked for, all he had dreamed of since childhood, gnawed at him, worry increasing with every exhilarating performance he gave, every mundane class he worked through.

'It doesn't have to be the end of the world,' Xenia said. 'There are other companies out there, you know. They might not bear the Romanov name, but they come with other things that might be even better.'

Luka grinned at her. 'Impossible.'

'What about the Ballets Russes? If you left the imperialists and joined the innovators, you'd be taking a path that let you explore a thousand different countries and a thousand different theatres. You could be the next Nijinsky.'

Luka shook his head and took another swig of his *sbiten*.

'Don't be so quick to dismiss the compliment, *malysh*. I don't give it lightly. Do you know how much I wish it were me with the talent to join the Ballets Russes? But it's nothing more than a distant dream. However, you, my young friend, should think seriously of it. If nothing else, it may alleviate your fears about your contract renewal.'

'I suppose,' Luka replied. Truth be told, as much as he admired Nijinsky, he'd never imagined following the man's footsteps into another company. The Imperial Russian Ballet had been the sole lifelong focus of Luka's ambitions.

'Another drink?' Xenia asked, pushing her empty glass away. 'Allow me this time.'

'Not at all. I still owe you for saving me. I can't think of anything worse than going onstage wearing those treacherous socks.'

Luka's smile faltered. 'I can,' he said softly. 'Last week we were waiting in the wings to go on when one of the coryphées pushed us all back. He had tears streaming down his face and was utterly distraught. Apparently his contract wasn't renewed, and he'd already been conscripted to the war.'

Luka doubted he'd ever forget that moment. The man had been doubled over, his arms wrapped around himself as he choked, 'I can't go out there and dance as if everything is alright, as if everything is the same as ever.' The orchestra's notes had softened, preparing to switch from the overture to the melody that would open the performance, but no one noticed. A tear had escaped and was trickling down the coryphées's cheek; Luka watched it, transfixed, his throat constricting so that it was hard to breathe. That tear seemed to hold everything he'd been afraid of; it was confirmation that all could go wrong in the blink of an eye and he would be powerless to stop it.

'What happened?' Xenia asked. 'I don't recall any of the performances being interrupted.'

'No. One of the other dancers talked him into going on. The coryphée said, "I'll die out there," but the other dancer gestured to the stage and said, "Then you should live out there first."'

Xenia was silent. That was what they did as artists: they put aside their own emotions and realities, even when their hearts were breaking, and performed.

Luka had followed the man on to the stage, leaving his own now heightened fears behind him, only to return when he entered the wings once more.

And now he waited for his own letter from the Imperial Russian Ballet, not knowing if the news it contained would be good or bad.

Luka patted himself down, even though his practice uniform had no pockets. As he was getting changed for the day he'd realised that his lucky gloves were not where he'd expected them to be. True, he sometimes stashed them among his things in the theatre's dressing room during a performance, so their luck was close by, but he usually returned them to his coat pocket afterwards. He tried to tell himself that they must be waiting for him in the theatre somewhere, that this wasn't an omen about whether or not his contract would be renewed. But he couldn't stop his hands from reaching for pockets that didn't exist, and so didn't see Xenia until she was almost on top of him.

'Finally,' she said, grabbing his hand and pulling him towards the studios. 'Come and see the noticeboard—the casting for *La Belle au Bois Dormant* is up.'

'Did you get a role?'

Xenia snorted. 'Of course not. I've tried long enough to get the notice of the company to know that's never going to happen.'

He stopped, making her stop too. 'Surely you haven't given up?' he asked her.

'Give it long enough, Luka, and you'll realise that your worst enemy here is yourself. Everyone has limitations, physical or otherwise, that hold them back; and eventually the hope of anything more becomes too much to live with. We're Romanov dancers; we're told our places. Trying to outmanoeuvre that is a game best left to those whose hearts can withstand the disappointment. Or those who have the talent to look at other options, such as the Ballets Russes.'

Xenia smiled as she nudged him, but behind the smile Luka saw the exhaustion of years of hard work that hadn't paid off in the way his friend had hoped. Her resigned tone made him wonder if one day he too would be telling a young dancer not to dream too much. Perhaps sooner rather than later if the letter he was waiting on from the company didn't contain good news.

'Anyway, let's not be melancholy,' Xenia said in a singsong voice, pulling him towards the noticeboard again. 'Not when we have good news to celebrate.'

Luka's eyes found the casting notice pinned to the middle of the board, and his gaze travelled down it slowly. There were no surprises really: Mathilde Kschessinska was cast as Princess Aurora—a role Luka thought her too old for; Pierre Vladimiroff was Prince Désiré; and Valentina Yershova was to be the Lilac Fairy. The roles of the other fairies, Gold, Silver and Sapphire, were given to Olga Spessivtseva, Lubov Yegorova and Felia Doubrovska; and the Bluebird was Anatole Vilzak. Still no surprises. Luka would have been shocked if their names *hadn't* appeared on the casting list.

Then he saw it. The reason Xenia had been so insistent on getting him to look at the noticeboard. There, beside the role of Puss in Boots, was the name Luka Zhirkov.

He looked at Xenia incredulously. Her hands were clasped together, and in her onyx eyes was an excited light that Luka knew mirrored his own.

'You got it,' she said. 'You got a role.'

Luka let out a shout and picked Xenia up by the waist, swinging her so the skirt of her ballet dress flared out around her like a snowy fan. Those nearby looked at them with disdain, but Luka didn't care. It was only a small role—a comic pas de deux in the wedding scene with the White Cat—and if Luka had been given a choice he would have preferred the Bluebird, where he could show off his virtuosity and draw the audience's eyes to him, not his partner. But it was a step out of the corps de ballet and it tasted glorious.

'Luka, stop!' Xenia gasped, her fingers clawing at his back through the fabric of his tunic. 'I'm going to hit someone!'

Luka gently put her down and she swayed, pink-cheeked, then took a couple of stumbling steps to the side. Luka laughed at her, his own eyes swimming with dizziness.

'Oh, sorry!' Xenia cried, straightening herself. She stepped aside to let the person she'd bumped into pass by.

It was Valentina Yershova. Rubbing her arm where Xenia had jolted it, she stared at them. 'Perhaps the corridor isn't the best place to be doing … that,' she said, her low voice holding a cool edge of displeasure.

'Sorry,' Xenia said again, looking anything but. 'Luka got cast in his first role and we were celebrating.'

Valentina's eyes flickered to Luka. She barely held his gaze for a second before she walked by. She didn't look at the noticeboard.

'You got the Lilac Fairy,' he called after her, thinking she would want to know. It was the most sought-after female role aside from Princess Aurora herself.

Valentina paused, but didn't say anything before sweeping into one of the studios.

Xenia grimaced at Luka. 'What a cheerful soul that one is.'

Luka laughed in agreement. Nothing could bring him down now. Not the surly demeanour of another dancer, nor the loss of his gloves. Their disappearance couldn't be an omen; not after this sign of recognition from the company. He would find the gloves again, and send up a prayer of thanks to his mother when he received his renewed contract.

CHAPTER FIVE

Winter 1914

Dismissed from her Lilac Fairy rehearsals for the day, Valentina roamed the halls of the Mariinsky, looking for a spare rehearsal room to continue practising on her own. She had a pair of long socks pulled over her pointe shoes, and a short fur cape wrapped tightly around her shoulders to keep the cold at bay. She paused at the doorway to one of the studios, saw it was taken, and went to move on. But then she recognised the person inside and hesitated.

It was Luka Zhirkov, the promising young corps dancer. His hands were held out in front of him, and in his reflection in the wall mirrors Valentina saw a frown. He was practising the Puss in Boots pas de deux; Valentina had performed it many times herself and recognised the playful steps. There wasn't much use in practising without a partner, though. Stepping into the studio, she cleared her throat.

Luka jumped, his hands falling to his sides as a blush crept up his cheeks.

'Puss in Boots pas de deux?' Valentina asked, pulling the collar on her fur cape higher.

'Yes. I … I was just practising …'

'A little difficult without the White Cat.'

'She preferred to sit next to the stage and knit.'

'Ah.'

Valentina had been in the wings when Luka had rehearsed the pas de deux in front of the ballet master. He'd only learned the choreography that week and was struggling with his timing. The woman cast as the White Cat had made her disdain for him clear. It made Valentina scornful. The woman had been in the company for nine years and was only now being given small roles. Luka had already matched her after just a few months. If she were smart she would foster a relationship with him instead of letting jealousy get the better of her. But that was the reason people like her stayed in the lower ranks, while those like Valentina rose through them.

Valentina thought it likely that Luka's timing was off due to nerves. She'd seen it in the way his movements became almost frenetic with energy when he stepped onto the stage. With practice and a few more roles behind him she doubted it would be a problem any more. As yet, the young man seemed unaware of his own talent, or the fact that the company had noticed it and no doubt had plans for him. Which meant he was ripe for cultivating as a partner. With luck and clever manipulation on her side, they might one day be a great duo, like Karsavina and Nijinsky. But first, she needed to test his skill for herself.

She undid the ribbon of her fur cape and dropped it to the floor. Luka drew back, as though he expected her to remove the rest of her clothes too. Valentina almost sneered. Luka Zhirkov was not the kind of man who could afford that pleasure. Bending down to hide her expression, she tugged the socks off her feet, then pressed first one foot, then the other, onto the tips of her pointes. 'Well, come on then,' she said, and strode to one corner of the studio. She stood there, arms ready *à la seconde.*

Luka was still standing in the same spot, watching her with a bewildered face. 'I don't ...'

'Don't what? Don't think I know the pas de deux?'

'No! I know you've performed it before.'

Valentina gave a nod. It always satisfied her when people remembered her performances. 'Then you also know that I know what the company looks for in the piece. So come on.'

Luka gazed at her, his expression still unsure, then slowly moved to the opposite corner.

With a couple of arabesques and some cat-like hand gestures, Valentina moved around the open space, the familiar steps igniting a spark in her that was rarely there these days. A moment later, Luka had joined her in the centre of the room. Valentina stepped into an attitude en pointe, and Luka's hands landed on her waist, his cheek pressed against hers. The roughness of his stubbled skin took her by surprise; she'd been thinking of him as a boy, naive and pliable. But of course, he was a young man. Valentina broke away, and Luka pursued her. She turned on him and chased him back with a series of playful pas de chat. Both their hands were curled in cat-like claws, which they unfurled at each other—and when Luka met her eyes she saw that he was smiling. She turned her face away.

Maxim would not like this. He was a possessive man, and Valentina did her best to please him. But she couldn't pin all her plans on him. Dimitri had left her before she became principal, and there was no saying that Maxim wouldn't do the same

if she failed to make him her husband. She was not going to
ignore opportunities to make useful connections of her own.
And besides, Maxim would never find out.

Luka moved to stand behind her again. Her leg was raised to
the side, and he ran his hand down it. Even through the thick
material of her stockings she could feel the warmth of his palm.
The smell of his soap mixed with sweat made her suddenly
aware of his masculinity again. Her weight almost shifted off
her pointe, but Luka sensed it and corrected it for her. That
was promising—a good partner should always be able to sense
the centre of balance of the other and help compensate when it
went wrong. His hands were on her waist again, and Valentina
unfurled her leg to the side in a long développé. Luka's hand
reached for her foot and she batted it away, perhaps a touch too
hard. His grip changed, one arm curling protectively around
the front of her body. Another développé, and another hit of
his hand, then she was turning to face him. She saw that he
was grinning.

'You're not supposed to laugh,' she said, lowering herself to
flat feet and running her hands down the skirt of her ballet
dress to smooth it.

'I know. I'm sorry. It's just the piece ...'

'It is a comical one. That's why the audiences enjoy it so, I
suppose.'

Their eyes met, and Valentina took an unconscious step
away from him. He no longer had the boyish softness the
young ones all entered with. She knew that in the years she'd
been with the Imperial Russian Ballet, her face had changed
too, becoming older, harder and yet more refined. She had
the urge to reach up and touch his features, to trace them, as

if that way she could understand the meaning behind their change, and perhaps find some answers to her own.

'Excuse me, do you know—oh!'

Valentina and Luka both turned to the doorway. Standing there, one hand on the frame, was the corps woman Luka had been flinging around in the hallway the day of the casting announcement.

'I apologise. I didn't realise you were in here,' the woman said.

'You were talking to an empty room, then?' Valentina couldn't help the retort. She didn't like the way the woman was looking at her. There was a superior glint in her eyes, and the way her mouth twisted up at one side spoke of disdain.

Luka was already crossing the room with eager steps. Valentina's chest burned. She was the highest-ranking dancer here; it was she who should be given favour. Not some rude little nobody who'd interrupted where she wasn't wanted.

'Xenia, you were looking for something?' Luka asked, meeting the woman near the door and taking one of her hands in both of his.

'You, actually. I thought you might need some help practising your pas de deux. That viper they paired you with wasn't exactly forthcoming.'

Luka laughed. 'You were correct. I was rehearsing by myself when Valentina Yershova came across me and offered to help.'

Xenia's eyes shifted over Luka's shoulder, and Valentina saw the way her mouth compressed into a grim line. 'She did? How very ... surprising of her. Well, I'm sure she has other things that need attending. I'll be glad to take over.'

A derisive laugh escaped Valentina's mouth. This woman had never performed outside of the corps. She was no match in skill for a soloist.

But the two of them looked at her as if they couldn't understand why she might laugh. It felt like an insult, and caused Valentina to tilt her chin up. She crossed the room casually, her pointe shoes tapping against the timber floor, picked up her fur cape and draped it around her shoulders, then threw her socks over one arm.

As she reached Luka, she turned her back to the woman, deliberately blocking her from view. 'It was lovely to dance with you. Perhaps we'll have the chance to do so again sometime, on the stage.'

She saw the way Luka's eyebrows lifted and left before he or the woman could say anything else. She'd achieved what she'd wanted: she'd experienced Luka's skill as a partner firsthand, and laid the first claim to him. That woman could have him when Valentina was done with him.

Not ready to go home in case Maxim had let himself into her house again, Valentina returned to the Mariinsky Theatre's stage to watch the rehearsals. But when she got there, the dancers had been dismissed or sent to the rehearsal rooms to learn further choreography. The theatre was unnaturally quiet, only the scene-shifters pulling up pieces of scenery on ropes disturbing the stillness. It made her restless; her body itched to be somewhere noisy, somewhere she didn't have to think too much.

She decided to stop by Leiner's, the delicatessen which was popular with the Petrograd elite, for a light meal. While there, she would pick up some of the prohibitively expensive Black Sea oysters Maxim preferred—that should take the edge off if it later turned out he had been waiting for her. She was leaving the theatre when she noticed a pair of gloves folded neatly over the top of a piece of painted scenery. She picked them up: they were small, no bigger than a child's, and had been patched so many times she could barely make out their original colour. She held them to her cheek; they smelled warm and distinctly human. She wondered who had left them behind; or who, for that matter, would be wearing so tattered a pair. It wasn't likely any of the Imperial Ballet School students would wear their gloves for more than one winter—Valentina knew that from her own experiences as an outsider among the wealthy.

Despite the gloves being so worn, there was something about them that made her feel comforted. She could almost see a mother lovingly darning them and promising that next year her child would get a new pair. The gloves didn't deserve to be left here in the theatre, tucked over a fake shrub; they deserved a real home. It was a silly thought, but it made Valentina smile, and she tucked the gloves into the bodice of her white practice dress.

Maxim was sprawled next to her, his breathing thick and wet from a night of drinking at one of his favourite restaurants. He was taking up most of the bed, and Valentina was curled uncomfortably next to him in the space left between his splayed arm and leg. Carefully, she slid out of the bed, landing softly on all fours like a cat. She glanced up to make sure he hadn't stirred. The floor was cold against the naked balls of her feet and hands.

Crouching down further, she felt along the underneath of the bed frame. She couldn't quite reach. She lowered her knees to the floor, stifling a gasp at the iciness that penetrated through her silk chiffon nightgown, and stretched out her hand. It brushed against something and she knew she'd found what she was after. Holding the box against her chest, she rose slowly to her feet, willing her overused knees and ankles not to crack.

Maxim was still fast asleep, and she tiptoed away from the bed, almost slipping on the newspaper she'd thrown on the floor last night. Even in the darkness, the headline—'Grigori Rasputin: Tsar in All But Name?'—screamed at her.

In the room next to her bedroom—a room her staff weren't allowed to enter—it was even colder. She'd have to be quick, otherwise the iciness of her skin would wake Maxim when she slipped back into bed. Pushing the door to, Valentina sat the object she'd taken out of hiding on a dusty octagonal table with gilt edges. It was a candy box; the kind given to children in the theatres on the Tsar's name day. This particular box was the first Valentina had ever received, and its once bright colours were faded now, its sides gone soft and malleable with age.

She opened the lid carefully, thinking, as she usually did, that she could smell the sugary sweetness of the long-gone candy, even though it was impossible. She would never forget that smell for it was the scent of her mother. Mamma had worked in a candy factory, coming home in the evenings with the smell of sugar clinging to her dress, and her fingertips raw and bloodied from wrapping endless pieces of candy in waxed paper. Valentina had known the smell of sugar her whole life, but this box from the Tsar was the first time she'd ever tasted it. Prior to then, candy had been a luxury for others who didn't have to concern themselves with how it was made. Holding that box in trembling hands, a hard sweet resting on her tongue, was the first time that Mamma's words about how money could buy you all sorts of things you didn't even know you wanted made sense to Valentina. She'd jealously guarded the box until every last piece of candy in it had been eaten, and still she hadn't been able to get rid of it. Now, of course, it had its own special use.

Nestled inside was a small group of mismatched objects that would make sense to no one but herself—treasures that had no worth when compared to her jewels, her house and all the fine things that filled it. A letter written in a childish hand and declaring schoolboy love for the sullen and silent child-Valentina rested on the bottom; a letter that had gone unanswered. In a corner lay a teardrop-shaped pearl snatched from when she had danced one of the Little Swans in the Danse des Petits Cygnes in *Le Lac des Cygnes*. And now, carefully laid inside with shivering hands, went a pair of tattered children's gloves.

Valentina took one last look at the contents of the box before closing the lid. She would leave it in this room tonight, and return it to its hiding place when Maxim was safely gone. For now, she was satisfied to have added to her little stash of treasures.

CHAPTER SIX

Spring 1915

It was almost the end of the company season. Since he'd been with the Imperial Russian Ballet, Luka's feet had bled and his muscles had ached, but his ambitious heart had never been happier nor more determined. He was shocked by how time seemed to move so quickly; it slipped through his fingers like grains of sand—and he still had not gotten either a renewal or notice of dismissal from the company. Puss in Boots was behind him, and although he'd received a brief mention in one of the newspapers, the company had not acknowledged his success. The gloves that were so precious to him remained lost, and he began once again to dread their disappearance as an omen.

As he sat uncomfortably on the polished seat of the tram heading towards the city's outskirts and his father, he tried not to think of his losses but rather to remember all he had achieved in the past few months. It seemed only weeks ago that he'd begun living this dream that had been years in the making. It had also served as an excuse not to visit his father: he was always too busy, or too needed. They'd both known it was a lie, but had both preferred it that way. Now, with the off-season on the horizon, Luka no longer had reason to put off the visit.

He disembarked from the tram near the Putilov Mill where his father worked and looked with trepidation at the forest of factory chimneys standing against a sky made dull grey by the endless billowing smoke. The sounds of his childhood, in those years before the ballet had rescued him, enveloped him: the rattle of enormous rollers, the clanking of iron bars, the hiss of escaping steam, and the never-ending hum of the steam boilers which vibrated the earth beneath your feet if you got close enough.

The building where his father lived was indistinguishable from those around it. On the stairs, Luka had to step over children with bare feet. He could smell their dirty hair, skin and clothes, and held his breath as though that might prevent him from catching germs. The company would not like him being here—they would consider the risk of illness too great— but Luka knew his father would never make the trip to the city to see him.

A grey mark ran underneath the unvarnished, splintered handrail, left by the fingers of decades of children. Luka's own hands had contributed to those marks. Forgetting to avoid the seventeenth step, he nearly twisted his ankle as the loose board buckled beneath him. He swore softly, then looked guiltily at the children at the bottom of the stairs, who ignored him. The stairwell was narrow, and as he heard footsteps coming the other way Luka stopped and pressed his back against the wall. A man appeared in front of him, and it took Luka a second to recognise him. He lived on the same floor as Luka's father, in a room with three other men, and they had played together in the street as boys. However, the older Luka got, and the shorter his visits back home from the Imperial Ballet School, the greater the distance between them had become.

'*Zdravstvuj*,' Luka said in greeting, and the man halted. Luka saw recognition flit across his face, then his jaw tightened and he shouldered past without responding. Luka watched him go, the man's silent resentment almost a physical presence. Trying not to feel slighted, he continued upwards.

'Why haven't you volunteered for the army?' his father asked as soon as Luka stepped inside the tiny apartment.

Despite the mild weather, it was colder inside than outside. Luka wondered if his father couldn't afford to buy coal to keep the stove burning. He tried to pull his light coat tighter around him without his father noticing.

'We've talked about this before,' he replied, stifling a sigh. 'I see no point in volunteering when I'd likely just die for my efforts. I'm no soldier.' The Russian words felt strange in his mouth after so many months of only speaking French or English.

'You don't need to be a soldier to volunteer. You just need to be a man. Like your brother. There's honour in fighting for your country.'

'And freezing to death in the trenches because I can't find some dead man's boots to steal? What honour is there in that?'

Despite directing the words at his father, Luka felt the cut of them himself. Here, in the room he'd shared with his brother, he couldn't stop seeing Pyotr's face. Not as it had been in childhood, when Pyotr's wide, grinning mouth had taught him dirty words, but frozen in a blue grimace, pale eyes staring unseeing at the sky after succumbing to the winter that still lingered on the Eastern Front. It was a nightmare Luka had woken from many times; and he was glad that he lived alone so no one was there to witness his shameful cries. He shuddered and dismissed the revolting image, reminding himself that he had received a letter from Pyotr only last week. His brother was cold, yes, and wishing for better food, but he was alive.

His father scowled. 'You don't know that's true.' He threw back a cupful of cheap vodka without offering his son any.

Luka rubbed his palms against his eyelids. He'd been up late the previous night dancing in a performance of *Le Réveil de Flore*, but he didn't think that was why he felt so tired. 'All the newspapers say it. There aren't enough weapons, food or clothing for the soldiers they already have. Can't you tell from Pyotr's letters? What would be the point in adding to the problem?'

'It's what a man would do.'

'You haven't.'

'Don't think I haven't tried, boy. They say I'm too old to fight, too unwell. If they'd let me, I'd be out there. I'm not afraid of war.'

'Well, maybe you should be,' Luka muttered.

His father eyed him moodily, but Luka didn't think he'd heard. If he had, Luka's face would be dripping with vodka right now. He sat up in his chair a little straighter and spoke louder this time.

'If I'm conscripted'—he tried not to shudder, knowing that would mean his contract hadn't been renewed—'I'll do everything I'm asked to for my country. Even now, I've volunteered for the Union of Towns in Moscow during the ballet's off-season.'

Luka kept his tone firm, but he was afraid his father might still sense the quaver of guilt that ran through him, hear his desperate need for approval. Approval from whom, he wondered. Himself? His father? The absent Pyotr? Luka didn't even know. Vladimir opened his mouth to deliver a smart reply, but instead began to cough. It was a rattling sound so fierce it shook the uneven chair he sat on. Luka wanted to slap him on the back to ease the cough away, but didn't. It would only earn him a clip around the ear. Instead, he looked carefully away, pretending he didn't notice.

The apartment was tiny; just one room in which a few steps had you touching every wall. It had once been the corner of a bigger apartment, but space was at a premium and it was common for people to erect more walls to create extra sleeping quarters. Luka's father had got the best part of the former apartment, though: at one end hunkered a clumsily built stone stove that provided warmth and survival. A curtain of furs, which had long ago lost any resemblance to their original animal, enclosed the warm space on top of the stove where his father slept; a space Luka, Pyotr and their mother had once shared too. There was no bathroom—that was two floors down: a hole in concrete that was considered quite a luxury—nor was there a kitchen. Meals were a group affair, with the building's residents pooling whatever food they had into one large *tyurya* or *shchi* to share. Still, Vladimir was lucky he didn't have to resort to sleeping in factory barracks or next to his machinery, and even luckier to have a place to himself, where the bed was not on shared rotation. As a metal-worker, he was considered skilled and ranked at the higher-paying end of the factory workers.

While he waited for his father's cough to subside, Luka stared at the water bucket in the corner of the room with the old peeling painting that served as a lid. The pockmarked surface of the table was rough beneath his hands, and he realised that for many months now he'd only touched surfaces that were polished and smooth.

Finally, the coughing died down, and his father scratched at his beard in irritation, bits of spit still damp on his lips. 'I suppose no one else in that company of yours is joining the fight against the Germans either?'

Vladimir never referred to the ballet directly, as if the word would poison his mouth. Luka wished that he could talk properly to his father and describe his life at the ballet: how he still felt like the *malysh* that Xenia teasingly called him, yet also how it was as though he'd been there forever. But if he could have done that, they would have been an entirely different father and son.

'Too busy spending money the rest of us don't have,' his father added. 'Relaxing in their palaces and playing with their diamonds and pearls, no doubt.'

'I've told you before, it's not like that. Mathilde Kschessinska has even set up a hospital for wounded soldiers and the Grand Duchesses themselves volunteer there, to help men like Pyotr.'

His father shrugged. Like many other factory workers, he considered the hospitals the wealthy had established a way of alleviating their bourgeois guilt. Luka had wondered whether paying for a hospital would assuage his own guilt if he'd had the means, then pushed the thought away, disgusted at himself.

'I'd wager your lot adore the mad monk too,' his father continued, in his element now. 'I've heard what he gets up to with those rich women while our sons and brothers are sacrificing their lives. Plain immoral if you ask me. Though no one ever does, of course. I'm just a poor factory worker—my opinion doesn't matter. Never mind that it's people like me who keep this country running and stop us all from becoming Germans.'

The visit dragged on in the same uncomfortable manner until finally Luka couldn't listen to his father's wet cough any more. He made his excuses and left, ignoring the visibly relieved look on his father's face. Unfortunately, leaving Vladimir's presence didn't mean he left his voice behind. Luka could hear it still as he travelled back towards the centre of the city and its clean buildings that glowed with electric light. Would a lonely death in a trench somewhere, hungry and far away from home, truly be a more honourable path? Pyotr didn't want that for him. In truth, Luka didn't want it for himself, either. Of course, one day that choice might be taken away from him.

Luka took the letter out of his pocket for what must have been the hundredth time. He ran his fingertip over the imperial eagle in the top corner, silently thanking the Romanov dynasty for understanding the need for ballet in a world that too often succumbed to ugliness.

The letter had arrived while he was in Moscow, filling his summer off-season with volunteer work for the Union of Towns. They were attempting to send munitions and food to the front, where a supply crisis was causing Russian troops to lose ground as well as lives. The heavy lifting had been a good workout for Luka's muscles while he wasn't dancing, but seeing the weapons, knowing what they were meant for, had unsettled him.

He was grateful the letter had been forwarded from his Petrograd address; he didn't know if he could have stood being in the dark about his future too much longer. He'd let out a whoop of elation when he'd read that his contract had been renewed—an expression of joy those in the Union of Towns hadn't appreciated. Now, as the taxi carriage trundled towards the noise of Kalanchyovskaya Square, he had to resist the urge to press the letter to his lips. Instead, he tucked it carefully back into his pocket, as tenderly as though it were a living thing.

The noise was increasing—they must be getting closer. But as the taxi carriage slowed, the joyful expression on Luka's face faded. This wasn't the ordinary noise of traffic and travellers. This was something else. The carriage halted. Chanting overwhelmed Luka as he stepped down. 'Down with Niemka! Down with the German woman!'

The women and men who swarmed over Kalanchyovskaya Square had their fists raised in the air, anguish and anger competing on their faces. Children weaved between them, playing games as though this were some sort of celebration— for them, it probably was: a rare day away from gruelling work in the factories. Most were without shoes, and their eyes were large in their thin faces. A few reached beseeching hands out to a woman who sprinted along the edge of the crowd, using her teeth to tear off mouthfuls from the loaf of bread she'd clearly stolen. Two women and a one-armed man chased her, screaming obscenities.

Beads of sweat sprang up on Luka's forehead. He'd read in the Moscow newspapers that protests were cropping up over the city: people were upset their Tsarina, ruling in place of her husband who was at the front, listened more to the whisperings of the monk Grigori Rasputin than she did to their cries. But seeing this angry mass, Luka knew it was worse than had been reported. The people of Moscow had had enough of loss and fighting. The prospect of triumph promised by the Tsar had faded, and instead they were left with gaping chasms of grief, and farms that were unmanned and thus unable to provide food. And to cap it all, their ruler insisted they must not, *would not*, back down.

Luka stared in the direction of the Nikolayevsky Terminal, but it was too distant to make out the clock tower's hands. He would have to hope he could get through the crowd in time to board the train home. The driver handed him his rectangular case, and Luka thanked him, wishing he could hop back into the carriage and be whisked to safety instead. He didn't think this crowd would be happy to know that he was exempt from the risk of losing his life to the increasingly unpopular war.

He put his head down and stepped into the crowd. Immediately, the hot odour of humanity swept over him as he was jostled from side to side. He could only move slowly, shuffling steps that often took him sideways instead of forward.

Two women grabbed his arms and linked them through their own as they lifted their voices high into the air. 'Send her away to a convent! Russia for Russians only!' They looked at him, faces split by wide grins; they were indistinguishable from the women Luka had grown up around, and he could easily imagine his father amongst their ranks should the protests ever arrive in Petrograd.

He forced himself to smile back, but the expression felt ugly. He pulled his arms from their grip and, ducking his head down, powered through the crowd towards the rusticated masonry of the train terminal, careless of who he knocked out of the way.

He needed to break free of this swirling, heaving mass and the treasonous shouts, back to where the world made sense again. He emerged from the crowd and gasped like he was surfacing from the ocean. The pilasters of Nikolayevsky Terminal loomed tall, and if he'd craned his neck he could have made out the time on its clock tower now. But he just wanted to be inside.

By the time he'd got his passport and documents verified and boarded the train, where the shouts could no longer be heard, his heartbeat was returning to normal.

Luka threw his bag into his sleeper compartment—one of twenty-five curtained cubicles in the carriage—but didn't crawl in after it. After the stress of the crowd, he didn't want to be in a confined space quite so soon. He stood in the corridor, leaning his weight forward to stretch his calf muscles. Outside the small windows white clouds of steam billowed, and slowly the train pulled forward, taking him north to Petrograd and another year in the Imperial Russian Ballet.

A strange hiccupping noise interrupted Luka's thoughts. He turned to see a boy of about thirteen trying to coax a woman into a sleeper cubicle. She was crying with such force that she couldn't see where she was going. Another boy, around ten, was holding onto her skirt with one fist, attempting to look brave.

'I know, Mamma,' the older boy said, his voice quaking with responsibility. 'Let us just climb inside the sleeper and then we can grieve together.'

Luka's heart lurched as though he too were feeling the woman's grief. Stepping forward, he took her arm, hoping to help, but at his touch she flinched. Her cries cut off abruptly and wet eyes turned to glare at him. With an expression on her face that cut Luka to the core, she crawled into the sleeper below his, pulling her younger son with her.

Luka turned to see another pair of dark eyes flaming at him.

'Why aren't you fighting at the front like my father did?' the older boy asked. 'Like all his friends are—and like I will as soon as I'm old enough?'

Luka opened his mouth to tell the boy that his brother was at the front. But he stopped himself. That would not ease the boy's anger. There was nothing Luka could say that would make things seem right in the young man's eyes. He knew that from dealing with his father. He knew it because there was nothing right about it. He was protected where others weren't.

Lowering his head, Luka turned towards his sleeper. But he couldn't stomach nineteen hours of this broken family's silent reproach. He would wait until they'd had enough time to fall asleep. He walked away down the carriage, feeling the boy's eyes boring into his back. It was a relief to get through one door and into another carriage, putting a barrier between them. But the weight in his chest was still heavy, the hollowness in his stomach still accusatory, and he kept moving, feeling the thrum of the steam locomotive underneath his feet as he walked the length of the train.

When he reached a door near the very front of the train, an attendant put up an abrupt hand to stop him. 'Sorry, sir, this is a private carriage. There's no entry.'

Luka's heart sank. He wasn't ready to return to his sleeper yet; he needed the distraction of movement. But the choice wasn't his and so he turned back.

'Look here, little Djibi needs to go—could you do something about that?' a woman's voice said.

The door had opened, and a short, very finely dressed woman was holding a small white dog with a black patch covering half his face out to the attendant. With a jolt of recognition

Luka saw it was Mathilde Kschessinska, the prima ballerina assoluta of the Imperial Russian Ballet.

The attendant tentatively accepted the dog, clearly unsure what to do with it. Mathilde turned away, straightening the necklace of walnut-sized diamonds that encircled her throat. She paused for a second, then turned back to look straight at Luka.

'I know your face,' she said.

Luka checked over his shoulder. There was no one else there, so it must be him she was speaking to. 'Yes, Mademoiselle Kschessinska. I'm an imperial dancer too. Only in the corps de ballet though.'

'Is that so?' Mathilde's eyes lit up with interest and she looked Luka up and down. 'Yes, you do have the look of a dancer, even if I hadn't recognised you. Come, join me and talk of the ballet. It will liven up this frightfully boring trip until it's time to sleep.'

Startled, Luka felt his feet grow roots, holding him to the spot. Mathilde was in the class of perfection, but he had never spoken to her before. She was far too above him. He couldn't imagine spending minutes in her company, let alone hours.

She had walked back inside the carriage, and a grey-haired man who must be her porter was holding the door open for Luka, waiting. Luka took a nervous step forward. The porter gently nudged him further in, then closed the door behind him, blocking out the chatter of the public carriage.

Luka stood in the corridor of a carriage that contained private cabins. A carpet of swirling, intricate patterns had been laid down, and a boy was stomping up and down it, chanting, 'Bored, bored, bored, bored,' over and over. He didn't even look at Luka. As he moved hesitantly forward, Luka saw the door to one cabin was open. Within sat two young ladies playing cards. They glanced up, surprised to see a trespasser. Luka nodded a greeting to them, but Mathilde was striding along the carriage and he hastened to catch up. He noticed that many of the other cabins, devoid of passengers, were packed with boxes, some spilling their tissue paper that caressed new purchases.

Mathilde went through an open door halfway along the carriage, and after a nod of encouragement from the porter, Luka followed her in. It was a two-sleeper cabin, not yet set up for the night. Mathilde sat on one of the long padded seats that would later become a bed and pulled a light rug threaded with gold around her. Propped behind her back were cushions embroidered with her monogram, and on the seat opposite was a large cushion with little white hairs clinging to it. Silver dishes for Djibi—one full of water, the other empty—stood on a small fringed rug on the floor. Gauzy material hung at the windows, allowing in a thin veneer of sunlight, and the cabin had been scented with jasmine perfume.

'Come into my private cabin—although you'll have noticed the whole carriage is private.' Mathilde laughed, as though it was some great joke, and kicked off her shoes to replace them with slippers. The toes Luka glimpsed under the hem of her long skirts were hard with calluses. 'I detest noisy carriages when I'm forced to travel, so I booked this entire one for myself, Denisov there, plus my housekeeper, and her two lovely daughters you'll have seen on your way in. And my Vova, of course.' Mathilde tilted her head to the doorway, where the loud complaints of her son could be heard.

Vova was around the same age as the boy who had challenged Luka outside his own sleeper, but the difference between the two could not have been more pronounced.

'Now sit and tell me your name, young man.'

Tentatively Luka perched on the edge of the seat across from Mathilde, their knees close to touching. She was fiddling with a pale pink cardboard box, and when she held it out to him the scent of sugar mingled with the artificial jasmine in the air. Luka took a piece of the hard candy, remembering as he unwrapped it the women in his neighbourhood who had worked in the candy factories. Their children had never complained of boredom; the ones too young to work in the factories had packed snow around the fingers of their mothers at the end of each day, watching the white turn pink with blood before it melted. He popped the sweet in his mouth, but barely tasted it. He was becoming more uncomfortable with every passing second. This woman was as close as one could get to the imperial family without actually speaking to a Romanov. She was the Tsar's former lover, current lover to two Grand Dukes, and mother to a boy who might have borne the name Romanov if Mathilde hadn't been so fond of fostering the mystery of who might be his father. Perhaps it would have been better to stay in his own carriage with the angry, grieving family.

Mathilde sat back, resting her chin on slim white fingers that sparkled with gems, and regarded him with satisfaction. The effect of her eyes shining at him through thick dark lashes made Luka want to shrink away. For the first time he understood why men were so drawn to her. It was the power of that gaze, and the knowingness within that was almost obscene.

'You know, I thought this trip to dance at a charity benefit with the Bolshoi Ballet would be unbearably dull. But I believe you, young Luka Zhirkov of the corps de ballet, are about to make it more interesting.'

Thankfully, Mathilde did most of the talking. She peppered him with questions about how long he'd been with the ballet, laughing when she realised they had attended the same class of perfection for months. She showed a great deal of curiosity about his casting as Puss in Boots, musing that she remembered watching his dancing from her position onstage. All the time, sweet mouthfuls of food came and went, carried by the silent Denisov, and Luka tried to think of a way to excuse himself and return to his sleeper.

'I believe I like you, Luka Zhirkov,' Mathilde eventually said. She seemed satisfied with this conclusion. Luka had no idea how to respond. He wasn't sure he could return the compliment.

'When the season commences, you must come for a weekend at my country house. No—no arguments. Think it over, if you must, then come back to me with a yes.' Mathilde leaned closer, cocking her head in a conspiratorial manner. 'You know, I only invite other dancers to my dacha when I'm sure they have a great future ahead of them. Or I find them too amusing a distraction to resist.'

Luka didn't know which he was supposed to be, and didn't dare ask.

CHAPTER SEVEN

Autumn 1915

Luka pressed his fingers to his eyelids, trying to stem the encroaching ache in his head. The weekend hadn't even started yet and already he wanted to run back home. He stood at the gate that led into the lush gardens of Mathilde Kschessinska's country house. A cool breeze tickled the back of his neck, and the taste of salt on his lips told him the ocean was nearby. He opened his eyes and squinted into the sunlight. A wooden turret rose against a backdrop of birch trees, their leaves turning gold. If he had a desire to do so, he could have crossed the small canal running behind the house and been in the grounds of the Konstantin Palace. But he would rather have been back in Moscow, loading carriages and trains with munitions, instead of embarking on this unasked-for weekend of luxury.

He knew there was no point delaying any longer; sooner or later, he would have to go through that gate. Its hinges sighed as he opened it and stepped onto grass so thick it was a carpet beneath his shoes. Before he could close the gate, Mathilde's dog appeared out of nowhere and zipped between his feet and onto the road.

'Djibi!' Mathilde, long ruffled skirt flying, came running from her dacha. '*Bonjour,*' she panted as she reached Luka, speaking in French as always. 'Excuse me for a moment—I just have to get Djibi.'

Darting through the gate, she ran down the road to where the little dog was waiting for her, his stub of a tail wagging. Just as Mathilde reached him, the dog took off again, running another twenty or so steps before stopping to wag his tail once more. Mathilde shook her finger at him, then crept closer, her delicate steps showing her ballet training. The dog tried to repeat his trick, but with a smooth glissade Mathilde caught him. Muttering in his ear, she walked back to where Luka was standing, strands of dark hair coming loose around the cabochon sapphires of her Fabergé diadem.

'My apologies, Malysh. Djibi here is a naughty little boy and insists on making a bad hostess of me.'

Luka started at the sound of Xenia's nickname for him in the ballerina's mouth. He wondered where she had heard it. She hadn't known it when they'd spent those few hours together on the train.

Mathilde closed the gate behind her with one pointed foot, then let the struggling dog bounce free of her arms. He promptly crashed through a bed of tulips, flattening them.

'Come, please,' she said. 'My other guests are enjoying a drink inside. Just leave your bag by the gate. Denisov will collect it.'

Luka dutifully placed his small bag on the grass. Djibi immediately came to give it a sniff. Mathilde clapped her hands to chase the dog off, then beckoned for Luka to follow her to the house.

'There are other guests joining us?' he asked, relieved at the news.

'Yes, a larger party is always better, don't you think? Valya is one of my dearest friends, and I can't go past any chance to indulge myself with her company. Especially now she has that charming man by her side.'

Luka stumbled, and some speckled goats in a nearby paddock bleated as if they were laughing at him. 'Do you mean Valentina Yershova?'

Mathilde shook her head at the goats. 'Ignore that lot. My pet goat is among them and he cries whenever he's away from me. It only takes one bleat before the whole group chimes in.' She turned her attention back to him, her bejewelled fingers twirling the curls around her face. 'What did you say? Oh yes, Valya—have you met already?' She didn't give him time to answer. 'It's a large company and it can take some time to get to know everyone, what with new people joining and leaving every year.'

Mathilde led him into her dacha. As they passed through two rooms, Luka attempted to take in his surrounds. But they were moving so fast all he saw was an impression of gilded frames, thick carpets and mosaic floors before he found himself in a room full of strangers.

'Malysh is here!' Mathilde announced, throwing her arms wide.

Luka cringed at being introduced by the nickname he'd thought private. He forced himself to stop fidgeting with his sleeve cuffs. His hands felt awkward dangling at his sides, but he didn't know what else to do with them.

Two gentlemen responded with polite nods, while a third, standing in a corner, simply raised an eyebrow. With cold unease, Luka saw it was the same man he'd asked directions of on his first day. The man whose presence made Valentina Yershova behave when she was working herself into a temper.

Valentina herself was reclining in a gilded chair with padded seat and arms. She glanced at Luka, her cool eyes not registering any recognition before she averted them.

'Malysh. What an interesting name,' Valentina's companion said. He took a sharp step towards Luka, then stopped, waiting for him to fill the rest of the gap between them. It felt like a challenge, one Luka wasn't sure he wanted to take.

'Actually, it's Luka. Luka Vladimirovich Zhirkov,' he said, staying where he was.

Valentina's eyes flitted towards the two of them, and this time they didn't move away.

'Everyone calls him Malysh, though,' Mathilde said. 'It's a company nickname. Charming, don't you think?'

Luka couldn't stop his eyebrows from rising. He caught the man's smirk before Mathilde darted out of the room to search for her housekeeper. Dislike rose in him, but he told himself to ignore it. He was just unsettled by the unfamiliar setting and company, and the shock of seeing the man he'd accidentally annoyed so long ago.

'A man who mistakes me for a dancer and carries the name of a baby.' The man cocked his head to one side, fingertips brushing his thick moustache.

Luka noticed his pink nails were perfectly trimmed; they'd probably never seen a day of real work. His dislike reared again, followed immediately by a sense of shame. Although Luka himself had been destined for the factories like his father, mother and brother, his acceptance into the Imperial Ballet School had meant he'd never set foot in one. Aside from his brief stint at the Union of Towns, he was no more a working man than this stranger. He was in no position to judge.

'It's rather an odd nickname, even if given affectionately,' the man continued. 'Wouldn't you say, Malysh?'

'I don't know. I'm not the one who made it.'

'No. You're just on the receiving end.'

'Maxim, my love, let the boy be. He doesn't know your name, nor those of the rest of us, and you're making fun of his pet name. You have him at an unfair disadvantage.'

Both men turned to look at Valentina. During their exchange, she had stood up and moved to one of the long windows overlooking the garden, her back to them. Her voice was melodious with a gentle, enticing appeal, but the fact she had called him 'boy' stung Luka.

Valentina turned and her dark hazel eyes met his. Luka remembered the time she'd helped him practise the Puss in Boots pas de deux. It had been a kind act from one who outranked him, but it had also made him uncomfortable. It had seemed wrong to put his hands on the waist and legs of the famous Valentina Yershova. Heat crept up his neck at the memory, a crawl he knew wouldn't end until it had reached the very tips of his ears.

'If no one else is going to do the introductions, I suppose I had better,' Valentina murmured. Luka wondered if he detected a hint of displeasure in her tone, but her face didn't show it. 'Please meet His Serene Highness, the Grand Duke Sergei, and His Serene Highness, the Grand Duke Andrei.'

The two men nodded at Luka. They were separated by the expanse of the room, yet inextricably joined by their bloodline and the woman they shared. Luka knew from gossip that it was rare for them to be in each other's presence.

'And the man who finds your name so amusing is Maxim Sergeivich Ilyn,' Valentina said.

Maxim didn't acknowledge the introduction. Quiet settled over the room, and Luka once again felt the urge to fiddle with his sleeves. He took a deep breath and tried to appear unconcerned.

'Before you came in, we were talking about the situation in Moscow,' the Grand Duke Sergei said, breaking the silence. He had to be as old as Luka's father, but instead of a persistent cough and a sour temperament, he sparkled with vitality. 'Shameful business, isn't it?'

'It'll all blow over soon enough.' Mathilde's voice preceded her into the room, removing the need for Luka to reply.

Behind her came a woman with an aristocratic face carrying a glass of fizzing champagne on a silver tray. Luka took the glass, thanked the woman's quickly retreating back, and sipped. The champagne was very different from the thick yeasty beer he favoured, and its bubbles were so light they tickled his nose.

Mathilde threw herself onto one of the upholstered chairs. 'What are Malysh's thoughts on the matter? You were in Moscow, after all; you must have seen the protesters. Do you think Niemka should be exiled to a convent?'

Luka flinched to hear the almost treasonous nickname in the mouth of one so close to the imperial family. Perhaps it was because the Tsar was away at the front that Mathilde spoke so boldly against their Regent. Or perhaps it was just a long-held jealousy for her rival.

'I can't say I know enough to have an opinion,' he replied.

'What a very delicate answer!' Mathilde laughed. 'Perhaps you're a diplomat as well as a dancer?'

Luka shook his head, denying the charge.

'Unrest isn't new to Russia.' Valentina's low voice cut through the room. She was seated again, and one arm dangled over the side of her chair, holding an upside-down empty champagne glass by its base. With her other hand she twisted the ends of her bobbed, honey-coloured hair. 'I've been caught in the midst of it before. The revolution that happened in 1905 was far worse than these impassioned grumblings. All the country believed murder had been royally sanctioned, and the people answered with whispers of revolution. But it all went away in the end.'

'That only settled because the Tsar agreed to create the Duma,' Luka ventured.

The new government had appeased the rage of the people after the imperial family had ordered their soldiers to fire on protesters who wanted better working conditions. Men like Luka's father had never forgotten though, and they'd raised their sons to remember the shame of Bloody Sunday.

'And we still have the Duma now,' Maxim said, as if putting an end to the matter. 'Not to mention Grigori Rasputin. With his divine powers we can hardly go wrong.'

Luka hesitated, but the words on his lips wouldn't be held back. 'We weren't given the government people thought, though. It wasn't the one we were promised.'

Maxim Sergeivich made a sound that was half-laugh, half-snort. 'The people got exactly what it said in the peace treaty. If they were too stupid to understand what that meant, it's hardly the fault of anyone but themselves. That's what you get when dealing with *muzhiki*, though.' Maxim looked Luka up and down and the inference was clear. 'Peasant brains in peasant people.'

The conversation turned stilted and dull after that, until Mathilde moved them into the garden. By then, the light had faded into the cool blue tones of an autumn evening, and she had decided such unseasonably fine weather meant the perfect opportunity to dine outside. Lanterns strung all around illuminated their faces, making their features seem soft and fuzzy. Or perhaps that was the Moët et Chandon Brut Impérial Luka had been drinking. The night was warm, and he could smell salty air drifting in from the sea. Mathilde owned a nearby beach and was planning to take them there for a picnic the following day.

The table, brought up from her cellar, was decorated with a Limoges porcelain dinner service, and such an array of knives and forks that Luka fiddled with his lace napkin until the others had picked up their own so he could copy their choice. They dined on salted cucumbers, partridge, mushrooms in cream sauce, and tiny sausages. Forget-me-nots in Imperial Porcelain Manufactory vases stood between the plates, waving gently in the breeze. Piano music drifted from the house, but was drowned out by the voices of the guests. Vova joined them for a while, stealing sips of champagne when he thought no one was watching, before one of the housekeeper's daughters took him off to bed.

'Superb dinner as always, *mademoiselle*,' Maxim said, bowing his head towards their hostess.

Mathilde smiled at him lazily. 'You'd never expect less, not from me. Now, shall we play some poker? You know I never finish a night without a game of poker.'

The guests laughed as if she had made some great joke. Luka opened his mouth to join in, but found he couldn't muster any sound.

'What about bridge?' Maxim asked. He slipped a cigarette into a mother-of-pearl holder and lit it, leaning back in his chair. 'I'm rather partial to bridge myself.'

'Absolutely not,' Mathilde said. 'I can't abide the game. It's poker, or baccarat if you prefer, but I won't have bridge played at my dinner party.'

The guests laughed drunkenly again, all but Maxim. His hand had frozen halfway to his mouth, and the smoke from his cigarette curled around his face in a way that made Luka think for a moment that it was coming from the man's own ears and nostrils. Realising he was being watched, Maxim bared his teeth at Mathilde in an expression meant to be a smile. His voice when he spoke was brittle. 'Of course. Poker we shall play, and I couldn't be more pleased about it.'

Luka thought he was poised to say more, but the group was interrupted by the woman who had brought Luka the glass of champagne when he'd first arrived: Mathilde's *dvornik*. She had been on the train from Moscow that day, but hadn't ventured out of her sleeper, leaving all the work to her daughters and the porter. She carried a chair with her now, which she squeezed in between Luka and the Grand Duke Sergei. She shifted her backside, making herself comfortable, then pulled out a packet of cards and looked at the group expectantly.

'What is it tonight then? Poker or baccarat?'

Laughing, Mathilde reached over to squeeze the woman's hand. 'You know me too well. We're playing poker. Won't your daughters join us?'

'I've sent them to bed. It's too late for decent young ladies to be up and about.'

'What a shame; they would have completed our little group. Oh, what am I thinking—I haven't introduced you to our Malysh. Malysh, this is Madame Roubtzova. Her husband was Nicholas Roubtzov, the artist.'

'Was, but is now just a corpse in the ground,' Madame Roubtzova said. She didn't look up at Luka, remaining focused on separating the deck of cards.

Mathilde made a sympathetic noise in the back of her throat. 'Such a sad business. He worked on the interior of my house, and it's some of the best work I've ever seen.'

'He was certainly a talented man,' Maxim said, his eyes still hard as he looked at his hostess. 'I don't think I ever had a bad word to say about him.'

'Who would? I was heartbroken when he passed away, and the thought of his wife and daughters having no one to look after them was too much to bear,' Mathilde continued. 'So I asked Madame Roubtzova to join my household, and insisted on her girls coming to live with us too.'

'In the servants' quarters.' The words were quiet, spoken through lips so tightly pursed they had almost disappeared.

The silence that followed would have been uncomfortable if the Grand Duke Sergei hadn't jumped in to disperse it. 'Mathilde dotes on those girls. She's always buying them pretty dresses or trinkets just to see the look of delight on their faces. Isn't that right, my sweet?' His smile was one of adoration, and Mathilde took the hand he held out to her.

While the other guests admired their hostess's generosity, the Grand Duke Andrei studied the garden intently, averting his gaze from his lady's other lover.

Luka's stomach churned. It was all too much: the champagne, the rich food that must have cost a small fortune, the cloying scent of cigarette smoke mingling with expensive perfumes. While the others toasted Mathilde's health with vodka in gold-painted glasses, Luka pushed his chair back and excused himself. He didn't wait to hear whatever snide comment Maxim responded with, or Madame Roubtzova's careless dismissal as she started dealing the cards. Luka made his way to the far end of the garden and gulped the air as if he could drink it. Its saltiness made his mouth dry, but the surrounding scents of jasmine and lilac calmed him. These were smells that he would be able to find in his own world. He brushed his hand along one of the squat bushes that lined a pebbled pathway, feeling the need to grasp onto something real, as though it would steady his spinning mind.

He walked down the path, trailing his hand along leaves that were almost blue in the darkness. A feather caught his attention, tangled up in a shrub. He plucked it out and twirled it between forefinger and thumb; it was small, neat and perfectly white.

'What have you got there?'

Luka didn't need to look to know that the voice belonged to Valentina.

'It's just a feather.'

'Can I see it?'

He turned and held it out for her. Her fingers brushed against his as she took the feather, and he almost jumped at the touch.

'It's white,' she said, and he heard the change in her voice. 'Do you know what it reminds me of? The white feathers Odette wears in *Le Lac des Cygnes*.'

It was not something Luka would have thought of. The world of the ballet seemed a long way from them tonight.

'I've always wanted to dance Odette, you know.' Valentina spoke in a low, distant tone.

Her back was towards the party and the light from the lanterns, so Luka couldn't see her expression properly; just the outline of her hand as she caressed her cheek with the feather. Her chin-length hair glowed a little, like an unearthly halo. He wondered how much champagne she'd had to drink.

'Perhaps it's a sign,' he suggested, and found himself lowering his voice to match hers, even though no one was near to hear them.

'A sign of what?'

'That you will dance Odette. One day soon.' He didn't know why he was saying it, but he had an uncanny feeling that this woman—the dancer who symbolised everything he wanted to achieve—needed comfort.

Valentina's hand stilled. 'Do you really think so?'

'I do.'

Without thinking, Luka took a step closer to her, and the hand that held the feather fluttered down to her side in an unintended port de bras. Luka's head swam dizzily, but he made himself stand still. He couldn't be sure, but he thought she was on the verge of saying something more to him, something important, perhaps that she couldn't share with anyone else ...

'What are you two up to?'

They both jumped. Maxim had circled around them, hidden by the shadows. His voice was jovial, but even the darkness couldn't obscure how his face had turned to flint. Valentina didn't appear to notice. She broke into a smile and leaned into Maxim so he had to tuck an arm around her to keep her upright.

'Look what Malysh found,' she said, waving the feather in front of his moustache.

'A feather. How thrilling.'

'Ah, but you don't know what it means. It's a sign.'

'A sign of what?' Even though he was talking to Valentina, Maxim didn't take his eyes off Luka.

'That one day I'm going to dance Odette. You know, from *Le Lac des Cygnes*.'

Finally Maxim broke his gaze from Luka and looked down at Valentina. He squeezed her with the arm that encircled her waist. 'My dear, you'd make a far superior Odile than you ever would Odette.'

Odile was the other side of the dual role in *Swan Lake*: where Odette was sweet, delicate and innocent, Odile was flashy and cruel. Her power lay in her ability to deceive and seduce, and every moment of her dancing was cold, calculated and brilliant.

Valentina was silent for a moment, then she gave a hard laugh that sounded like it could break the night air. 'You're right, of course. It's lucky I have you to remind me of these things.'

Maxim leaned down and kissed her, but his eyes once again flickered to where Luka was still standing, watching.

'Let's go to bed,' he said, breaking away from the kiss. 'Mathilde has won all the money from me that I'm comfortable losing tonight, and I'm tired.' He pushed Valentina ahead of him towards the house.

Luka watched them go, not sure what had just happened. It was as though he'd been caught up in some kind of game to which he didn't know the rules nor how to win, and hadn't wanted to play in the first place.

He didn't belong among these people. Tomorrow he would make his excuses and leave, no matter what Mathilde Kschessinska said.

Valentina sat in front of the mirror, dabbing perfume onto the insides of her wrists. The scent was muskier than she usually liked, but Maxim had given it to her, so it was prudent to wear it. Besides, she'd sweat it off once she got on the stage in a couple of hours. The company hadn't ended up performing *La Perle* the previous year, as had been rumoured. But they were now, and Valentina had indeed got the role of one of the two Black Pearls. Maxim was triumphant. It was he who had made noises about the role being perfectly suited to her, whispering in well-placed ears and buying timely flutes of champagne.

He stood behind her now, watching her dress, as he so often did. She pretended not to notice.

'How is my Odile feeling? Prepared for the big performance? Black Pearl now; Black Swan next perhaps.' Maxim rested heavy hands on her shoulders.

Valentina saw her face tighten in the mirror and forced it to relax. He didn't mean anything by it.

'Careful, or I'll trick you into falling in love with me,' she said, leaning her head against his hand.

His fingers twirled the short waves of her hair. 'Perhaps you already have. That is Odile's trick after all, isn't it?'

Valentina could only hope so. Men these days were less inclined to marry without love, not unless the marriage brought them something valuable. She knew she had no such thing to offer.

Maxim kissed her on the temple, then told her to hurry up lest she be late. Valentina was relieved the edge had finally gone from his temper. He'd been agitated ever since they'd come back from the weekend at Mathilde's dacha. That feather incident had been a rare slip-up. She could imagine how it must have looked to Maxim, but it was not what he thought.

Since returning to the ballet, Valentina had noticed how Luka Zhirkov's dancing had moved from the realm of talent into something far more exquisite. He really might become someone worth knowing, not to mention a superlative dance partner. That was why she'd followed him into the garden: she'd decided it was worth making an attempt to build a connection with him. Instead she'd foolishly made a drunken confession about a dream only Maxim and Dimitri had ever known about. Luka's assurance that the feather was a sign had ignited the spark of hope she so desperately tried to keep in its hidden place, and she'd lingered too long, indulging herself.

She couldn't explain any of this to Maxim though. Only another dancer could possibly understand. And now the feather was hidden away in her candy box, where he would never find it.

CHAPTER EIGHT

Luka stood in the wings, nervously rising to demi-pointe and back down again. It was the opening night of a double performance of *Chopiniana* and *La Perle* and the company had already performed the former. He had been given the short but vital male part in the Yellow Pearl pas de deux in the latter. A million reminders raced through his mind: keep the shoulders low and free of tension; rotate from the hips and not just the feet; lengthen the torso so his head reached towards the ceiling.

His first few steps onto the stage made his knees weak, and he felt he might collapse in his ballet slippers. Then he was moving over the black expanse, forgetting all thoughts as he turned trust over to his body and the hours of training and rehearsal. The footlights faded, the harsh make-up on the faces around him became the features of various sea creatures, and the painted scenery brought to life an underwater grotto. If he'd cared to notice he could have seen the gleam of white shirt-fronts in the audience. But he was focused on his partner, the Yellow Pearl, and no longer realised there was an audience.

La Perle came to a close and the audience rose to its feet in rapturous applause. Luka's heart swelled as he took his bow, the applause bubbling over him the way champagne did over his tongue. He knew his dancing had been at its best that night: his body had obeyed his every command and he'd felt elation run through him when, at the height of every jump, he'd seemed to hover mid-air for a second. There had been a tense moment when his sleeve had ripped at the seam, but even that hadn't been able to dull the triumph that thrilled through his arms, legs and torso with every movement.

The way the audience cheered when Luka took his bow was almost as intoxicating as the dancing itself had been. He didn't want it to end, but one bow was enough. There were other, more important people who had to take the stage. He waited in the wings, watching the soloists and principals take their turns, repressing the urge to run back out and drink in the audience response again himself.

Finally, it was Mathilde's turn to curtsey. Although the role of the Yellow Pearl had been created for her, tonight she had danced the larger White Pearl. In the past the role had been given to international guests, who would perform with the company for special limited runs. Mathilde had report-edly been determined that one day it would be hers. And, as with most things, she'd got her wish. Roses, violets and tulips landed at the ballerina's feet as she bent her knee. It should have been a joyful moment, but Luka could see the cold look in her eyes as she glanced at the flowers. A bad taste formed in the back of his throat.

The applause continued, and Mathilde curtsied deeper, her knee not quite touching the floor as no royalty was pres-ent. Finally, the entire company took their last bow together, and the dancers began to trickle away to the dressing rooms to wipe the thick greasepaint from their skin and transform themselves from mythical characters back to their everyday selves. Luka hovered where he was, still watching Mathilde. She had walked offstage with her smile in place, but the second she was hidden by the black curtains of the wings, it dropped. She threw down the bouquet of roses she'd only moments ago picked up.

'Stupid halfwits,' she spat, her painted lips lifting in a sneer. Those around her froze, the sudden sharpness in her voice making them uncertain. 'Can't anyone read a newspaper any more? I asked for no flowers while the war continues.'

'Perhaps the people wanted to show their gratitude anyway,' the *régisseur* suggested, his tone placating.

'Yes, but you know who the newspapers will hold at fault. This will be just another example of my excess. I'll be deemed unpatriotic.' Mathilde's eyes were flaming, and she looked especially impressive in her exaggerated stage make-up with elongated brows. Unlike the rest of the dancers, the jewels on her white tutu and in her delicate tiara were not just coloured glass.

Not wanting to hear more of the prima ballerina's ingratitude, Luka slipped away to join the other male corps dancers in their shared dressing room. He liked to move slowly after a performance, taking time to rid himself of his character with every piece of his costume. Tonight he slowed his pace even more than usual. Luka knew that his own performance would receive little, if any, attention in the newspaper articles that would appear the following day. But if his father read them he would still know that his son had been part of an evening that seemed to ignore the increasing poverty of the war-restricted country; a direct insult to those who were fighting to save it. He thought of Pyotr's letters and the light tone he tried to maintain as he described squabbles over barely edible food and competitions to see whose boots could hold together the longest. How many pairs of boots, how many meals, would the money spent on those flowers tonight have bought?

Such thoughts dulled his exhilaration as he put on his ordinary clothes. The dressing room was empty by the time he had finished changing, the others either rushing off to join the party Mathilde was holding at Kiuba, or heading home. Jamming his hat on his head, Luka made his way out of the dressing room. His intention was to go straight home, tuck himself into bed and try to forget the worries that plagued him. He wanted to relive his performance in his mind, to pick apart every last movement to see where he could improve.

Just as he got to the stage door, he realised he'd left the latest letter from his brother in the dressing room. He hesitated; the company carriages would be waiting outside, the other corps and low-ranking coryphées and soloists impatient to get going, not ranking high enough for a private company carriage. But to lose the letter would be just as bad as losing his gloves had been. The doorman eyed him curiously; with a sigh, Luka asked him to signal to the carriages that he wouldn't be long, then made his way back to the dressing room.

His bench space was littered with spare pairs of shoes and pots of face paint, and he shifted them aside to search. A program for that evening's performance lay beneath the detritus, and between its pages was tucked the letter. Luka gratefully slid it underneath his clothes, next to his chest. Turning to go, he was halted by the sound of raised voices. They were coming from Mathilde's dressing room.

The only way out was past the open door to the dressing room. Treading as lightly as if he were once again on stage, Luka swiftly passed by, hoping not to be seen. But at the last minute, curiosity got the better of him and he glanced back. Valentina and Maxim were standing inside the room, at an angle to the doorway, Mathilde and her dresser apparently already gone. Valentina's back was pressed against the make-up strewn bench, her face obscured from view by her protector. Maxim had a hold of her shoulders, his fingertips disappearing into the folds of her dress. His face, blotchy and ugly, was thrust into hers. Valentina's hands were against his chest, patting him in an awkward soothing motion.

'Why didn't you tell me not to?' Maxim snarled at her. 'Did you think it would be funny to make a fool out of me?'

'No one thinks you're a fool, Maxim. It was all my fault. I just didn't think.' Valentina's voice, in contrast to Maxim's, was oddly devoid of emotion.

'I know you didn't think!' He shook her shoulders.

Luka's first instinct was to intervene. He took a step forward, then hesitated. Valentina was a proud woman who, according to Xenia, liked to remain superior; she might not appreciate someone witnessing this vulnerable moment. But how could he walk away after seeing such violence in her protector's manner?

Before he could make a decision, Valentina's head shifted and her mouth dropped open into a little 'o' of surprise as she spotted Luka. She instantly tried to cover it, closing her lips tightly and looking back at Maxim, but it was too late. He'd seen her shock of recognition.

He turned to face Luka. Never in his life had Luka seen a man's face contort into such an ugly expression. Maxim's bottom lip drew down unhappily, while the top one lifted in a sneer. The angry red blotches on his face deepened, and he breathed through his nostrils so raggedly that Luka could see the hairs of his moustache shiver. His eyes were as cold and hard as stone.

He stared at Luka for a moment, then with a deliberate effort pulled his face into a smile that was even uglier. 'Malysh ... I might have known it would be you. Would you excuse us— we're going to be late for Mathilde's party.'

He reached behind him, grabbing Valentina's forearm so abruptly that she jumped. Her feet automatically followed her protector, her eyes carefully trained away from Luka. He moved to the side to let them pass, afraid to brush up against either of them. It was obvious that it was costing Maxim a great deal of effort to keep a grip on his emotions.

'What about ...?' Valentina gestured at the now empty dressing room. The floor was littered with colourful petals, confetti surrounding the naked green stems they'd been torn from.

'Leave it.' Maxim's voice was cold. 'Someone else will clean it up. And like you said, there were mountains of other flowers, so no one will notice.'

The last word sounded like a challenge. Valentina raised her eyes to meet Maxim's and they stared at each other for a moment.

Eventually, she nodded. 'Right.' Her tone was soft, compliant.

With a sharp tug on her arm, Maxim pulled her down the corridor. Neither of them said goodbye to Luka. He waited another moment after they'd disappeared from sight; he wanted to make sure he was alone before he dared to move again.

Once sure of his solitude, he stepped into the flower-strewn dressing room. He kneeled and picked up a couple of soft pink petals, rubbing them between forefinger and thumb. He couldn't tell what kind of flowers they were, but by the sheer number of petals he was sure it had been an expensive bouquet. He ran his fingers through the mess, searching for the card he knew must be there somewhere. The edge of his hand brushed against something thin and hard; he barely had to read it to know it was from Maxim. It contained the usual generic congratulations a ballerina of Mathilde's status would expect.

Luka stood up and ran his finger along the edge of the card, staring at the wreckage of the bouquet that had accompanied it. Such a small thing to get upset over, and such a violent reaction.

Valentina chewed the inside of her cheek as she followed Maxim away from Mathilde's dressing room. Her shoulders hurt from where he'd dug his fingers into them, but she paid it no mind. She'd learned that Maxim's temper rose quickly, blowing in like a snowstorm no one saw coming, but it also disappeared just as quickly, leaving little trace that it had ever been there in the first place. It was an uncomfortable but fleeting price to pay for the kind of influence and roles she could never have got by relying on her talent alone. Besides, it had been her fault really. She should have told him about Mathilde's patriotic wish not to receive flowers. Of course, there had been the announcements in the newspapers. But Maxim wrote for the newspapers; he couldn't be expected to read them too.

'Where's your cape?' Maxim said abruptly, stopping.

'My cape?' She'd been wearing a sable fur cape earlier, but it wasn't around her shoulders now. 'I must have left it in my dressing room before ... before we went to Mathilde's room. I'm sorry. I'll fetch it. It won't take me a moment.'

'No.' He stilled her with one hand. 'I'll go. You wait here.'

He kissed her on the cheek; his lips were cool even though his skin was still flushed. Valentina could tell he was already coming off his temper. By the time they got to the party he would be back to his usual self, probably suffering remorse for the way he'd spoken to her.

She leaned against a wall as she waited for Maxim to return, absent-mindedly practising some petits battements. Her movements were restricted by her heeled boots, but she didn't really notice. She was too busy remembering Luka's expression. He was too young to understand what life was like for a man of Maxim's status; how quickly it could all crumble if he made even one wrong move. She hoped Luka would have the decency to keep what he'd witnessed to himself. If he didn't and Maxim found out, the shame of it would be almost too much for him to bear. And much of the blame would land on Valentina.

Luka was placing the card on Mathilde's dressing table when a voice made him start. 'That doesn't belong to you.'

He turned to see Maxim Sergeivich leaning in the doorway, a woman's fur cape draped over one arm. His face was shadowed by the doorframe and Luka was glad he couldn't see his expression.

'I know, I was just returning—'

'What is it you think you saw tonight?'

Luka faltered. They both knew what he had seen. Did Maxim want him to detail it, or was he looking for a way to forestall damage to his reputation? Luka chose his next words carefully.

'I suppose I saw something that isn't my business.'

'Close, but incorrect.'

Maxim took a step into the dressing room. Luka had expected his face to be contorted into fury, as it had been during his confrontation with Valentina; but it was cool and detached, that superior glint Luka disliked so much lighting his eyes. The impulse to step back gripped him, but he resisted.

'You saw nothing.'

'Nothing?' Luka couldn't keep the disdain from his voice.

Maxim's lips twisted into a wolfish smile. 'You are still so new to this world. It would be a shame for one so promising to find himself released from his contract.'

The earth began to fall away beneath Luka's feet. His breathing quickened, and his fingers reached for the bench behind him to steady himself. Maxim didn't really have the power to do that. Did he?

'You know Valya wouldn't be with me if I didn't have the power to influence the ballet,' Maxim said. He ran two fingers over his moustache, his gaze fixed on Luka. It seemed he wanted an answer.

Luka swallowed, willing his throat not to stick, his voice not to shake. Fear and loathing were battling inside him, but he didn't want this man to know he had rattled him.

'I saw nothing.'

Maxim laughed. Of course he knew he'd rattled Luka. The predatory edge dropped from his smile; he had what he wanted

now. He reached forward, making Luka flinch, but all he did
was slide the card off Mathilde's dressing table and pocket it.
He turned away, the heels of his shoes loud in the empty space,
then paused in the doorway.

'Oh, and Malysh? There's no need for Valya to ever know
about our little tête-à-tête. Not unless you want to encoun-
ter an unfortunate accident which will damage your precious
dancer's feet beyond repair.'

Luka's jaw tightened so much he thought his teeth might
break. He was burning with rage towards this man: for his
threat to undo all of Luka's dreams on a whim, and for the
cowering fear he'd incited. He managed to choke out a sound
that Maxim took as an affirmative.

'Good boy.'

Luka had to stop himself from hurling one of Mathilde's
unwanted bouquets at the man's retreating back.

CHAPTER NINE

Winter 1915

Xenia sat smiling between Luka and his father in the troika, her legs tucked under the seal fur coverlet Luka had given her to keep warm, hands hidden in an ermine muff. The buildings around them, normally stained black from the factory chimneys, had taken on a new beauty under the crisp snow. People were everywhere. Most were on foot, and Luka watched them through the cloudy mist of his own breath, reminded of Christmases past. His family had never been able to afford transport, instead trudging over the icy roads, the noise of the crowds around them amplifying their own silence. Luka wished Pyotr were here to experience this. From his comfortable spot in the troika, he was able for the first time to truly enjoy the spectacle of Petrograd's midnight streets blanketed in snow, yet alive and swarming with crowds. The view reminded him of the Kingdom of the Shades in *La Bayadère,* where the entire female corps came onto a blue-lit stage in frothy tutus and slowly performed a series of repeated lilting steps—posé arabesque, fondu—over and over again until the stage was covered with a snow-white swaying crowd.

The sleigh jostled Luka closer to Xenia, and the warmth of her skin seemed to filter through her heavy coat to his own. As he watched the steam rising from the flanks of the three side-by-side horses before them and breathed in their earthy, hard-working smell, Luka felt that perhaps the world wasn't such a bad place after all. Their prayers would be heard, and the men would come back from the war victorious, his brother among them. Pyotr would find a way to make him laugh at Maxim's threats and they'd fade into nothing more than a distant, unpleasant memory. Food would become plentiful, and Russia would be at peace. On a night like this, it could almost be believed. It was, after all, a night for miracles.

Initially, Luka had regretted asking his father if Xenia, whose own family was ill and therefore off-bounds to someone in the Imperial Russian Ballet, could spend the Christmas celebrations with them. But his father had warmed to Xenia after she spoke about her own father being at the front— oblivious to the fact that he was in the artillery department and not likely to see a day of fighting. He hadn't snapped when Xenia had taken over setting the table with the white tablecloth, hay, candle and *pagach*. Perhaps he'd been glad of her presence to fill the gap left by Pyotr. They had made the blessings and thanksgiving with quiet solemnity, and when the time came to break their fast, his father had refrained from declaring that it was greedy and wasteful to serve all twelve of the traditional dishes in this time of shortage. Luka had paid triple the usual price for the food, but as they'd dined on slow-cooked beans, mushroom soup, fresh dates, figs, nuts and *kutya*, washed down with wine so dark it stained their lips, he'd thought it a worthy way of giving thanks for all this year had brought him.

The troika lurched to a stop near the red-brick façade of the Temperance Church of the Resurrection of Christ, and Luka stepped down, his ankles disappearing into the snow. He could smell the ice in the Obvodny Canal behind. He reached up to help Xenia, but she was already being handed down on the other side by his father. Luka was surprised the old man remembered chivalry. He'd always been gentle towards his wife, but Luka had thought it a result of her influence. Her kindness had been infectious even to the most hardened of souls.

The church's wide interior was bare of ornamentation, and the overhead concrete arches supporting the central cupola lent an appropriate gravity to the occasion. The pews were only filled to halfway up the nave, and Luka realised the worshippers were mostly women, children and old men. Xenia's hand slipped into his to give it a reassuring squeeze, and he wondered if she had noticed too.

They slid into one of the pews, the hard wooden seat cold beneath their legs even through their clothing. Luka was making sure Xenia was comfortable and didn't see the woman standing before him at first. It was Xenia's odd expression, a widening of her eyes as the corners of her mouth tightened, that made him look around.

The woman was dressed in a worn sheepskin *shuba*, and Luka knew instinctively she was a factory worker. She had that perpetually underfed hollowness to her face and a lack of hope in her eyes that made her fit in with this crowd in a way Luka no longer did. He offered her a smile, wondering if perhaps she had seen him dance and wanted to say hello. It would be the first time anyone had ever recognised him and it coming from the area he'd grown up in would be some kind of validation. But the smile died as he saw what she held in her hands, and his stomach flipped like he might vomit. It was a white feather, so like the one he'd handed to Valentina at Mathilde's country house. But this was not a symbol of a dream waiting to be fulfilled.

The woman silently held the feather out. Trembling, Luka lifted one hand. Xenia put her hand on his arm, trying to stop him, but he didn't hesitate. With face burning and insides emptier than they'd ever been despite the earlier feast, he took the feather. The woman took her seat, and Luka lowered the feather into his lap. His eyes prickled, but he would not let any tears fall.

'You shouldn't have accepted it,' his father growled.

'Why not? It's true, isn't it?'

'It's not her position to say so.'

The fact his father hadn't disagreed with the woman didn't escape Luka. The service began and he kept his head bowed; not giving thanks, but looking at the symbol of cowardice that had been bestowed on him.

As soon as they left the church, Xenia snatched the feather out of Luka's hand and thrust it into the snow, where it got lost among the sea of white. But she couldn't rid him of his shame, which was a greasy layer coating his insides. The ride back home had lost all its magic. The feather was burned on his palms, and he kept checking them for welts. No one spoke until they were almost home, when his father broke the thick silence.

'Have you received a letter from your brother recently?'

Luka sensed the concern underneath the casual tone. He tried to think back to the last time he'd got word from Pyotr. 'Not for a number of weeks. Why?'

His father scratched at his beard; his eyes were scrunched, but was that fear Luka saw lurking within them? 'I haven't heard from him since then either.'

The troika came to a stop. Luka was shivering, but he didn't move from his seat. Neither did his father.

'I'm sure it's not easy getting letters out,' Xenia said in a quiet voice. 'Or perhaps he's even on his way home.'

'Perhaps.' His father dismounted.

Ugly thoughts were trying to creep into Luka's mind. He hadn't questioned the long stretch since Pyotr's last letter for he knew his brother wrote to their father more often. But to know that he hadn't written to him either … it was impossible not to think of the horror stories from the front, the increasing number of deaths being reported every week. Enemy bullets competed with frostbite and starvation to steal a soldier's life first. His chest was tight, and Luka distracted himself by paying the man he'd rented the troika from, then headed inside. His father was stomping snow off the *valenki* that had been a Christmas gift from Luka. Snatching up the bottle of vodka Xenia had given him, he nodded to their guest. 'That's me finished for the night.' He clambered up the few rickety wooden steps to the platform on top of the stove, and pulled the curtain closed with a hacking cough.

'*Spokoynoy nochi*,' Xenia called after him.

She stood next to the stove as Luka silently lit it. He would have liked to have left it burning while they were out so they'd have a warm room to come back to, but his father hadn't had enough coal. Luka had offered to go out to buy some, but was told in a sharp voice that if any were readily available Vladimir would have bought it himself.

'I look a wreck, don't I?' Xenia said softly. She put a hand to her hair, smoothing down the dark strands that had come up when she'd taken off her rabbit-fur turban.

'Not at all.' Luka took the hat from her and placed it on the table. He removed his own coat, lost in thoughts that were too bleak to share.

'You seem withdrawn,' Xenia said, surveying him with concern. 'Is it your brother?'

Luka nodded, and tugged off his gloves to warm his hands on the stove. Even this small action pierced him with guilt, knowing there would be no hot stoves for Pyotr and the other men at the front.

He lowered his voice so his father wouldn't hear, even though he'd begun a slight, rattling snore. 'Xenia, do you look down on me for not going to fight in the war?'

She sighed, and Luka hated the look of pity on her face. 'Damn that feather and the silly woman who gave it to you. Don't pay any attention to it.'

'Why not? Even before she gave it to me, I've been struggling with myself. Why should I be exempt because of my talent for dance? Why don't I volunteer anyway, like a good patriot?'

'Luka, don't you think that if they needed more men out there, they'd call for them? That not even the ballet could prevent you being conscripted then?'

'I suppose so. But my father says—'

'Your father has high notions about how this country should work. That doesn't mean they're right, or even possible.' Xenia rubbed her hands together, chafing the cold out of them. 'There's nothing to say that you won't be conscripted anyway. Perhaps you've been given this time as a gift.'

'What for, though?' He wanted to believe what she was saying, but it was difficult when he couldn't think of one reason why he should be granted such a gift when others weren't.

'I didn't say the gift was just for you ...'

Luka stared at her, trying to understand what she meant.

A loud chorus of song interrupted the quiet moment, followed by an answering cough from his father.

'*Kolyadki*,' Xenia murmured, her dark lashes fluttering with amusement. She grabbed Luka's hand and pulled him to the apartment's single tiny window.

Luka pushed it open to the freezing night air, hoping the creak of the hinges wouldn't disturb his father. He was lucky to have a window—not many others in the building did. He and Xenia pressed themselves together so they could both peer at the ground below. A group of women dressed in costumes to resemble manger animals stood there singing carols, as Xenia had guessed.

As they watched, Luka was conscious of Xenia still holding his hand. Hers was delicate and warm in his, and when the time came to pull away so he could throw a few coins down to the singers, he was reluctant to do so. The coins collected and their thanks shouted up, the singers trailed away. Luka pulled the window shut once more, blocking out the frost. He could still hear the women's voices travelling across the frozen night air.

When he turned around it was to find Xenia watching him, her eyes unreadable. The intensity of her gaze made him flustered.

'Will you be ... That is, I don't think you should go. Home. Tonight, I mean.' Almost immediately he realised his words could be misunderstood and rushed to correct them. 'I mean, it's so cold out there. And it's almost three o'clock. I don't think it would be safe for you to go back to your apartment at this time of night. We've already seen how on edge people are, and in such fine clothes you won't entirely blend in ...'

'Why Luka, are you worried about me?' Xenia teased. She was standing so close to him now that her long skirt brushed against his trouser legs.

'Of course I am. I ...' Luka didn't know what to say next. He stared at her pink face, the heat from the stove finally beginning to seep through his clothes, and felt an urge to lean in closer. He struggled with himself; the food and wine, his father's unusual lack of resentment, and his desire to push away the memory of the white feather were addling his mind. He shouldn't do anything stupid.

'If I don't go home, where will I stay?' she said softly.

Luka wondered if she could possibly be thinking the same thing he was.

'I sleep on the floor when I stay here.' He gestured as if Xenia wasn't able to see the floor for herself. 'It's not as warm as on top of the stove, of course, but it's quite comfortable with a few blankets and pillows.'

'That's you sorted then. What about me?' She moved closer. One of her legs was bent so her knee was resting between his.

It was strange. Xenia was his friend, the only one he had at the ballet—he didn't count Mathilde's patronising companionship, and the men were one another's competition, making friendship difficult—yet Luka wanted to run his hands over her neck, her shoulders, down to her waist. He wanted her to lie down on the blankets in front of the stove with him. He wanted it so much he ached, but still he didn't say anything. For underneath this desire was a fierce terror that lust was clouding his mind. She could be disappointed in him for thinking of her like that; perhaps she might refuse to be his friend any longer. His body quivered with indecision and he was unable to make a sound.

'It looks like there's room for two,' she said.

When he didn't say anything in response, she gazed at him steadily and undid the top button of her sailor-collar blouse.

Luka ran his fingers over Xenia's bare arm, enjoying the way her skin erupted into goosebumps at his touch. She was soft, like some expensive fabric that could only be bought in Paris. Leaning in close, he kissed her elbow and was rewarded with a soft laugh.

'You're supposed to be sleeping,' she whispered.

'I know. But I find it hard to sleep when you're beside me like this.'

'Hush, your father might hear now we no longer have our heads buried under the blankets.'

Xenia rolled over to face him, and for a second her features were those of another dancer—one more used to the feel of fur and lace against her skin than his father's rough blankets, her face discoloured with old bruises. Luka jerked back. He didn't know where the vision had come from.

It was true that the scene he'd witnessed between Valentina Yershova and her protector had played on his mind ever since, unsettling him. He'd made a forced promise to keep it secret, but had been unable to stop himself from scanning the soloist's face for bruises whenever he caught a glimpse of her. He had never seen a mark on her; that ugly moment might have been an aberration. Still, Luka found himself pondering it in the most unlikely moments. Like now.

Xenia, registering his shift away, tried to disguise her crestfallen look. 'Is something the matter?' she whispered.

'No. Nothing at all.' Luka bent his head to kiss her. But it was awkward, the imagined picture of Valentina disturbing the intimacy of just moments ago. He suddenly felt like his nose was in the way, or perhaps his lips were too dry.

Whatever it was, Xenia must have noticed, but she didn't say anything. She just lay in his arms, breathing rhythmically. Their heads were tucked underneath the *yolka*, its branches criss-crossing above them and the pine scent curling around their nostrils. Their feet almost touched the table at the other side of the small room. It was exactly how Luka and Pyotr used to lie in the days leading up to Christmas, each tucked against one side of their mother as she told them stories to a backdrop of their father's snores. Vladimir always slept the sleep of the exhausted.

'This isn't exactly what you want, is it?' Xenia whispered. She pushed her fingers through his damp hair, the gesture delicate, almost sorrowful.

Luka caught at her hand to kiss her knuckles. 'What do you mean?'

'Well, it might have been *what* you wanted,' her eyes crinkled at the corners in the dim light, 'but only in that moment. It's not what you really want.'

Luka spoke against her skin, tasting the sweat that had dried now they were still again. 'Of course it is.'

The words sounded hollow, but he was telling the truth. He knew he could live a good life with Xenia. She understood him: how conflicted he was about his brother, the war and his own desire to dance—an internal force that felt like it came from some otherworldly place. She was his best friend; she could be his family too. This was what he wanted. He was almost sure of it.

As if able to hear his thoughts, Xenia spoke again. 'I know you think that right now, Luka. But I'm older than you, and perhaps that's why I can see things with more clarity. And I know: this isn't what you want.'

'Oh, really?' Thinking she was joking, he added lightly, 'Tell me then, what do I want? Seeing you know so much better than I do.'

Xenia changed position so she was lying on her front, her chin resting on her folded-up arms. She was no longer looking at him. 'Passion.'

'Didn't we just share that?'

'Not that kind. Tell me, Luka, have you ever had to question your love for the ballet? Or is it just there, burning so brightly you know it can't be ignored?'

He didn't answer.

'How could a woman ever compete with that, unless you felt the same passion for her?'

'It's not a competition,' he said.

'All of life is a competition, my Luka, and I've been playing at it long enough to know when I'll be on the losing side.'

Luka lay back. Through the scented boughs of the *yolka* he could make out the few ornaments his mother had made. They were cheap and hadn't worn the passage of time well, but his father still placed them on the tree every year. He knew Xenia was right. He didn't love her the way he loved dancing; nor the way his father had loved his mother.

The sweet pleasure that had lingered in his body had almost faded as he said, 'What do we do now?'

'This wonderful night, this precious moment—' Her voice caught and she looked down, her unfashionably long hair making a thick curtain that masked her face.

Tonight was the first time Luka had seen her hair down; usually it was tied back for classes and rehearsals, or hidden underneath a wig for performances. Only moments ago he'd enjoyed its long silkiness, running his fingers through it and twining it between his fists. Gently, he pushed it back over her shoulder; it stayed there briefly before sliding back.

With a sound like a laugh, Xenia shook her hair out of her face and looked at him again. 'Tonight is just that, Luka. Just one night.'

'You mean you don't …?'

'No, I don't. If we leave it as just tonight, my heart remains protected. I can pretend that for one night I had everything I wanted, that everything was perfect.'

They lay together in a silence marred only by his father's staccato cough. Luka wondered how he could have believed, even for a moment, in the possibility of miracles.

'I suppose this isn't quite what you wanted either then,' he murmured.

'Not quite. But I got to experience every last bit of you. That's enough for me.'

Xenia moved closer again, her face resting on his neck. Their naked bodies were pressed together so tightly that her heart beat rapidly against his own.

'I should leave, before your father wakes and finds me still here,' she whispered.

'Alright,' Luka said, but he knew his day would be far emptier without her.

CHAPTER TEN

Winter 1916

Valentina swallowed the bile that was swimming at the back of her throat and pressed the handkerchief she'd soaked in lavender to her nose and mouth. It didn't block out the sweet, rancid smell, but went some way to covering it. A nurse had just finished lancing the raw wound where the remainder of the soldier's leg had been, and the Grand Duchess Olga was now bathing it with warm water from a chipped china basin. The white *apostolnik* she wore left only her face exposed, and her dark tapered eyebrows were drawn together in concentration over her strikingly pale blue eyes. Her nursing uniform and apron were stained with substances Valentina didn't want to identify. She wondered how this young woman who had grown up in palaces could stand the sights or stench of the hospital.

'Perhaps you would like to hold his hand while I finish?' the Grand Duchess Olga suggested. 'It might help to ease his pain having something to squeeze.'

Valentina's eyes widened. The man's curled fingers looked clean, but she was frightened of touching him all the same. Still, Maxim was by her side—he'd assumed any invitation from the imperial family must include him—and he wouldn't be pleased if she refused such a small request from the Grand Duchess. Reluctantly, she peeled off her glove and stretched trembling white fingers towards the soldier's hand. His fingers were cold and didn't curl around hers the way the Grand Duchess Olga had suggested they would. The soldier's eyes opened and a brief flash of accusation told her he knew her concern was not for him, then they squeezed tight again as he twisted in breathless pain.

Valentina turned her head away, but there was no better place to look. To her right the hospital's matron was keeping a watchful eye over a man waking from the anaesthetic he'd been put under while surgeons tried to repair his shrapnel-torn face. On the other side were the rest of the twelve beds that made up Mathilde Kschessinska's hospital for wounded soldiers. The building had originally been a house, and the patterned wallpaper made an odd backdrop to the iron beds with their white linens, and the distraught expressions of the men who inhabited them. Mirrors and other glass surfaces had been removed from the building, so the soldiers would not be disturbed by their own shattered, unrecognisable appearances.

'I understand it can be confronting,' the Grand Duchess said gently. 'I asked you here to see if you might help me with another matter, though.'

'Your Imperial Highness?'

'I have been thinking that perhaps it would be nice to give a special ballet performance for the injured and recovering soldiers, to lift their spirits. You have been so kind to my sister Anastasia in the past, making her laugh, and Grigori Rasputin speaks highly of you.' Valentina sensed Maxim's smirk. 'I knew you were just the person to ask. I'm sure I could persuade Mamma to open the Hermitage to the soldiers were you to agree.'

Valentina's heart skipped, and she breathed slowly through her nose to hide her excitement. The Hermitage was the Romanovs' private theatre inside the Winter Palace, and dancers could only perform there by special invitation from the imperial family. It was an honour that all in the Imperial Russian Ballet aspired to.

'Your Imperial Highness is most generous,' Valentina said. 'I would be honoured. Perhaps I could dance some of the favourite variations from the classics, and a few pas de deux. I know someone who would make a wonderful partner.'

She carefully avoided looking at Maxim as she responded to the Grand Duchess; not because she was afraid of his expression, but because she didn't want him to see hers. It was Luka Zhirkov she was thinking of as a partner. She knew Maxim didn't like him, but his dancing held such promise. And, if she were honest with herself, she found him interesting. A man who didn't seem to fully realise his talent, who occasionally spoke his mind and was a terrible liar—his weak excuses to leave Mathilde's dacha that weekend had shown her that—was someone she rarely came across in her own circle. She pushed the latter thoughts away, though, telling herself her interest was only in how she could tie their names together in the eyes of the company, so that when his star began to rise, hers would be strengthened too. Just as Maxim did with Grigori Rasputin.

As little as he liked Luka, even Maxim would have to recognise this as a shrewd move. It was the kind of thing he himself would do, and Valentina thought with satisfaction that it would show him what a powerful team they could be. A wife who understood how to get ahead was a wife worth having.

Luka leaned against the gallery rail, watching the Imperial Ballet School's senior class below. Like him, many of those students would spend their lives going over the same exercises, striving for a perfection that would never come. Only the lucky ones, though. Those who didn't have the skill or the correct body would have to move on to something else, the ghost of that which they'd tried yet failed at evident in the grace of their posture and everyday movements.

Behind him, heeled shoes tapped against the floor. Luka didn't need to turn around to know it was Valentina—he could smell her musky perfume. As she came to stand beside him, her cool presence indicated that she'd only just entered the building. Spring was around the corner—the sound of the ice cracking in the River Neva heralded its arrival—but the air still held the last cold dregs of winter and people's skin and clothes carried the crisp scent of snow.

Luka wished Valentina would go away. He hadn't forgotten Maxim Sergeivich's threat; in fact, he'd been thinking a lot recently about how the great Vaslav Nijinsky had been expelled from the company and wondering if he too had been the victim of someone's dislike. If Nijinsky wasn't immune from being ordered to resign, no one was.

'Bringing back memories?' Valentina murmured. The necklace that hung to her waist clattered against the gallery rail and she put her pale hand up to still it.

Luka didn't answer at first, but the growing silence made him uncomfortable. It wasn't easy, like the silences between him and Xenia; rather it felt as if it was saying too much.

'Look at how the teacher can't take his eyes off the two front and centre,' he finally muttered.

Valentina's gaze went straight to them. 'It's understandable. They're very good.'

'They are. But now look at the young man second from the right in the third row.' He waited while Valentina's eyes found the boy; he wasn't as easy to pick out as the other two had been, his movements not demanding the same attention. 'He's not hiding in the back row because he hopes no one will see his faults. He's pushing forward; he wants to be seen so he can improve. But the teacher only has eyes for the front two, who are already skilled and don't need the extra help. Has it always been that way?'

He turned to look at Valentina. Her skin, always pale, had a washed-out sallow look to it, and dark circles like bruises were imprinted beneath her eyes. Perhaps the demands of both the ballet and pleasing a protector were taking their toll on her.

'Of course,' she said, and he heard the tiredness in her voice. 'Perhaps you never noticed when you were at the school because you were the one front and centre.'

'Perhaps.' Luka wasn't sure he liked the thought.

'Watching them reminds me of my audition day,' Valentina said softly. Her dark hazel eyes were still trained on the young dancers but they'd taken on a distant quality, as if she wasn't really seeing them. 'Mamma bought me a new pair of socks for it. They were the first new thing I'd ever owned, and when I put them on I was sure they'd transformed me into a glamorous adult. But when I got to the school and saw the other girls in their fancy ruffles and lace-trimmed dresses, the socks embarrassed me. Funny, isn't it? Nothing had changed, but all of a sudden my socks weren't beautiful any more.'

She paused, and seemed to realise that she was speaking about her personal life, a past usually kept tightly to her chest. An almost visible veil came over her as she turned to Luka. It reminded him of the first time he'd seen her in rehearsal—how quickly she'd changed from angry and confrontational to smiling appeasement. He felt the urge to stop the change, to expose the Valentina underneath, the person she'd allowed him to see for a second. But he didn't know how, and a second later it was too late. The Valentina Yershova the public knew was back in place.

'I've been looking for you,' she said. 'That friend of yours told me you might be here.'

'Looking for me?' he echoed in surprise.

She nodded, diamond and turquoise earrings swinging. 'I have a proposition for you. One that will no doubt assist in your career. I've been invited by the imperial family to put on a performance at the Hermitage for wounded soldiers. I would like you to partner me for a few pas de deux.'

Luka's mouth almost dropped open. An invitation from the Romanovs, a rare chance to dance at the Hermitage—Valentina had been understating it when she said it would assist his career. His mind flashed to Maxim and his threat. Luka would almost be guaranteed another contract renewal were he to dance at the Hermitage. Maxim wouldn't dare to openly criticise a dancer who'd been shown public approval by the imperial family.

Warily, he said, 'You could choose any man you wanted from the company to partner you.'

Valentina shrugged. 'Yes. I chose you.'

Luka didn't ask why. It didn't matter. There was no chance he would turn down this opportunity and the security it offered him.

They chose the Black Swan/Prince Siegfried pas de deux from Act III of *Le Lac des Cygnes* as the pinnacle of their Hermitage performance. It surprised Luka that Valentina didn't choose a White Swan piece instead. True, this pas de deux was one of the most spectacular in the entire ballet repertoire, but he knew how she yearned to dance Odette. Valentina was adamant, though. She said audiences responded with wild applause to the brilliant, sharp movements and daring risks the danc-ers took; and the wounded soldiers deserved such a spectacle, not the aching tragedy of Odette. The Black Swan would make them forget their pain, their nightmarish memories, if only for a moment. It was a touching sentiment, and one Luka didn't quite believe. He thought that perhaps she didn't want to dance the role of Odette by her own choosing. She wanted the recognition of the company bestowing it on her. If that were the case, it was something Luka could understand.

'Are you able to keep up?' Valentina asked him during their first rehearsal.

They were using one of the rooms at the Mariinsky, and she had somehow roped in a pianist—not the one who deliberately played too fast when she danced—to accompany them. Luka had only learned half of the pas de deux so far and Valentina's comment could have been seen as an insult. But as she stood before him, hands on her hips, damp curls springing out from beneath the scarf tied around her head, he didn't think she meant it as one. She wanted them both to be the best they could be. Nothing else was as important.

'I'll admit, it's more difficult than anything else I've danced before,' he said. 'But I will perfect it. I won't rest until I do.'

A rare smile blossomed on Valentina's face, and Luka thought he might even have heard a chuckle. He wanted to remind her that she'd once admonished him for laughing when they were practising, but decided against it. Who knew how long her good humour would last if he tested it.

'An admirable sentiment. I believe I made the right decision choosing you, Luka Vladimirovich Zhirkov. Now, over here, please, and place your hands on my waist.'

Luka obeyed.

CHAPTER ELEVEN

Spring 1916

'Are you mad?' Luka's father stared at his son as if he didn't recognise him, then grabbed his shoulder and pulled him inside the apartment.

Luka almost fell, but managed to catch himself with one hand on the back of a chair. His other hand held a half-loaf of bread.

'What? What did I do?'

His father ignored the question. He slammed the door, then crossed the tiny room to peer out the window. Luka asked again, but his father batted an impatient hand at him, still looking outside. Frustrated, Luka sat down at the dining table, dumping the bread on it.

'Look at that fool out there,' his father muttered. 'Strutting around thinking we don't know he's a member of the secret police. Like the green of his overcoat and galoshes don't give him away.'

He pushed away from the window, coughing as he walked to the table. Luka kicked out the chair opposite him, but his father took a step to the side and sat in a different one. His arms were folded across his chest, his hands tucked into his armpits.

'Is that what you're worried about?' Luka asked. 'The *okhrana*?'

'Of course not. They're always out there somewhere, trying to stop us from wanting more than this pitiful lot.' He gestured at the apartment. 'That'll never change. But you—do you know what could have happened because of that?' He nodded at the half-loaf as though it were something muddying up his table. 'You could start a riot carrying bread around so openly.'

The bread had cost Luka many hours in line, trying to ignore the wailing children behind him whose parents hadn't arisen as early and would likely miss out by the time they reached the front. When he'd finally wrapped his hands around the bread and breathed in its yeasty smell, it had been hard not to start breaking it up to share with those children right away. But even if he'd ripped it into the tiniest chunks possible, there wouldn't have been enough to go around. So he'd kept it to share with his father, knowing he had probably gone without bread for a long time too. He shouldn't have bothered.

Now, Luka wanted to snatch it and run back to the bakery's line where the loaf would be received like the gift it was supposed to be. But he forced himself to stay where he was, staring down at the table, marking its surface with his thumbnail. His father tore off a crescent of fingernail with his teeth and spat it on the ground. He began grumbling about the war, and Luka noticed the way he spoke had changed: there was no more pride in his voice; no more demands for Luka to join the fighting forces. There was only resentment. Neither of them had heard from Pyotr for months now, and each time Luka thought of this, panic tightened every muscle in his chest until he could barely breathe. The feeling of being able to do nothing, of knowing nothing about his brother's whereabouts or state, was an ache too difficult to confront, and he'd been glad of the distraction of the long hours spent rehearsing with Valentina for the Hermitage performance.

'I'm sorry,' he said, standing abruptly. The chair scraped on the floor, and his father winced at the sound. 'I should be going. I just wanted to give you that.' He gestured to the small loaf.

'Take it with you,' his father spat. 'I don't want it. It'll only make me a target for thieves.'

The words sounded hard to get out, and Luka saw hunger barely disguised beneath his father's anger. He was tempted to push the matter, to remind him that refusing the bread would not mean Pyotr wasn't going hungry, wherever he was. But he knew his father wouldn't take back his words now that he'd spoken them. He'd rather the bread go stale or mouldy. Irritation burbled within him, and Luka snatched the loaf off the table and stalked out of the apartment without saying goodbye.

Outside, he paused and looked around, hesitating. He didn't want to believe what his father said, but Vladimir knew this area and its people better than Luka did. It wasn't his home any more; he was no longer one of them. He tucked the bread under his coat so it was hidden from view. Just in case.

The streets of Petrograd bustled with people as Luka disembarked the tram to walk home. The air was balmy and soft, the pale evening light filled with an excited buzz. Nearing the cream-coloured Palace Theatre, Luka saw a crowd assembled outside. They were clearly patrons who should have been filing through the timber-framed doors to collect glasses of champagne and deposit coats and capes instead of milling around outside. Curious, he edged his way into the crowd, pushing past a tall lady who sent him an angry glare. He grimaced an apology at her, but kept moving until he emerged at the front of the crowd, where he finally saw what they were all staring at.

The crowd had formed a semi-circle around a young peasant woman who was wringing her hands and calling out forlornly in Russian. The rough brocade of her dress, once thick and warm, had worn away so much that in some places the lightness of her skin showed through. Her face, framed by a dark scarf, reminded Luka for some reason of his mother.

'*Khleb*,' the woman cried, her voice jagged. She spoke quickly, the words almost tripping over one another as she begged for a little money to buy bread.

'What is she doing here?' a disgusted voice next to him murmured. Luka looked around; it was the woman he'd accidentally jostled before, who had also made her way to the front of the crowd. Her hands were folded neatly on her stomach, and she didn't seem to be talking to anyone in particular. 'Don't they usually stay on their side of the city? Why on earth would she come here to beg? Dirty thing.'

It was true that beggars were rarely seen in this area. There was an unwritten law in Petrograd that, until now, had always been obeyed: the poor would stay within their own areas, moving from home to work to markets, and never venturing into the glistening inner-city world of the rich and privileged. They belonged where the tram tracks stopped and you had to wade through mud to get anywhere; where there was no electricity, and the nights were as black as the insides of your eyelids.

Both rich and poor had silently agreed on this so long ago that no one noticed the division any more—until now, when that border was suddenly crossed by one that didn't belong there.

A few people laughed and turned away from the begging woman as she reached out her hands to them. Others jumped back, frightened that her poverty might be catching.

'The police will be here soon,' a man behind Luka muttered. He sounded satisfied at the prospect.

The beggar was crying now, tears running silently down her face as her hands dropped to her sides in defeat. Luka thought of those he had ignored in the line at the bakery. What if this woman had been one of them? What if she had children waiting for her at home, not knowing if their mother would come back empty-handed?

'Here,' he said, stepping forward.

The sound of another voice speaking their native Russian made a few people arch their necks in surprise. Others gaped as Luka approached the woman, digging in his jacket.

'Please, take this,' he said, his voice soft as he held out the half-loaf he'd tried to give his father.

The woman's tears stopped flowing, resting on clean cheeks where she didn't bother to wipe them away. But she eyed him warily, poised to take flight if he moved too quickly or tried to hurt her. She half raised her hand, wanting to take the bread but afraid he might be playing a trick on her. He nodded encouragingly. The woman's hand darted out so quickly that Luka almost didn't see it, only felt the loaf slipping from his grasp.

A ripple of noise spread through the crowd, but Luka ignored it and smiled at the woman. She regarded him for a moment, then broke into a smile herself.

'*Bol'shoye spasibo*,' she said, taking a step forward and clutching his hands gratefully, one arm curled protectively around her loaf.

'*Pozhaluista*,' Luka replied. He glanced at the crowd and lowered his voice to a whisper, 'You should leave now, quickly. They'll have the police coming to take you away.'

She nodded, but didn't let go of his hands.

'Go now. Please.'

She thanked him one last time, her voice breaking with the weight of her gratitude—which only made Luka's guilt more intense—then turned to leave.

The crowd parted, afraid of touching her, and she walked through them, her feet making barely a sound. Her steps became more rapid as she hurried away. Luka wondered if she could feel the eyes of the crowd on her back as they watched her go. He thought he felt another set of eyes—those of the police, or perhaps even the *okhrana*, arriving with guns swinging at their sides—and he willed her to move faster.

When she finally turned a corner and was out of sight, Luka released the breath he'd been holding on to so tightly. He turned to go, not wanting to hear the angry accusations of encouraging the poor to come begging in the city that would surely be thrown at him. He wanted to get away from this scene and return home. But before he'd taken even four steps, two faces he hadn't noticed before came into view, and he stopped short.

Valentina was standing at the front of the crowd, her hand tucked into Maxim's elbow. She was staring at Luka, her eyes dark and unreadable. Maxim had one lip lifted in a sneer beneath his moustache, regarding Luka as if he were something dirty.

Luka wiped the palms of his hands against his trouser legs, and immediately wished he hadn't. It was as if he'd given Maxim exactly what he wanted.

The other man looked at him with a satisfied smirk, then whispered something to Valentina. He gestured towards the theatre. Valentina followed, but her head was turned over her shoulder, her eyes appraising.

Luka tried to smile at her, but either she didn't see or didn't want to respond.

Valentina stood backstage, nervously twisting her fingers together. Maxim had volunteered her to be one of the models for the Evening of Russian Fashion at the Palace Theatre, in which artists from all over the country were showcasing designs. The idea was to boost the morale of the people—or at least those who could afford a ticket—with a display of the best in Russian design and textiles. Valentina's dress had been designed by an artist under Maxim's patronage and she'd hated it from her very first fitting. The dress restricted her movements so that only her hands and wrists were free, reminding her of the winter coats, nicknamed 'penguins', they'd had to wear at the Imperial Ballet School. Ugly and impractical. Maxim had assured her the dress was a work of art, ahead of its time, but she couldn't remember ever feeling so ridiculous in a garment. The panels didn't match up, the lines of stitching were crooked, and worst of all the skirt was far too short to be decent, showing her ankles. Fine if she were a factory worker trying to save money on fabric, which was in short supply these days. But she wasn't, and neither was anyone who would be viewing the dress that night.

She sighed, and tried not to think about the dress. Around her were many faces she recognised. Tamara Karsavina and Lyudmila Mesaksudi-Barash were there, both of whom she'd shared the stage with before. Their dresses, to Valentina's eye, were ugly too. Karsavina's was at least a daring scarlet shade, but Ludmila's looked as though it had been made from old quilted scarves stitched together. Valentina snickered, but the sound died as she glanced down at her own dress again.

She turned her mind to the scene outside the theatre earlier, frowning as she recalled Luka Zhirkov handing his bread to the tear-stained beggar woman. She had learned during their hours rehearsing together that he was conscientious and determined, with a true passion for his art, yet she'd been surprised by his bold compassion in front of so many peers. His actions made her question her own disregard of the woman's plight. For although Valentina now belonged to the people who had ignored or laughed at the peasant woman, she could just as easily have found herself in the woman's place. If Mamma's petition for her to audition for the Imperial Ballet School hadn't been accepted … if she hadn't passed the audition … if she hadn't been accepted into the company … if her contract wasn't renewed every year …

A familiar tremor of fear ran through her, accompanied by a voice that told her her rightful place could still catch up with her one day. She knew the voice well. She could no longer tell if it belonged to Mamma or was her own—but it didn't matter. She listened to it every time it spoke to her, and used its message to renew her determination. She would please her protector so he never wanted to let her go. She would not let this life be snatched away from her.

Valentina moved into the wings and peered out at the vast expanse of the Palace Theatre's stage. Karsavina was walking towards her onstage, and with a lurch Valentina realised it was her turn to go on next. She ran her hands down her skirt, knowing it would do little to improve the look of the dress; then, with a steadying breath, she stepped out where the audience could see her. Chin tilted high in a deception of pride, Valentina walked to the centre of the stage, marked by a painted dot on the floor, and twisted right and left to allow the audience to see the dress from all angles.

She knew Maxim was out there somewhere; his eyes were a burn across her skin even though she couldn't see him. Much easier to make out was Grigori Rasputin. Comfortably ensconced in the imperial box and wearing his customary black coat, he sat with his hands folded neatly in his lap, leaning forward.

Valentina turned her back to the audience. She thought she heard a noise, but ignored it as she glided upstage, then downstage again, this time avoiding the stare of the monk. This was always how it was for her onstage; even when dancing, she was aware of the eyes upon her. She could never quite lose herself the way others seemed to, could never forget that she was just Valentina Yershova, born into a nothing family. The only time she succumbed fully to movement and character was when she was alone in her private studio, often in the dead hours of night when there were no sounds of life to distract her. This inability to let go was, she knew, the reason she would never be a truly great dancer.

Her attention was called back to the theatre by the sound of stifled laughter. It was muffled in a cough, but she recognised it for what it was. Her step faltered. Another quiet giggle followed, then another.

Valentina wanted to raise her chin even higher, but if she did she would be looking at the ceiling. Instead, she swept regally towards the wings, taking measured steps so no one would think she was running away from their laughter.

Maxim didn't even wait for Valentina to dismiss her dresser before unleashing his temper. He raged and snarled and spat insults at the audience, the artist, Valentina herself. Unable to rip the dress off her—it was too tightly fastened for that—he instead swept her belongings off the dressing table in one swift movement. Then he closed his eyes, taking deep breaths.

The dresser cowered against the back wall, eyes wide, mouth hanging open. Valentina knew that money would have to change hands again tonight to ensure her silence.

'Come on,' Maxim finally growled, marching to the door and yanking it open so forcefully it banged on the wall behind. 'Let's get this over with.'

'What ... what do you mean?'

Valentina's voice was tiny in the presence of her protector's fury, and he closed his eyes for a second, as if bracing himself against her stupidity.

'We have to stand out there and receive false compliments as though we can't hear them whispering behind our backs. You know that's how it's done. If we were in their position, we'd do the same, and damn well enjoy it too.'

He left, not bothering to close the door behind him.

After changing into her evening gown and paying the shaking dresser, Valentina followed Maxim into the warm golds and bronzes of the theatre's interior. Electric chandeliers, their lights made to look like candles surrounding a softly glowing orb, illuminated a crowd that competed with the elaborate glamour of the theatre's black and gold balustrades. Valentina's cheeks hurt from holding her false smile. Maxim was right— she could hear the whispers as she walked through the throng, detected the notes of vicious enjoyment. She kept moving, trying to avoid talking to anyone. She wasn't sure she'd be able to keep up her charade of unconcerned confidence if she had to speak.

She bumped into a very tall figure. As she turned, the hairs on her arms rose and it was no surprise to see Grigori Rasputin looking down at her in satisfaction. His lips twisted into a smile that would be more at home on the face of a snake, and his heavy brow was menacing as he held out his arm to her.

'Valentina. Your company for a moment?'

The monk's familiarity in using only her first name made Valentina squirm, as did the watchful eyes of those around them. She had no choice, though; she linked her arm through his and followed the path that opened up through the crowd.

'It was a pleasure to see you onstage again, even if not dancing. You cut a fine figure.'

'Thank you.' She had to force the words out of unwilling lips.

'I thought tonight would be an opportunity to discuss your Hermitage performance for the wounded soldiers.' Valentina shot him a questioning look, and he replied with an indulgent nod that was both paternal and patronising. 'The Tsarina has tasked me with overseeing her daughters' arrangements for the event. You know, it was I who suggested you model Maxim's artist's creation tonight. I can be a very beneficial friend.'

Valentina said nothing, and they continued to walk in silence, Valentina dwarfed by the man's great height. They passed Maxim, and she saw the quick jealousy flit across his face then disappear. Grigori Rasputin was the one man her protector could tolerate her being arm in arm with; his power and connections were valuable.

But what would the rest of the crowd think of her right now, she wondered—the artists, and the princes and grand duchesses who bore the name 'Romanov' but didn't consider Rasputin divine the way the imperial family did? It was no secret that the monk's popularity with the general public was declining. Too many felt he'd made himself far too comfortable in the Tsar's absence and was ruling through the Tsarina. Valentina noticed shoulders being turned slightly away, painted lips pressed together. They would not dare to do more, but it was enough.

Rasputin, however, seemed either oblivious to the tiny snubs, or didn't care. His interest was only in what pieces Valentina was intending to dance at the Hermitage.

Maxim hovered at the edge of her vision, clearly waiting for an invitation to join them. For a moment the tight muscles at the back of Valentina's neck relaxed. This evening might still be salvaged for her protector. But the monk never turned towards the man who had worked for him numerous times before, and Valentina couldn't find an opportunity to interrupt and make the invitation herself. And so the cloud on Maxim's brow darkened, and she knew she would have to face yet another rage when they were alone.

Valentina split the lemon neatly into two equal halves. Putting one aside, she picked up a silver spoon and scooped the pale flesh out of the other. The acidic smell stung her nostrils, and she tried not to breathe it in. There must have been a time when the smell of lemons hadn't made her stomach turn. But that time was long gone. She discarded the last of the flesh onto a delicate china saucer, then dipped the peel into a bowl of water. Once the remaining juice had been soaked from it, she rinsed it with vinegar to ensure it was as sterile as possible; then placed it on a piece of soft cloth to dry.

She realised she was slouching and forced herself to sit up straight. Developing rounded shoulders would be disastrous for her career. Besides, she should know better than to let what she was feeling on the inside affect her so obviously on the outside—but an invisible weight was pulling at her chest. Maxim was waiting for her to call him to her bed when she was finished. It was the only way she knew to placate him after he'd got himself so worked up, but her thorough preparations always caused him extra frustration and he refused to be in the same room until she was done.

Valentina sighed. She wished her mother were there. Registering what she'd just thought, Valentina made a sound that was only vaguely a laugh. She dug the silver spoon into the flesh of the second lemon half, wondering what was wrong with her. Her mother would slap both her cheeks for being self-indulgent; perhaps lock her in a cupboard until her self-pitying attitude had disappeared and obedience had taken its place once more.

No, what she truly missed was the sense of belonging to someone. Not the kind of belonging that came from the exchange of money or jewels, but something deeper. The way families belonged to each other, even if they sometimes wished they didn't.

Valentina placed the second lemon half next to the first, then sat cross-legged on her bed and pulled the blanket around her knees. 'Riches,' she whispered to herself. 'Money. Security. Safety.'

Looking at the bright yellow peels, she wondered what she would do if they stopped working. Did all children turn women into cold-minded, sharp-fingered shrews, or was that just what she'd done to her mother? *Baudruches* weren't an option, of course. They were supposedly effective at preventing babies, but had a reputation for being low class because of how widely used they were by prostitutes. They were also said to dull the man's pleasure. Valentina couldn't ask that of Maxim—why would he pay a fortune for her if he couldn't fully enjoy her? Rather than make her his wife, he'd just find some other dancer all too willing to satiate his desires.

Valentina wondered if Luka had ever had cause to use a *baudruche.* The thought had jumped into her mind before she could stop it, and her cheeks flamed. Luka was merely on her mind because she'd seen him outside the theatre.

She stood and stalked into the private room adjoining her bedroom. On the dark octagonal wooden table with gilt edges stood a framed photograph, and next to it a candle in a silver candlestick that had been a gift from the Mariinsky gallery a few years ago. Wax coated the top end, dripping down it like grotesque fingers. Valentina kneeled on the bright oriental rug that covered the entire floor, and lifted the candlestick, leaving a shining circle where it had stood. The table was coated so thickly with dust that she sneezed, and a little grey puff flew into the air and danced in front of the photograph. There was only a stub of candle left, and the wick took some time to catch. She exhaled softly, letting her breath cross the flame so it danced, then placed it back on the same dust-free circle and turned her attention to the framed photograph. It was a portrait of her mother. Cracks ran through the glass, splitting Mamma's eyebrows so she looked as though she were furious at the camera for daring to take her picture.

'Mamma?' Valentina whispered.

She held her breath, willing the candle flame to bring the photo to life. The sounds of the house faded around her, her entire concentration focused on the portrait. *Any minute now*, she thought. *Just a little while longer and she'll talk to me ...*

Nothing happened.

Valentina sighed. The exhalation almost extinguished the candle. Irritated, she licked her forefinger and thumb and squeezed the wick so the flame disappeared. She'd known it wouldn't work. Whatever magic the photo had held for her as a child was long gone. But still she was disappointed.

When Mamma had given eleven-year-old Valentina the photo, she'd told her it was to watch over her at the Imperial Ballet School; that through it she'd be able to see every action of Valentina's and know when she misbehaved. Valentina had been so convinced that she'd shied away from everything and everyone she thought might induce Mamma's anger. She didn't make friends, and was too scared to join in passing letters in class or sneaking into the maids' pantry to steal extra food. The other students found her cold and odd, and eventually they'd given up trying to tempt her to join their fun.

And then Mamma had died, right in the middle of Valentina's graduation performance. The shock of the sudden loss was compounded by the discovery that Mamma had already arranged for Valentina's first protector, despite her being only eighteen. Dimitri guaranteed Valentina's acceptance into the company, but there was a moment when she'd thought she might resist. With Mamma's death she was finally free of her watching eyes. Perhaps for the first time, her life could be her own to live.

But when Valentina had picked up the photo to pack it away, Mamma had glared at her. Or so Valentina had thought. That's how it had become cracked—she had dropped it in fright when she'd seen Mamma's eyebrows lower in the way they so often had in real life. She'd run to Dimitri and the safety of a position in the company. Now, enough years had passed to dull the memory, and she knew the moment to be nothing more than the imagining of a lonely girl immersed in confusion as she stood on the cusp of womanhood. But somewhere, deep down, she had always hoped that maybe that wasn't true. Maybe the photo really did hold some magic, and through it Mamma would one day come back and order her life for her again.

'That's enough being silly,' Valentina muttered, pushing herself back to a standing position. Maxim wouldn't like being kept waiting for so long. It didn't matter that she was tired, that she didn't enjoy the way his lovemaking became forceful and almost violent after a temper. She wasn't paid to satisfy her own wants.

Not allowing herself time to think about it, she went back to her bedroom and the hollowed-out lemon halves. She slipped off her undergarments, snatched up one of the halves and rubbed it in both hands to soften and warm it. Placing one foot on the edge of the bed, she lifted her skirt to her knees and carefully folded the peel so it would be easier to get inside. She held it between her legs for a moment, closing her eyes to steel herself.

'Riches, money, security and safety,' she whispered once more.

CHAPTER TWELVE

'Do we really have to do this?' Luka asked. 'We could turn around right now and go somewhere else—have a quiet dinner, just the two of us. It'd be much more enjoyable, I'm sure.'

He didn't say it, but he was fretting about his brother. Still there had been no letter from Pyotr. The end of his second season with the ballet was getting closer and Luka didn't know how he was going to face the worry of his brother's silence without classes, rehearsals and performances to keep him distracted. He didn't want to admit this to Xenia though, lest it seem he was using his brother as an excuse for gaining his own way.

'You're not getting out of this,' Xenia told him. She didn't slow her steps to match his dragging pace and after a minute or two he hurried to catch up with her.

Ahead of them was the restaurant Kiuba, with the word 'Cubat' spelled out in electric lights on the rooftop to celebrate its famous chef. The place looked decadent, but to Luka, not very welcoming. Inside, Mathilde Kschessinska would be seated with a group of nobles and high-ranking company members, getting drunk on Moët et Chandon Brut Impérial and eating caviar by the spoonful. It was a celebration of Mathilde finally, at age forty-three, dancing her most coveted part: the title role in *Giselle*.

'You know I wasn't technically invited,' Xenia reminded Luka as they paused outside the door so she could tuck stray hairs into place under the little beaded cap she wore. The sounds of laughter and silver cutlery carelessly hitting china plates floated out to them on a breeze of warm air that smelled of slow-roasted pig, garlic and cigarette smoke. 'I'll never get the chance to see one of Mathilde's infamous parties unless I arrive on your arm. Give it a year or so and she'll be ordering the company to partner you with her, and you'll be beyond my reach then.'

Luka stifled a sigh. He was tired of the joke. In truth he could never imagine being beyond Xenia's reach, not after that Christmas night they'd shared together. Since then she had acted as though nothing had changed, yet Luka wondered if she felt the same sparks of regret and desire that he did every time they touched.

'Alright,' he said, unable to meet her eyes for long. He was afraid his feelings about his brother might show, and he didn't want to give them voice in case that made them real. 'But don't blame me if the night doesn't turn out as you expect. These people aren't like you and me.'

It wasn't strictly true. Xenia came far closer to the people inside than he ever could. Not in company rank, but in a societal one.

With an enchanting smile, Xenia slipped her arm through Luka's and together they entered the French restaurant. Most of the tables, draped in crisp white tablecloths topped with ornate place settings, were set for two and lined up in rows that had a military precision to them. A man in an impeccably tailored dark coat led them between the rows, underneath chandeliers shaped like upturned parasols, and past long vine-like plants that stretched up the walls towards the ceiling.

Luka whispered to Xenia, 'How many parties do you think Mathilde has thrown this year?'

'I don't know,' she whispered back. 'But I can guarantee one thing: those newspapers that think they're being so clever by over-exaggerating the number probably don't know the start of it. I heard she threw a soirée when an abscess disappeared from her foot.'

This last remark was spoken just as they reached Mathilde's table, and Xenia switched her face and tone so quickly to an enthusiastic greeting that Luka almost laughed.

'Malysh, my dear!' Mathilde cried, leaning down from her end of the table. She spoke in French as always. It had become the more respectable language since the uprisings against the English-speaking Tsarina, which thrilled Mathilde, who both detested the Tsarina and was not fluent in English.

In a sapphire blue gown with matching jewels around her neck, Mathilde was radiant. Her setting was opulent too. The table stood in an octagonal-shaped annexe to the main dining room, with walls that alternated between long windows and floor-to-ceiling paintings in gilded frames. Above, a heavy chandelier reached down from an ornate carving, so low the diners could have almost touched it where they sat. Unlike the other chandeliers, this one resembled a mass of candles that would have surely rained wax down on everyone if they hadn't been electric.

Seated to Mathilde's left, framed by the green fan of a rare palm tree, Luka recognised the critic and author Konstantin Skalkovsky, a man who liked to pretend he was French and sneered more than he smiled. Next to him sat Princess Zinaida Yusupova. To Mathilde's right was the Grand Duke Andrei. Luka noticed his relaxed posture and knew it must be because the Grand Duke Sergei was with the Tsar at the Stavka, sent there as Field Inspector General of Artillery. Although the Grand Duke Andrei was officially the chief of the 130th Infantry Regiment of Kherson, most of his time was spent in Petrograd, idling with Mathilde.

'Malysh, who is this charming companion you've brought with you?' Mathilde asked.

'Xenia Nicholaievna. She's a member of the corps.'

'Ah, of course. Welcome to our little soirée, Xenia Nicholaievna.' Mathilde opened her arms wide, laughing loudly; the gathering was anything but little.

Xenia was laughing as well, but Luka didn't think it was because of Mathilde's joke; rather because her choice of words mirrored Xenia's own when she'd made fun of the ballerina not five minutes earlier.

'*Merci*. And may I congratulate you on a glorious performance as Giselle tonight,' Xenia replied.

Luka cringed to hear the exaggeration come out of Xenia's mouth. But the compliment worked as intended, and Mathilde pretended to blush while insisting Luka must bring Xenia to more of her events.

When Mathilde's attention shifted to Princess Zinaida Yusupova, Xenia turned to Luka with a carefully schooled smile. 'See, it's not so hard to fit in,' she murmured. 'You just have to pet them a little.'

Luka shook his head.

He was disturbed to find himself seated almost opposite Maxim Sergeivich, who was careful to ignore him, and Valentina, who sat at her protector's side. It was the first time the two men had been so close since Maxim had threatened him, and the memory of how that calm, arrogant face could twist into something ugly and violent made Luka lose any appetite. He sat back in his chair and let the dinner carry on around him. Conversations overlapped up and down the table, quieting only when meals were placed in front of them.

A few of the men were smoking and the smell reminded Luka of his father. The scent of tobacco had been a permanent background to his and Pyotr's childhood, until Luka had left home for the ballet school. He wondered what his life would be like if it had been Pyotr who had the passion and skill for ballet. Would Luka be in a trench somewhere right now, fretting that he wasn't able to get a letter to his family? Or would he be dead? It was the very thing Luka didn't want to think about, and he closed his eyes briefly in an attempt to make it go away.

Maxim's amused voice broke through his thoughts. 'They're calling it the "Ministerial Leapfrog", because of how quickly ministers are named then removed. Rather a novel name. It must be difficult for Grigori Rasputin to find men who can live up to his just and righteous expectations.'

'Novel?' Luka couldn't stop himself.

Maxim's laughter was cut short and he turned to Luka with narrowed eyes. 'That is what I said.'

The condescension in his tone irritated Luka. 'You think it's fine for Grigori Rasputin to treat Russia's politics as if they're a game to amuse himself with, when others are dying for those politics?'

'You dare to question the Empress's authority in leaving such matters to Rasputin?' Maxim gave Luka a smile that exposed all of his teeth. 'But then the only game you would know about is *gorodki,* a game for children. Right, Malysh?' He slipped a cigarette into his mother-of-pearl holder, lit it and popped the end in his mouth, smirking at the smothered laughter around them.

Luka felt Xenia's body stiffen next to him. He wished he could reach across the table and smack the cigarette holder out of the other man's mouth. Instead he pretended to laugh with the others, hating himself for it and wondering what his brother would think of him if he could see.

'Tell me, Malysh,' Maxim continued, 'you come from *muzhiki,* don't you? That's why you can't understand the complexities of the aristocrats.'

He exhaled a stream of smoke at Luka's face. Xenia leaned forward and waved the grey cloud away. Luka wished she hadn't. It only drew more attention to it.

'My family aren't peasants,' he muttered, then was angry with himself for allowing the accusation to seem like something shameful. He sat up straighter and said loudly, 'My father is a factory worker, as was my brother until he became a soldier. And you're right when you say I don't understand the actions of the nobility. Perhaps my background does have something to do with that. Although I'm not the only one here who comes from a working family.'

A stillness settled over their end of the table. Luka got the distinct feeling everyone was avoiding looking at Valentina.

She herself had raised her head from her plate and was staring at him with darkened eyes. As Luka met her gaze, the frustration in him swelled to a hot little ball that sat heavily in his chest. Why didn't she say anything? Why didn't she defend her people? But all she did was stare back, her eyes flashing with a thousand different thoughts, none of which made their way out of her mouth.

'I don't believe the peasants and workers have it as bad as they like to pretend,' Maxim said, breaking the spell that held them all. 'On my work travels I see plenty of them, and they're often smiling and singing.'

'They aren't a Zinaida Serebriakova painting,' Luka retorted.

Maxim's answering expression gave him a stab of grim satisfaction. No doubt the man hadn't realised Luka would know anything about art. But his education at the Imperial Ballet School had taught him more than just dance, and seeing the response gave Luka all the encouragement he needed to carry on.

'Those people sing to comfort their children when they're hungry, and smile so they don't cry. They don't have thousands of pieces of cutlery, made of wasteful silver or gold, to do the exact same job.' He slapped the table in front of him, and a knife clattered to the floor. Xenia bent to pick it up, but Luka didn't stop. 'And those stoves that you disguise behind painted screens and decorative tiles, which for you never run cold? They're a source of life for most of the country. Entire families sleep on top of them, praying their supply of coal will last through the night so they don't freeze to death.'

There was a pause while Maxim took his cigarette holder from his mouth. Luka, his heart pounding from his impromptu impassioned speech, thought he might have finally got through to the man.

'How very primitive,' Maxim said.

A few who had turned to listen to Luka laughed. The hard lump that appeared in Luka's throat felt like it might choke him.

'Excuse me,' he muttered, pushing back his chair and standing up. 'As you have so helpfully pointed out, I am "Malysh". Which means it must be well past my bedtime.'

He turned to go, and felt fingers grab his arm. 'Luka—'

Luka didn't let Xenia finish. 'No, don't. You stay here and enjoy the rest of the party.' Her face was troubled and he tried to remove the anger from his voice. 'Please, I mean it. Stay. I want you to have a nice evening.'

He walked away before she could argue or try to follow him. He couldn't stand to be there any more, with people who were so ready to ignore those who had already lost so much and were desperately trying to survive off less food than was left over on the silver plates they dined from. What was more, he needed to get away from them so he could try to convince himself that he wasn't becoming one of them. That he wasn't ignoring his hungry, hurting country just because his own life had been made easier thanks to the ballet.

Luka didn't want to see any more faces that night, rich or poor. He just wanted to be surrounded by the quietness of his shabby apartment. There was something comforting about the cheap furniture, scuffed floors and simple curtains. Perhaps because it was the first time in his life he'd had his own space in the world; not shared with others like his childhood home and the dormitory of the Imperial Ballet School had been. It made it special; and knowing it was money earned from his dancing that afforded him this luxury imbued the otherwise plain apartment with the glow of achieved ambition.

But when he entered his building and climbed the two flights of stairs, he found someone waiting for him in the hall outside his door. It was his father, dressed in a dark *zhilet* with copper buttons. He was leaning against the wall, thin face glowering as he stared at the uncovered floor.

He looked up at the sound of Luka's footsteps. It must have taken him a minute or two to recognise his son for his face remained frozen until Luka stepped into the light offered by one gas wall lamp. Then his frown deepened. 'Are you happy with yourself now?' he snarled, pushing himself off the wall and staggering towards Luka.

Luka reached out to right him. Vladimir swatted his hands away, then swayed on the spot, running the back of his sleeve over his face. Was he drunk? Luka couldn't imagine him drinking in the city, but nor could he imagine him taking the tram all the way here if he was already drunk.

'What are you doing here? What's the matter?' he asked. His hands hung uselessly by his sides, wanting to do something but not sure what.

His father leaned closer; yes, there was definitely alcohol on his breath. But that wasn't what made Luka hiss through his teeth. His father was crying. His eyes were red-rimmed and swollen, which meant the tears now coursing down his grizzled cheeks had been making such tracks for a while. Luka's stomach dropped so suddenly his knees almost buckled. He took a step back; he'd only ever seen his father distraught like this once before.

'No,' he choked out.

'Pyotr.' The name ripped from his father's chest, as though his son was being torn from him in that very moment.

'No,' Luka said again, shaking his head. Something hit him from behind; he'd backed into the opposite wall without realising. 'He can't be ... he isn't ...'

'He is dead.'

The only sound in the hallway was Luka's rough breathing. He closed his eyes, then buried his face in his hands, trying not to think, not to feel.

'Don't you dare hide your coward's face from me,' his father snarled.

'That's not what I—'

'Your brother gave everything he had for this country— because people like you won't give a single thing!'

Luka dropped his hands. 'People like me? I thought you no longer supported the war, that you didn't want me to—'

'Of course I don't support a war that took my only decent son away from me!' His father was shouting now. 'But that is no excuse for cowardice. I know it, Pyotr knew it. Only little Luka, with his precious ballet slippers and dancing feet, had to hide away in his borrowed, gilded life. You should be ashamed! Ashamed you weren't there for him, ashamed you couldn't ... you couldn't ...'

Luka thought he might vomit. He couldn't hear more. He turned his back and fled down the stairs and out the building's door, gasping in the night air as if it were the only thing that could keep him alive. It wasn't, though. He needed movement. He began running, hoping he could outpace the truth of his father's words. Undo them and make his brother alive once more.

He paid no mind to where he ran, nor how many people stopped to yell at his strange behaviour, focusing only on putting one foot in front of the other. Eventually, his chest burned with something easier than the pain his father had inflicted, and he slowed down. It must have rained in the short time he'd been in the hallway, for now he saw the glowing light of the gas streetlamps reflected in shallow puddles. The sound of carriage wheels on the wet roads made it hard to think, but for that he was grateful. His head felt as though it weighed as much as the grand curtain that hid the Mariinsky stage from audiences when it was closed. He forced it up anyway and took in his surrounds. He thought he recognised the area—and making a few turns, found himself at the entrance to The Wandering Dog. He pushed the door open, walked along the gloomy hallway, and descended the stairs into the club.

Tonight, the patrons of The Wandering Dog seemed to share his mood. A man, bearded and hard to make out in the dim, smoky light, was singing a slow, sad song, not even bothering to get up from his chair so the crowd could see him. His voice was round and mellow, only occasionally marred by a crack when the emotion became too much for him. He was sipping a beer as he sang, timing the swallows so his song was never interrupted.

'You're new here, aren't you?'

Luka, still standing at the foot of the stairs, realised the voice was addressing him. He turned and saw the club's host smiling at him. He found it impossible to return the expression.

'Sort of. How did you know?'

'I make it my business to know. We have a fairly regular crowd, so it's not too hard to spot newcomers.' He scratched at his chin, and Luka saw that the stubble covering it was at that awkward point between clean-shaven and becoming a beard. 'You an artist?'

'A dancer. At the Imperial Ballet.'

The words held a sense of shame after all Vladimir had said, but the host nodded his head in satisfaction.

'We have another dancer come here sometimes, when she's in the country. Tamara Karsavina. You know her? Our patrons love it when Tata dances.'

'She dances for you here?'

Despite his dark melancholy, Luka felt a twinge of surprise. He couldn't imagine the star of the Ballets Russes making her way between the crowded bodies and mismatched furniture to dance among the dropped ashes of cigarettes. It was certainly not something an imperial dancer would do. Perhaps that was one of the reasons Karsavina had left the Imperial Russian Ballet.

'We push the chairs and tables right back against the walls,' the host said, 'and she dances in her bare feet. Perhaps you too will dance for us one day?'

Luka looked around at the unusual crowd, who were now half listening to an actor delivering an especially morose monologue. These people were exposing the depth of their heartbreak, sharing the burden between them all.

'Yes,' he said, nodding slowly. 'Perhaps one day I will.'

Maybe it could be a way of easing his pain.

CHAPTER THIRTEEN

Valentina adjusted her raspberry-pink skirts, causing the layers of tulle to rustle against each other. The sound reminded her of the draped romantic tutus worn in ballets like *Giselle* and *Les Sylphides*. This dress was a costume of sorts too, she supposed, only not in the same way. Every detail of it—the fine cut that showed an expanse of shoulder, the gold embroidery on the bodice and sleeves, the matching golden beads on the skirt that looked like a sprinkling of stars—was designed to be seen up close, so it could be admired and whispered about in jealous tones by those who didn't have the same good taste or money.

Valentina stifled a sigh. The thought of costumes reminded her how much she was going to miss the ballet. It was nearing the off-season again, and as always she both looked forward to the few months' reprieve and was nervous of it. What if her back should curve, or her ankle break? And then there was the prospect of a fresh batch of dancers joining the company at the end of the break. It was hard not to view the holiday as a threat to her position every year.

Maxim stood next to her, holding the jewelled staff he'd had especially made for tonight's ball. The fingertips of his other hand rested on the small of her back, quivering with impatience as the staff tapped out a beat on the ground that matched the music floating out of the Alexandrinsky Theatre.

Mathilde's Renault idled in front of the pale mustard-coloured building with its imposing white columns. The strange rumble of its engine was making the nearby horses nervous, and Valentina thought they might rear like the four horses that topped the building, tumbling the carriages they were strapped to. Pushing such nervous thoughts aside, she slipped her arm through Maxim's.

In response, he leaned down and brushed dry lips against her temple. 'You look like a Bakst painting,' he said.

His eyes were on her bright dress, which was a shimmering mirror of the stars in the velvety darkness above. The darkness wouldn't last much longer—the white nights would arrive soon, lighting up the sky so no one had anywhere to hide. Then the sky would be decorated with streaks of soft pink and peach, purple-tinged clouds resting like bruises on scrubbed-clean flesh—a glorious sunset that would last beyond midnight, before the sky finally cooled into a series of pale blues.

'Thank you,' Valentina said.

She checked the lace veil hanging from the back of her bejewelled *kokoshnik,* using the movement to cover her disquiet. She never looked forward to balls the way others seemed to; had never experienced that thrill of casting her eyes around upon entering to see who she might make a match with. She'd had her first protector before she'd ever attended her first ball, and to her they were just another event during which she stood by a man's side, dancing only when he wished to, leaving when he decided it was time. Tonight, though, her reluctance came from something more than mere boredom at the repetitiveness of it all. She couldn't pinpoint what was bothering her, but had the sense that something was inappropriate about this evening. Not that she was about to share that feeling with Maxim.

They entered the theatre, and the noise, which from outside had only just been audible, increased with every step they took. Valentina smelled the crowd before she saw them: sweat, perfume and tobacco mixed to create the aroma she knew so well—the scent of the social season.

Inside the auditorium was a world of dazzling colour and jewels, of rich scents and lush music swelling beneath excited chatter. Despite her trepidation, Valentina drew in a sharp breath. The ball was worthy of the Romanovs themselves— although they wouldn't be here, of course. They had taken to appearing in public only rarely as a mark of respect for the war.

The stage, which only hours earlier would have been populated by performers, had been transformed into an exotic Turkish tent. A rainbow of silks draped in deep curves from the ceiling, fringed rugs were layered on the floor, and cushioned benches lined the wings. Upstage, a gallery had been erected and a group of costumed musicians were perched there playing music. Hundreds of wax lights lined every flat surface, causing the auditorium's red and gold trim to glitter in their wavering light. Staircases led from the *parterre* to the finest boxes, where makeshift doorways had been created. The theatre's shining chandelier hung above it all like a giant crown.

Dancing couples swept past, so close that Valentina and Maxim had to take a step back to avoid being trampled. The movement was automatic for Valentina, who was used to finding herself in pressing crowds. She caught sight of an Oriental hat, and a jewelled staff similar to Maxim's, before he pulled her to the side to manoeuvre their way around the edge of the room. Servants dressed in livery embroidered with the imperial eagle stood with their backs to the walls beneath the branches of orange trees in oversized blue and white china pots; their job was to discreetly scatter perfume from copper vessels onto the floor. Valentina caught its bitter orange and rosemary taste in her mouth and grimaced. She was tempted to pluck an orange from one of the branches and sink her teeth into it to replace the artificial taste with a real one.

'Valechka, I think I see Grigori Rasputin.' Maxim pointed ahead, the pearl-encrusted cuff of his jacket shining against the colourful crowd.

Valentina arched her neck to try to see better, her heavy headdress making the movement difficult. She needn't have bothered. At that moment, a gap in the throng opened before them to reveal the tall, dark figure of Rasputin. Even in the crowded room she had the unpleasant feeling she was suddenly naked under the monk's eyes.

Maxim had already raised a hand in greeting, and was taking a step towards the monk. 'Let me go alone,' he said. 'I don't need you taking all his attention for yourself again.'

His shoulder bumped into that of another man and the two grabbed each other, righting themselves. Valentina's breath caught.

'*Excusez-moi*. Are you alright?' Maxim asked, brushing down the younger man's lapels without really looking at him.

He hadn't recognised Luka. Perhaps it was the half-mask he was wearing, or the shifting light from the candles and moving crowd. Whatever the reason, Luka didn't say a word in reply; he simply nodded and gave a tight smile.

'Good man.' Maxim patted him with one hand, then kept moving through the crowd, leaving Valentina behind.

Luka came to stand near her, his masked face tilted downward. Valentina smiled at some people who passed by, but no one stopped to talk.

In quiet Russian, Luka said, 'Do you know who I am?'

It was almost enough to make her laugh.

'Of course I know. My protector might not have recognised you, but it takes more than a mask to fool me, Luka Vladimirovich.' She turned a pointed expression on him. 'Besides, you're speaking Russian. You might notice no one else here is.'

'Yet they wear traditional peasant costumes and headdresses,' Luka returned, tilting his head at Valya's *kokoshnik*.

'It's considered patriotic,' she replied evenly.

Luka snorted, and Valentina's lips twitched. The young man still hadn't learned to cover his feelings in polite society.

'Nothing about this night is patriotic,' he said.

'And yet here you are.'

The part of Luka's face that was exposed coloured. Valentina felt a little sorry for teasing him. He'd been unusually quiet in their last few rehearsals, sullen even. She'd thought the confrontation between him and Maxim at Mathilde's celebratory dinner was bothering him, but given he had so rudely reminded their peers of her own upbringing, she didn't feel the need to offer him sympathy. Now, she wondered if she should tell him that it wasn't his fault if he was seduced by the more glamorous side of life in the Imperial Russian Ballet. Countless before him had been, herself included.

He spoke before she had the chance to. 'I just thought, with the season coming to an end, tonight might be ...' He didn't finish.

'A good opportunity to meet people who could help your career?' He looked away, as if ashamed of himself, and she added, 'You needn't be so coy about it. We all have our ways of getting ahead.'

He glanced down, adjusting the unadorned cuffs of his jacket. 'Why do you pretend not to have come from the same world as I?' he asked abruptly. 'It's not a world to be ashamed of. They are the people who are dying to keep our country whole.'

Valentina stifled a sigh. She didn't care for questions of this sort. 'If you'll excuse me, I should find Maxim,' she said, and took a step away. But Luka grabbed her arm and pulled her into the dancing crowd in the centre of the room. 'What are you doing?'

He placed one hand on her back, in the same spot Maxim's fingers had rested earlier, and took her jewelled hand in his other. 'I'm dancing with you. I should think you'd recognise that by now.' His feet moved to the valse à deux temps the musicians were playing, and without thinking about it Valentina fell into time with him. 'And I'd like you not to dash off before you've answered my question.'

Valentina averted her gaze, staring over his shoulder at the crowd that surrounded them, wondering if their smiles concealed inner turmoil the way hers did.

'You know why. You've been part of this world long enough to understand,' she said softly.

Luka leaned closer to hear her better and the proximity of his face made her turn her gaze back to him.

'Why is it so important to you?' she asked.

'You really don't understand, do you?' He sounded aggravated, and there was something like pain threading his voice.

Valentina kept her mouth closed. Her feet continued to move in time with Luka's, a gentle ebb and flow, and somewhere in the back of her mind she thought they would indeed make a fine couple on stage.

'When I was a student at the ballet school, things weren't always ... easy,' he continued, as she'd known he would. Most people filled a silence if you let it rest for long enough. 'You know what it's like there for people like us. We don't belong, but nor do we belong in our old homes any more. We betrayed our families, neighbours and friends by trading them in for a better life.'

Valentina's hand clenched at his mention of their similar past, but she released it almost instantly. Luka's eyes, visible behind the mask, flicked to her own, then away over the top of her head.

'But I had someone to look up to,' he said. 'You were just like me, yet not only had you made it into the Imperial Russian Ballet, you were becoming more famous, more accepted in that world, with every passing year. You symbolised what was possible.'

'And I don't now?'

Valentina had worked so hard to erase her past that she'd never for a second considered anyone might not see it the same way she did—as something to be ashamed of; an unchangeable fact that would always make her an outsider no matter how hard she tried to become one of Petrograd's elite.

'No. Now I know that you didn't get where you are by merit and hard work. You traded your way there.'

Valentina's feet stopped—but only for a second, because Luka curled his arm around her waist to force her to keep moving. She looked up at his masked face and wished that she, too, were wearing a mask; not a domino, but something large and ornate so she could be sure that the sting of his words wasn't showing on her face.

'I'm sorry my life has disappointed you so, Luka Vladimirovich; and even more sorry that, as a student, you gave such significance to a trifling matter. It's an amusing connection that you and I share a similar background, that's all. It certainly doesn't mean we're the same. I have to live my life the way I see fit, and you should do the same.'

'You're right.'

Now it was Luka's turn to stop dancing, and he did it so suddenly that Valentina had taken another two steps before she too came to a halt. His hands dropped from her and her body felt cooler without his touch.

'I've been foolish,' he said. 'I apologise. Good night.'

Deserted amid the crowd, aware of people giggling at her behind raised hands, Valentina watched him go in astonishment. Who was this young man who acted on his every feeling and didn't hesitate to say what was on his mind? Who, even when he was angry, kept his hands on her gentle? Without thinking, she took a step after him. People were still looking at her, aghast at the sight of her being left alone mid-dance, but she ignored them. She wanted to defend herself to Luka, or perhaps prove that he hadn't been wrong in his lofty boyhood opinion of her. She wanted to make him understand that she'd made the only choices she thought she could.

By the time she caught up to him, they were both outside. The air felt like cool water sliding over Valentina's skin after the oppressive warmth of the Alexandrinsky.

'Malysh,' she said, her voice an appeal that was tinged with anger she hadn't expected. He continued to walk away from her, his long legs taking rapid strides. 'Luka.' With effort, she softened her voice; it was enough to make him stop.

He turned to her and in the darkness his mask looked part of his face. Valentina took quick steps up to him, then paused. What had she come out here to say?

'Will you take that domino off please?'

Luka hesitated, then raised one hand and pulled the mask off. It had covered so little of his face that with it gone, his expression was barely any easier to read.

'Don't accuse me of not working to get where I am. It might not be the kind of work you consider worthwhile, but believe me when I say it's still work.'

There was a waver in her voice as she spoke; she'd been remembering all the times she'd had to deny herself in favour of pleasing others. Luka, who knew how it felt to wonder when your next meal might be or if there would be enough of it, should have understood.

He fiddled with his domino, refusing to look her in the eyes. Suddenly irritated, Valentina grabbed the mask, forcing his hands to still. When he did raise his head, the look he gave her was reproachful, the young hopeful boy he had been staring out of a man's eyes.

'Look at what it makes you, though,' he said. 'I just … I don't know how you live the way you do.' His voice had gone softer, gently questioning.

Valentina stared down at their hands, both still grasping the domino mask. 'Sometimes I don't know either.'

The words seemed to hang in the night between them. She could almost see them written in the air, gold like the embroidery on her dress, and wished she could grab them and stuff them back into her mouth where Luka couldn't see them.

Slowly, Luka drew one hand off the mask. A moment later she felt it on her face. It was just one finger, resting on her chin, and its unexpected warmth made her look up at him. He was frowning, his expression one approaching curiosity.

Valentina felt an urge to step towards him, to close the gap between them so he was forced to stop looking at her that way. She wasn't some amusement you could see in a circus sideshow.

She took the step.

Luka's eyebrows rose a little, but he didn't move away. His hand, too, stayed where it was. The dark centres of his eyes were swelling, and Valentina thought that if she continued to look into them, they might swallow her up completely.

She tilted her chin up. *Go ahead*, she thought defiantly, *show me what my paid-for life can't give me*. She parted her lips, the tiniest movement daring him to be bold.

Luka answered her invitation. He lurched forward, pressing his lips against hers, almost crushing them. The kiss was hard, too hard, and for an instant Valentina regretted it. But then his mouth softened and she was able to respond. The unfamiliarity of his lips was thrilling.

Luka moved his hand to grasp the back of her head, pulling her closer, and his tongue darted into her mouth. A pulse swept through Valentina's body; she knew it was desire, that eternally unsatisfied ache. Without thinking, she pressed her whole body against his, trying to feel him through the combined layers of their clothing. He was the first man who hadn't paid for the privilege of her kiss. It gave her an excitement she hadn't experienced before.

When he tried to pull away for air, she grabbed fistfuls of his coat to keep him where he was. *Not yet*, she thought. *Let this one moment of fantasy go on just a little longer.*

But in that slight pulling away, the spell dissipated and Maxim was in her head. The thrill of the kiss was already turning into heavy, burning guilt. Valentina reluctantly turned her face away. She had to be the first to speak. She couldn't let him say something that might change this moment from what it was—a reckless impulse—into something more.

She smiled at him, but she knew the expression wasn't a joyful one. 'Please don't do that again.' She had to force the words out. Her lips, still tingling from the touch of his, didn't want to say them.

'Why not?'

He didn't sound hurt or surprised, and the thought that she was so predictable made Valentina ache.

'You know why. You can't have what you don't pay for.' A bitterness crept into the playful tone she'd been aiming for.

She realised she was still holding onto Luka's jacket and made herself let go, taking a step back from him as she did. The domino fell to the ground between them. She bent to pick it up, wishing that her hair was long so it would fall forward and hide her face, giving her an instant of freedom from his gaze.

When she held the mask out to him, Luka didn't take it. Her hands fell to her sides, the domino resting limply in one of them.

'I should go back inside,' she said. 'Maxim will be wondering where I am.'

Never had she wished more for her words to be true. Her protector was probably still at Rasputin's side, hanging on for any favour that might come his way. Valentina had to find him. She had to remind herself of all that she'd worked for and all that her moment of impulse could have cost her.

Rasputin's presence would feel all the more invasive after the warmth of Luka's kiss, but it was a punishment she deserved.

CHAPTER FOURTEEN

The kiss with Valentina had aroused an unexpected exhilaration in Luka, akin to the feeling he'd experienced as a child when he'd disobeyed the school's rules and got away with it. The memory of her lips against his; her warm body, so pliable and inviting—and how his own body had been quick to respond. It never left his mind for long, even when thoughts of Pyotr's death sent him plummeting into bleak depression. Luka couldn't make sense of it: how it had happened, or why; nor his reaction to it.

The season closed—this time with his contract renewal already secured. The Hermitage performance was scheduled to take place during the off-season, but Valentina had not organised any further rehearsals. He assumed she would get in contact with him soon, although he'd not received word from her yet.

When the off-season began, it became his habit to go for long walks around the city. He wanted to keep his muscles as supple as possible, but also couldn't bear to be alone in his once comforting apartment with his grief and memories of his brother.

During one of these walks, he passed Leiner's, a cosy delicatessen whose price signs had been scribbled over more than once, each time signalling an increase that would only matter to those who couldn't afford to eat there in the first place. As he glanced in the window, he saw Valentina sitting alone, her feet absent-mindedly drawing circles in the sawdust on the floor.

Luka's heart jumped into his throat. The temptation was to slowly back away. She was so deep in thought it would be easy to slip past without notice. But another, stronger temptation immediately came on the heels of the first. Not quite sure what he was doing, but unwilling to question himself, Luka walked into the delicatessen and sat down in the empty chair across from her.

Valentina's attention snapped back to her surroundings and her features opened in surprise. For a second, it was the Valentina he'd only ever seen once or twice. Luka wanted that Valentina to stay before him, but already she was disappearing behind a schooled demeanour.

'What are you doing here?' Her voice was careful; not loud enough to draw attention, but not so low that passers-by might think she was being clandestine.

'Where's your protector?' The words were rude, but that was easier than telling her about his brother.

'Maxim left this morning for some business in Moscow.'

Luka didn't care about Maxim's work in Moscow. What he wanted was to ask her about the kiss. He wanted to know if she was as unsettled by it as he was.

'He should take you with him everywhere,' he said.

'Why? Because I might get kissed by some corps dancer the moment he isn't looking?'

A laugh escaped Luka, the first since he'd received news of Pyotr's death. He hadn't expected such directness from her.

'Well, that too. But I meant that if he's so concerned with your value, it would make sense for him to keep you with him at all times.'

Valentina pushed away her half-empty plate and wiped her hands with a linen napkin. 'Easy to say when you've never had to put a price to your own worth. Trust me, Maxim knows my value, and he pays every *kopeck* and *rouble*. And then some.' She tossed down the napkin, grabbed her gloves from the table and stood. 'You might as well make yourself comfortable. I'm leaving anyway.'

'But I just got here.'

'It's fortuitous timing then.'

She gave him a pointed look as she did up the buttons of her gloves. Her small embroidered hat framed her face in a way that was pretty, and Luka wondered why he'd never thought of her that way before. Perhaps it was because she was always covered by expensive materials and glaring jewels—he'd never been able to see past them.

Curious about what else he might see if he continued to look closely, he got up and followed her out of the delicatessen.

'What are you doing?' she asked, pausing just outside. She pulled her silk dust-coat closer around her even though the air was warm, buckling it at her waist.

'I'm coming with you.'

'To Cartier, to pick up some jewellery? For that's where I'm headed.'

Luka felt himself shrink. They both knew he wasn't able to afford such riches. He kept eye contact with her though, not allowing himself to succumb to embarrassment.

'Don't you have someone to do that kind of thing for you? Or why don't the jewellers deliver to your house?'

Valentina's fair, tapered eyebrows lowered. Luka didn't think that was the reaction she'd been expecting.

'It's a beautiful day and I felt like a walk,' she said finally. 'It's not that unheard of.'

Luka could relate only too well; in fact, he was surprised they had something so mundane in common. He didn't say this, though. Instead he looked up at the sky, where only a thin sliver of sunlight was managing to break through the drab grey clouds.

'The sun was shining when I left,' Valentina protested, turning sharply and striding away from him.

Luka took a few rapid paces to catch up with her, then slowed so their footsteps were in time. He knew he was being beyond rude now, and when Valentina stopped and faced him, she confirmed it.

'What are you doing? I said I didn't want you walking with me.'

'Actually, I don't think you did.'

'If I didn't, then I meant to. Please leave me alone. You could get me in trouble.'

'There's nothing wrong with a man escorting a woman on her errand, particularly when they work together.' Luka could see that irritation was making her eyes narrow and he dropped the teasing edge from his voice. He didn't want to upset her. 'You shouldn't carry jewellery around by yourself. Someone could steal it.'

'You do have a poor idea of the city's people, don't you?'

She walked off again, shaking her head. Luka followed once more, and reached out to touch her arm gently. She jumped as if he'd hit her with a cold handful of snow.

'Valya, please.' It was the first time he had called her by anything other than her full name, and they both seemed to realise this at the same moment. Luka didn't know where it had come from, except that a spark of genuine worry had taken hold of him. 'I know you saw that woman outside the Palace Theatre weeks ago, the one begging for money to buy bread. What do you think someone like her might do if an opportunity to snatch a fine jewel presented itself? The city is no longer the domain of only the wealthy.'

Valentina stared at him as though taking his measure. Her carnation-pink lips pressed together and she gave a curt nod. 'Come on then.'

Wordlessly, Luka followed her down the street.

'You weren't truly going to carry this around the streets of Petrograd by yourself?' Luka asked.

'Hmm?' Valentina wasn't listening. She was holding the brooch in her hand, inspecting it for flaws she knew she wouldn't find. 'It's supposed to be the white swan,' she said. She held it out for him to see. 'Odette.'

It was a large piece, half the size of her palm, and studded with clear white diamonds. Its setting was pure gold, twisted into the shape of a swan, its wings weighed down by the precious jewels. Underneath, clutched in its golden feet, was a large teardrop-shaped pearl, representing the lake made of the

King's and Queen's tears for the daughter they'd lost to the evil Von Rothbart's curse.

'Oh,' Luka said.

Valentina knew what he was thinking. Odette was supposed to be a fragile, ethereal thing who simultaneously hoped to be rescued and despaired of it ever happening. The glittering brooch of gold and diamonds hardly reflected that.

'Maxim had it made for me,' she said, handing it back to the jeweller to be wrapped. 'Remember at Mathilde's dacha, when we found that white feather? He wanted a surer sign for me, something more solid.'

'I thought he said you'd make a better Odile.'

Valentina only just stopped herself wincing. She wished Luka hadn't remembered that. 'He says a lot of things.'

When the brooch was wrapped, she passed it to Luka, who hid it somewhere inside his jacket. The thought of it being so close to him unsettled Valentina, and she found she could barely speak as they walked to a tram, then travelled on it together. His proximity made her anxious. Could he see the way she kept remembering how it had felt when he'd slipped his tongue into her mouth, the lingering pleasure it brought her?

It was with great relief that she saw her own front door being opened by Madame Ivkina, her housekeeper. She halted before they entered the portico.

'Thank you, Luka. I don't need any further escorting now.'

'You wouldn't leave a man outside in such weather, would you?' he asked.

Valentina froze; then she tilted her head back to look at the sky. A fat raindrop landed on Valentina's cheek, right where a tear would fall. She brushed it away, stifling a sigh as she looked across the portico at her housekeeper. She could hardly refuse

Luka's request without appearing either cruel or suspicious. And one could never be sure of one's staff's silence, not when *roubles* were always changing hands behind closed doors.

'Of course not,' she said. 'Please, come inside and wait out the weather.'

Valentina entered the wide foyer and began unbuckling her dust-coat with fumbling fingers, trying not to think about how odd it felt to have Luka inside her house.

'Madame Ivkina, would you tell the cook to bring us something to eat? I believe my guest hasn't had lunch yet. We'll be upstairs in the reception room until this storm clears.'

Madame Ivkina took her coat and hung it up in silence, then assisted Luka with his. Valentina was glad of the moment to regain her bearings. She took a stack of envelopes from a silver tray and rifled through, not really seeing them. She needed to forget that stolen kiss. It didn't seem to be affecting Luka the way it was her, and she'd make a fool of herself if she showed how much it was playing on her mind.

When she turned back, she saw that Luka's hands were fiddling with his sleeve cuffs. She gestured for him to follow her across the tiled foyer to the stairs. As they made their way to the first floor, Valentina couldn't help seeing the surrounds through his eyes. The walls, decorated with floral patterns in diamond shapes, heavy paintings spread across them at even intervals. The floors that alternated between dark tiles and light wooden boards to create a lush mosaic effect. The solid silver candlesticks and lamps that sat on the many polished surfaces. They were the spoils of her many years of hard work; physical evidence of what she had achieved through her manipulation of male desire. Would Luka be impressed, or judge them?

Valentina led Luka into a reception room decorated in varying shades of soft blue. It was the room she always used to receive guests, and was kept in crisp perfection by her housekeeper and maid.

'Sit,' she said, perching herself on a chaise longue whose quilted pattern matched the wallpaper.

Luka took a chair opposite, tapping the tips of his fingers together as he watched her unpin her hat. She gave her bobbed hair a shake, running her hands through it as Madame Ivkina entered with a tray laden with caviar sandwiches and grapes. Valentina told her to leave it on the low table between them so she could serve the food herself. She wanted to do something with her hands.

'Do your lot ever eat anything else?' Luka asked after the housekeeper had lit the cut-glass lamps and left them alone.

'Pardon?'

'Since I began attending Mathilde's events, I could swear I've eaten my own body weight in caviar.'

'Don't you like it?'

'It's not that. It's just I'd never had it before joining the ballet, and now I seem to …'

He trailed off, leaving Valentina feeling as if she'd done something wrong. She thought about telling him that the bread for the sandwiches had cost more than the salty delicacy, but decided against it.

'Never mind,' he said. 'Thank you for letting me wait out the weather here.'

She waved a hand. 'It would have been too cruel to send you back into that miserable day.'

As if in response, a crack of thunder sounded overhead. Valentina cried out, startled, then pressed a hand to her chest and laughed.

'Are you alright?' Luka asked.

He leaned forward, reaching for her hand, but couldn't quite grasp it. His hand came to rest on her knee instead, his fingers gentle against the white flounces of her dress.

Valentina pressed her fingers to her wrist to try to stop the sudden quickening of her pulse.

'Of course. I just got a fright, that's all. It was the thunder. I didn't expect ...'

Luka, his eyes fixed on hers, shifted off his chair until he was kneeling on the floor in front of her. His hand was still on her knee. Valentina's heart raced as she watched him come closer. This was just how it had been outside the Alexandrinsky. She knew she should pull away, tell him to leave regardless of the weather. But the memory of that kiss, how intoxicating it had been, stilled her.

Slowly, Luka raised both his hands and cupped them around her face. *One kiss can't hurt*, she thought. Just one more, then she'd make him go.

She waited, heart pounding, and the kiss came. His lips were sweet from the grapes, but it wouldn't have mattered; there was sweetness enough in his touch. The desire she'd felt last time ran through her again, its spark quickened by anticipation.

Luka pulled back from the kiss to breathe her name against her lips, then his mouth was on her neck. This was where she should stop it. The one kiss she had promised herself had ended, and so should this intimacy.

But she didn't speak up.

'Valya,' Luka said again. He was softly, tantalisingly, kissing the place where her neck met the slope of her shoulder. Slowly, he trailed up her neck and along her jawline.

His hands moved downward, and Valentina made a small sound in protest; she'd liked the protective feeling of them against her face, the way his fingers played with the soft curls at the nape of her neck. But when they stopped, one was curled around her back and the other resting on her breast, and she left off her complaint.

Lightning flashed, illuminating the room with a brightness that gave everything a razor-sharp edge. Luka's hands trembled against Valentina's clothing.

'Kiss me again,' she whispered, her voice thick. Somewhere in her head, another voice was telling her to stop, that she'd already gone too far. But her body was alight now, hungry, and she'd had enough of denying it.

'I can't,' he whispered. 'If you make me go on, I won't be able to stop.'

Valentina knew this was her last opportunity to cease what they were doing. She knew because she had seen it a thousand times before: the growing hunger in a man, the way he resisted until he was sure of her, then the uncontrolled release of his full desire.

She looked at Luka. His face was twisted, showing his eagerness for her body in the same way as the men before him. There was one difference this time: she was just as eager. She could feel it, the ache between her legs that she was sure would never go away if Luka left her now. She'd never been on this side of it before, had never felt how desperate the longing to have their bare skin touching and their bodies enveloping each other could be.

Wordlessly, she grabbed Luka's hand and drew him up onto the chaise longue with her. Eyes never leaving his, she lay back and brought his hand to her breast again. Only this time she slipped his fingers underneath the lace of her dress so they were touching bare skin.

He froze for a moment, his eyes fluttering closed, then began to trail his fingertips over the soft, small curve. Valentina arched her back in an effort to press herself more firmly into his hand. She was used to having control of her body, but here, with Luka, it had a mind of its own.

His lips met her skin again as his weight settled on her, and she couldn't think of anything but his name. She breathed it out softly, her voice lost in the whispers of their clothing peeling away from their skin.

Luka sat on the cool timber floor, his bare shoulders against the plush edge of the chaise longue. Valentina's fingers were resting on the back of his neck. She was lost in thought, unaware of his sweat dampening her fingertips. Her white dress was around her waist, exposing her naked torso so that she looked like a mermaid rising from a frothy, wild sea.

Luka wished he could think of something to say to her. Afterwards with Xenia, his silence had come from contentment. This was different.

'That was … it was unlike …' Valentina's voice trailed off.

'Yes, it was.' Luka shyly took her hand and kissed it. He understood why she couldn't find the words to explain what had happened between them. They had been overtaken by an intense and unexpected need, yet even in their desperation there had been gentleness, a delicate respect that had surprised Luka even more than the strength of his desire for her.

Just thinking about that tenderness aroused him again, and he turned to face her, tentatively encircling her small waist in his bare arms. 'Somehow I find myself wanting more.'

'You've only just put your trousers back on,' she teased.

'I know. But with you sitting there, your dress around your waist ...'

Valentina glanced down as though she hadn't realised she was still half naked, but she didn't make any move to cover herself. Luka pulled her closer. He wanted to press his face to her nakedness, to tease her skin with his tongue. He wanted to make her cry out the way she had only moments before. He wanted to forget all complications, forget his grief, and just enjoy her for a while longer.

'Luka.' His name was a sigh escaping her. 'That was wonderful, but we can't do it again. I have a protector, and he pays very highly for the privilege. I can't risk that for ... for what?'

Luka didn't reply. Anything he said would only be an admission of his own selfish desires. Of course he knew she had a protector.

'Just one last kiss then,' he murmured, gently resting his lips against her neck.

He could taste the saltiness of her skin, could feel the way her body responded to him as her breathing quickened.

CHAPTER FIFTEEN

Summer 1916

Valentina stood before the wall of mirrors in her home studio, her foot pointed to the side. Shifting it behind her, she planted her weight firmly down so that both knees were bent. She pushed off, whipping around in a sharp turn. As she came to face the mirror again, she lowered the foot she was standing on so she was no longer on her toes, straightened her other leg to the side, then flicked it back in so the force of the movement turned her around again—all within the space of a second.

She counted each time she turned, trying to ignore the dizziness that threatened to overwhelm her.

Eight. Nine. Ten.

She was sure she was travelling sideways instead of staying on the one spot as she was supposed to, but that didn't matter for now. She'd get the number first, then concentrate on the rest later.

Thirteen. Fourteen. Fifteen.

With the last turn, she toppled over sideways, only just managing to catch herself with her hands before her face hit the timber floor. She stayed in that position, willing the spinning in her head to stop.

It was the same every time. She started off executing the fouettés perfectly, then slowly the feeling of control slipped away from her. She always knew the moment when she'd lost it: her centre of balance shifted, and no amount of tightening her stomach or shortening the movement of her legs would bring her upright again.

The thirty-two fouettés from *Le Lac des Cygnes* were a newly iconic feature that perfectly showcased Odile's cruel attack against the unknowing Prince Siegfried and his love, Odette. Only a handful in all of Russia had been able to complete the full thirty-two, and Valentina was determined to become one of them by the time she performed at the Hermitage.

Biting down on the curse that wanted to roll off her lips, she picked herself up and walked over to a balled-up piece of fabric in the corner, using it to wipe the sweat off her face. It seemed, in this particular moment, that she had as much control over the fouettés as she did over her life. A tremor of fear ran through her at the thought, and she pressed the sweat rag to her abdomen as though that might suppress it.

She didn't know what was happening to her. All those years of schooling herself to only follow the desires that could further her position, and now she was acting like one of the love-struck characters she danced onstage. She didn't want to be Odile in life, as Maxim so often accused her; but neither did she want to be Odette, losing everything because of a man. Her fascination for Odette and her desire to dance the role wasn't because of how Odette stayed true to her feelings until the bitter end; rather it was because of the way those feelings betrayed her and caused her downfall. It was a role Valentina thought she could capture in a way that made it fully her own; as Pavlova, Kschessinska, Nijinsky and Karsavina had done with other roles.

She would not make Odette's mistakes in real life, though. What she needed was to unlock the secret of the thirty-two fouettés: if she did, she would be the first dancer in all of Russia to have done so without first attaining the rank of principal. Then she would be back on the track Mamma had set for her all those years ago. Money, power and connections—those were the things Mamma had taught her to count on, the only things that mattered. Valentina had had her own thoughts on the matter as a child, but eventually she'd fallen in line. She could remember the exact moment she'd finally reconciled with her mother's ambitions. She was fifteen, in her fifth year at the ballet school, and there was a step she couldn't get right. It had plagued her for weeks, and her teacher had almost given up on her. She'd been terrified of telling Mamma, and had practised until her feet bled. And one day she got it. She'd been in a studio surrounded by young girls in their practice dresses, watching herself in the mirror. Her outer self looked relaxed and at ease, a bead of sweat dripping down her face the only evidence of how much effort the movement cost her. An ecstatic tremor ran through her limbs as, finally, she executed the grand rond de jambe en l'air perfectly, receiving a small nod from the teacher in recognition. It was proof, demonstrated by Valentina's own body, that if she strove for something long enough, she would achieve it in the end. And that realisation made her begin to believe in Mamma's plan of a protector and influence and amassing wealth beyond dreams.

A plan that had, only a few years later, come to fruition without Mamma there to see. A plan she was now risking—for what? A few hours of fun with a man who would never pay?

She'd made a foolish mistake. It wouldn't happen again. She would let Luka Zhirkov know that never again would they go beyond dancing with one another. The privilege of her body was for Maxim alone. Then she would be in control once more.

Valentina kept her eyes closed, silently counting the rhythm of Luka's breathing next to her. The distraction of pleasure had died down and she was aware now of her dewy skin and the dampness between her legs. She could hear in her mind the cries she hadn't meant to make but had been unable to stop. Shame at her weakness in not being able to let this young man go, despite the danger he posed to her goals, threatened to overwhelm her.

'Why do you close your eyes like that?' he asked, his voice a soft whisper.

How was she supposed to answer? When she watched Luka, it was like she had never seen a man before. She drank in the fragile skin of his eyelids, the line where his hair met his forehead, the creases on his knuckles when he reached up to caress her cheeks, committing every last part of him to memory. There was always something new to look at, and every time it gave her the same strange tightness in her chest, almost like pain. So she did what she always did when emotions threatened to interfere: she tried to block it all out. It was the only way she knew how to keep winning at these difficult games.

'It doesn't matter,' Luka murmured.

The bed dipped underneath his shifting weight. Valentina tried to turn her face away, conscious even with her eyes closed that Luka's were on her. But his hand cupped her cheek, turning her back to him with a touch that was as gentle as the warm night air on her skin.

'You are beautiful,' he whispered.

Valentina had heard those words so many times they'd long ago lost all meaning. But never had anyone said them when she was like this—naked, unclean—and they pierced her. She was afraid that if she opened her eyes, the tears now stinging them would find an escape. Then they would both start asking questions she couldn't—didn't want to—answer.

She rolled over so that her back was to him. She felt him shuffle closer, the warmth of his solid torso against her back. He draped an arm over her, and she opened her eyes to see his square hand resting on the sable coverlet. She resisted the temptation to take it in her own.

'Luka?' she said softly.

She was trembling, knowing she was about to speak the words she shouldn't; words that would expose the Valentina Yershova she had been running from for so long.

'Do you think it's possible to have been lonely your whole life, only not know it?'

Only silence answered her. Luka had fallen asleep.

Valentina and Luka ran onto the small stage together, her a little ahead, their hands joined. In her black tutu and gold headdress, Valentina felt as she should: haughty, calculating, confident that this moment would be hers. A tremor ran through Luka's fingers clasped in hers. *Good*, she thought, *Prince Siegfried should be nervous*. He believed himself on the verge of getting all he wanted, but in reality he was about to lose everything, Odile's clever deception destroying the love between him and Odette.

Flirtatiousness raced through Valentina's veins as she danced. She couldn't stop herself flashing a grin each time her eyes met Luka's. Whenever she faced the audience, she saw the hulking figure of Rasputin in one of the large reclining chairs normally occupied by the imperial family, and the disfigured outlines of the soldiers spread in semicircles behind him. Grimness would grip her for a second; then she was looking at Luka again and her smile reappeared. The conflicting expressions made her the perfect Odile. Maxim would have been gratified.

Valentina took a wild lunge forward into an arabesque penché en pointe. Only Luka's hand holding hers stopped her from toppling forward onto her face, but she had total trust in him. As he pulled her back and turned her into a jump that sent her soaring higher than his head, she could feel the strength of him. She had been right: he was going to be one of the great dancers; a man who would elevate every partner he danced with, whose name would become almost as famous as the great female dancers.

The music slowed, and instead of her triumphant taunts, Odile became tantalising. Valentina's heart was racing, the slower movements somehow reminiscent of the many hours she and Luka had spent in bed together. And then she was pulling away, letting Prince Siegfried wallow in confusion, wanting more. Ensuring he came to her as she mimicked Odette's gentle movements, fooling him. He was on his knees and she couldn't help being cruel in her triumph. She drew him to her with nothing more than a look, then was whipping around in eight rapid pirouettes, until they stopped together in a final arabesque.

They held the position as the music died away, waiting for the applause. Valentina's mind was already racing ahead. Luka would be dancing Prince Siegfried's variation next, then it would be her turn. They would alternate: he celebrating what he thought was the culmination of his love for Odette; Odile celebrating her victory. The movements would become ever more difficult, showing off their virtuosity, culminating with the triumphant thirty-two fouettés before a final flourish that finished with one last lift.

Mathilde had divulged the secret of the fouettés to Valentina—a fact that not only told Valentina their friendship was true, but also that she wasn't considered a threat to Mathilde's career—and she had worked tirelessly in her studio since, perfecting the motion of keeping her head looking forward for as long as possible before whipping it around to look at the same spot again. She had managed to get to thirty-two only a couple of times, and tonight would be her first attempt in front of an audience.

Valentina was so focused on what was to come that it took a moment for her to realise that only one pair of hands were clapping. Luka released her from the arabesque, handing her forward to curtsey to an unresponsive crowd of at least two hundred. The small Hermitage Theatre was so quiet that she could hear her footsteps echoing beneath Rasputin's solitary applause. As she bent her knee in thanks, she saw the monk stand up.

'Why do you not applaud?' he demanded of the soldiers, his voice booming in the silence of the room. 'You should show your gratitude.'

Valentina straightened from her curtsey. Luka came up behind her, taking one of her hands, the other on her waist; ordinarily they would curtsey and bow together now, but they both hovered where they were, indecisive. Peering into the darkened auditorium Valentina could see the Grand Duchesses perched on seats either side of Rasputin. Olga's face was stricken, those of her sisters etched with nervousness.

'Well?' Rasputin demanded. His heavy brow was sinking, making his eyes almost disappear.

Many of the soldiers refused to look up. They stared at their feet, or picked at their nails. Finally, one stood. His position on the tiered seats made him almost the same height as the monk, although they were separated by quite a distance. He leaned heavily on a crutch, and pointed one shaking hand directly at the stage. Valentina could see his fingers were gnarled and discoloured from old frostbite. Amputation was likely around the corner. Her stomach churned, and she leaned into Luka, grateful for his solid presence.

'It's unnecessary spectacles like this that keep the rest of the country poor,' the man said in a surprisingly strong voice. 'Why should we be grateful for this peek into their sheltered lives?'

Those around him murmured in agreement, lifting their heads to shoot looks at Valentina and Luka that had an almost physical impact.

'You dare to question the generosity of the Grand Duchesses and the Imperial Russian Ballet—the Tsar's own daughters and dancers?' Rasputin spoke calmly, but his eyes were wild.

At a flick of his wrist, guards appeared out of the shadows along the curved back walls, where they had blended in between the sculptures of Apollo and his muses. With rapid steps they leaped down the tiered seating, making for the Grand Duchesses.

'The mad monk shows his true powers,' the standing soldier yelped.

Most of the other men were on their feet now, some even advancing on Rasputin. The Grand Duchesses were being ushered away by the guards, and as Luka pulled Valentina back from the edge of the stage she caught a glimpse of the distraught white face of the Grand Duchess Olga.

'I think we should go,' Luka whispered urgently in her ear.

'Who is the real Tsar? For we see no Nicholas here, only a monk giving orders!' the soldiers were now shouting.

'Arrest them,' Rasputin responded in a commanding tone.

The guards who weren't escorting the Grand Duchesses jumped into action, tackling soldiers who were barely able to fight back. Men with damaged limbs and scarred faces were dragged outside where a trip to the prison awaited them. Rasputin stood tall among the chaos, a smile hovering on his angular features, looking every bit the ruler he wasn't supposed to be.

Luka's arm wrapped around Valentina, crushing the black tulle skirts of her tutu, and he guided her into the wings and towards the dressing rooms. It took a moment for her to realise he was speaking.

'What is the monk thinking? His response is so far outside the realm of rationality.'

'What are you talking about?' Valentina pulled herself free. She no longer needed Luka's support; they were safe backstage, especially with Rasputin's guards taking such swift action.

'Rasputin! How could he arrest those men after they've given so much for our country? They're soldiers, and most of them crippled at that!'

'They insulted us,' Valentina said, stopping outside the door to her dressing room.

Luka had stopped too. She didn't think he would come inside and rage, the way Maxim would have, but he was giving her an incredulous look she didn't like.

'They chose not to applaud, that's all. And can you blame them, if you really think about it? Isn't there truth in what they were saying?'

'I don't care to think about it. We were honoured to be invited to dance here, as they should have been honoured to be invited to watch something that would otherwise be out of their reach. Grigori Rasputin's response might have been a touch heavy-handed, but what else was he supposed to do?'

'A touch heavy-handed? Valya, those men out there gave their limbs for us. They gave up their brothers and sons and friends so we can be safe. And you and Rasputin are offended by a little rudeness and some valid questioning?'

'Don't oversimplify the matter so,' Valentina snapped before she could stop herself.

She braced herself thinking she'd feel the quick sting of skin on skin. But Luka was not Maxim. With a disgusted look, he turned his back on her and marched to his own dressing room. He didn't even slam the door behind him.

CHAPTER SIXTEEN

Luka lay on his back, Valentina's weight numbing his arm. Sweat clung to them both in trembling droplets. He was staring at her ceiling, noticing how it didn't bear any stains of previous owners as the one in his apartment did.

'We should get moving,' Valentina said, and sat up.

Her bobbed hair was standing out on one side, and laughing he pushed it back down gently, savouring the silky feel of it against his fingertips.

'Will Maxim be returning?' he asked.

Valentina had taken to sending word for Luka to visit her whenever she was sure of a few hours free of her protector, but there was always the possibility he would return early. She had pointed out a number of places Luka could hide should that ever happen.

'No. I meant that we need to make sure we don't weaken over the off-season. Now that we no longer have the Hermitage performance to rehearse for.'

She avoided his eyes as she said this. Neither of them had spoken about their disagreement since the performance. Luka hadn't changed his opinion about Rasputin's actions, and didn't want to discuss it in case she hadn't either.

'You know I love to dance given any opportunity,' he said. 'But the Mariinsky studios seem so far away today, and I'm so relaxed ...'

'We don't need the Mariinsky. I have a studio.'

Luka sat upright so suddenly he almost knocked Valentina off the bed. She glared at him, and shifted so she was further away.

'What do you mean you have a studio? Where?' His body tingled with anticipation, the ghosts of the movements he knew so well already teasing his limbs.

Valentina waved her hand casually in the air. 'Here, of course.'

'Why didn't you tell me before? We could have interspersed our rehearsals for the Hermitage with other enjoyable activities.' He was teasing, and Valentina picked up on his playfulness.

'That's exactly why. Do you think my body could have kept up with such exhaustion?'

As if to demonstrate, she flopped facedown on the bed. Luka poked her in the backside. She squeaked, slapping a hand around to stop him, and he laughed.

'It's easy for you to be energetic. You've only got one person to please,' she mumbled, her voice muffled by the pillow. A second later, she rolled over and sat up, her white skin flushed pink from pleasure, and swung her legs over the side of the bed. 'Come on then.'

They dressed quickly, then Luka followed Valentina out of her bedroom to a green and yellow wallpapered dining room. A heavy timber table stood in the centre with velvet-seated chairs circling it. Along one wall was a pair of wooden double doors, which opened on smooth hinges. Behind them was a small ballet studio. A long wooden barre lined one wall, and mirrors reflected back at them at the front of the room. A piano stood in one corner. There were no windows, but paintings of dancers hung on the walls in heavy gold frames.

Luka stepped into the room and breathed in deeply. He took long, slow steps around the space, running his hand along the barre.

'I don't believe it,' he murmured. 'It really is a proper ballet studio.'

'What were you expecting? I said it was.'

'I know. But to have one in your own house ...'

'Anna Pavlova had one when she still lived in Russia. I didn't see why I shouldn't too.'

Luka faced the barre and rested his feet in first position. He bent his knees into a demi-plié and it was like greeting an old friend. He looked at Valentina, who was still standing in the doorway. She was regarding him with a peculiar expression.

'What?'

'You should see your face. You've barely taken one dance step and already it's come over all ... I don't even know the word for it. But it makes me sure you'll rule the ballet world one day. Perhaps even have your own company, like Diaghilev.'

'I rather like that idea. Perhaps I will. And when I do, for having been the first believer, you can be its star.'

'Don't make promises you don't intend to keep, for I'll hold you to them anyway.'

'I'll keep it. There'll be a rule in my company though, a rule not even Diaghilev has. No dancers will have protectors.'

The moment he said it, Luka knew he'd gone too far. Amusement fell from her face as though it had been slapped away. He drew in his breath, wondering what he could say to undo the slight. But then she began to laugh. It was a laugh that lacked mirth, true, but it was a laugh nonetheless.

'Good luck finding dancers for your company in that case,' she said.

She joined him in the studio, and talk stopped for a long time as they went through exercises ingrained in their bones. Then, a couple of pas de deux they'd experimented with but chosen not to perform at the Hermitage. Valentina showed off the thirty-two fouettés she'd never got to dance on stage, and Luka applauded with genuine awe. It was perhaps the longest amount of time they'd ever spent together alone, and he found himself wishing there were more days when Valentina was guaranteed of Maxim's absence for such a long stretch.

'I've just remembered something, and if I don't get it now I know it'll slip my mind again,' she said after some time.

Luka was lying on the floor, arms and legs splayed. Valentina stood over him, her face red and glistening with sweat beneath the colourful scarf that kept her bobbed hair in place. She poked him in the side with her toes, and he grabbed her foot and pretended to yank it. She had taken her pointe shoes off and he could feel the calluses beneath his palm.

She yelped, then gave him a soft kick. 'I'll be right back. Wait here.'

Luka forced his liquid muscles to clamber to a standing position. If he sat for too long, his limbs would stiffen. Already, the sweat that dampened his clothes was making him feel chilled. He paced the studio while he waited for Valentina, his feet making only the barest of sounds on the timber floor.

'Here it is,' she said, slipping back through the doors and holding her hands out in front of her.

A coil of hair had escaped her scarf, and Luka longed to reach out and touch it. Instead, he made himself look at her hands. In her palms was a small green velvet bag with a draw-string top.

'What is it?'

'A gift. Open it.'

Luka took the bag tentatively from her. It was soft and supple to touch, heavier than he would have thought. He glanced up at her, waiting with her fingers steepled together, then slowly opened it. Nestled inside was a rose-gold pocket watch. Luka tipped it onto his hand, and sunlight danced up the chain's links. A curling intricate pattern was engraved on the top, and the little door on the front popped open on smooth hinges.

'It's a Buhré watch,' Valentina said, as if Luka would know what that meant. 'A thank you. You know, for the Hermitage.'

She gave a one-shouldered shrug, and Luka wondered if it was a thank-you gift or her attempt at apologising for their argument.

He ran his finger over the glass covering the watch face. 'I've never owned anything so fine in my life.'

Valentina seemed pleased by this. 'You can also use it to keep track of the time until I arrive back at the ballet.'

The higher-ranking dancers often delayed their return to the new season as a way of reminding everyone of their stature.

Transfixed by the unexpected present, Luka closed the little door and spoke without thinking. 'I'd prefer it if you just came back with the rest of us, so I could see you more.'

Valentina made a little sound, and he looked at her. Her smile had disappeared. Perhaps it was because he hadn't thanked her properly and was instead seeming to ask for more.

'Thank you for the watch,' he rushed to say, but his voice suddenly sounded awkward. He tipped the watch back into the velvet bag and pulled the string tight, but that too somehow looked dismissive.

'You're welcome.' Her smile was back in place, but it was the false smile Luka was beginning to recognise.

He didn't want her to go cold and reserved again. On impulse, he grabbed her around the waist and kissed her. She remained stiff against his body for a second, then relaxed, twining her arms around his neck, not minding he was still damp with sweat.

His heart gave a flicker. It was not the usual surge of desire, but something more. He told himself to ignore it and enjoy the moment.

CHAPTER SEVENTEEN

Luka and Xenia were seated on crates at The Wandering Dog, lunching on pâté and salad. In one dimly lit corner a man with a violin was trying to get a melody right, and failing miserably. No one seemed to pay him much mind.

'How was the Hermitage performance?' Xenia asked. She had already filled Luka in on her unsuccessful attempts to get a placement with a foreign company for the off-season, and was now turning the conversation over to him. 'I read in the newspapers that some arrests were made due to a riot or uprising of some sort. Is that true?'

'As close to true as it can be without telling the full story,' Luka responded.

He winced as the violinist hit a note too sharp. The sudden thought of how much Pyotr would laugh at the man's pitiful attempts took hold of him and a chuckle tickled his throat. Then sadness took its place as he remembered Pyotr would never laugh again. He tried to focus back on Xenia, and what she'd been asking.

'The soldiers didn't feel grateful for the performance as they were expected to, and Rasputin didn't take kindly to it. So he arrested a group of unarmed men with missing limbs.'

Xenia's eyebrows rose and she gave a low whistle. 'That must have been something. I can't imagine how Valentina Yershova responded. Probably by holding them down for Rasputin so they couldn't get away.'

'No, she's not like that at all.' It was true Valentina hadn't exactly been full of sympathy for the soldiers, but Luka felt the need to defend her anyway. 'She put so much work into the performance, and it was all for their benefit. So yes, she was a little disappointed with how it came off, but that's understandable.'

'All for their benefit? Come, Luka, you don't believe that.' Xenia laughed as she raised a *granyonyi stakan* of vodka to her lips.

When Luka didn't join her, she lowered it again, staring at him. He had the uncanny feeling she was trying to read something in his face, and he shifted his gaze to his own glass.

'*Bozhe moy*,' she whispered. She glanced around them, then inched her chair closer. 'Luka, please tell me you've been nothing more with her than dance partners?'

Luka raised his own glass and threw its entire contents down his throat in one swift movement. It was good quality vodka, and he signalled for a second one.

'Luka, would you look at me?'

Unable to avoid her any longer, Luka met her eyes. He tried to keep his expression neutral, but his face was beginning to warm.

'Oh, Luka, why? Don't you know who that woman's protector is?'

'An art critic. He has nothing to do with me.'

'But he wields mighty influence because of who he knows. Why would you play such a dangerous game? And for her?'

Luka knew Xenia was right about Maxim. The man had already threatened his career once. But it was harder to feel the threat when it was the off-season and he'd received another year's contract.

'I can't explain it. I suppose ... I don't know how, but she makes me forget, Xenia. About Pyotr, and my father. My grief and anger and guilt fade a little when we're together.'

Xenia shook her head, lips pressed together. 'I should have known something was happening from the moment I saw you. Since that Christmas we spent together, you've often looked at me like a hungry man looks at a piece of bread. Oh, yes, I noticed, and I'm not ashamed to admit I liked it. For a while I even questioned if perhaps I was wrong about us, that it could be different. But today when you walked in, you didn't look at me the same way. I should have known instantly.'

Luka's second vodka arrived, and he was glad of the inter-ruption. He didn't know if he should apologise to Xenia or attempt some comforting words. Instead, he said nothing.

Xenia sighed and straightened up, crossing her arms over her chest. 'Just promise me one thing, Luka. I know you would be able to "forget" with any other woman. Valentina's charms aren't unique to her, and another woman would come with a lot less danger. Promise me you will think about that.'

Her gaze was steady, challenging. Luka knew it was because she cared for him that she asked this. It couldn't hurt.

'I promise,' he said.

Luka stood on the sidewalk, hat pulled low over his face. He fiddled with his jacket sleeves, trying to look as though he'd paused to adjust his clothing instead of surreptitiously watching the attractive wealthy couple making their goodbyes outside the pale brick building.

A child darted past, almost crashing into Luka's legs, and he stepped back so she wouldn't fall over. His gaze was averted for only a moment, but when it returned, Maxim was kissing Valentina. Her face was tilted up to receive the kiss, and when Maxim pulled away he said something that made her smile.

It was like an ocean wave crashing over Luka's head, taking his breath away. What was he doing? Watching while another man kissed Valentina in the hope it would be his turn next? Xenia was right. He was playing a foolish game that he could never win.

He turned his back and stared down at his polished shoes. In them he thought he could see the reflection of a man who had become indistinguishable from Mathilde and her cohorts. A man who made excuses for himself so he could satisfy his own whims. This was not the man he wanted to be.

He'd already taken a few steps away from his source of shame, when he thought of how Valentina looked at him as they peeled their clothes off each other. In his mind's eye he saw the way she studied him so intently, as if she had never seen a man before. And he felt the undeniable draw of her, the intoxicating pleasure of being admired by a woman whose notice he should have been below. Xenia wasn't right about everything: no other woman would be able to offer him that. Perhaps it was ego; perhaps it was his desires taking hold of him. Whatever it was, Luka wasn't sure he was able to let it go. Not yet anyway.

He turned slowly back to face Valentina's house, glanced up under the brim of his hat, then froze. Not thirty paces from him strode Maxim. He hadn't seen Luka, but another few steps and he wouldn't be able to miss him.

Luka leaped onto the road. A carriage nearly knocked him over, and the driver swore at him. Heart racing, Luka hunched his shoulders to try to hide his face and ran to the other side of the street. He didn't turn around to see if Maxim was watching. He kept walking, right past Valentina's front door, and took the first corner he came to, wanting to be out of sight, hating himself for being the coward his father had accused him of being.

Luka breathed in the familiar smells of greasepaint, worn shoes, ropes and paint in the backstage area of the Mariinsky Theatre. Even the pieces of scenery seemed to buzz with life as he took in that indefinable thrill only familiar to those who performed onstage. He felt euphoric to be back for the new season. He had been cast as Arthur in the three-act ballet *Barbe-Bleue*. Arthur, a page, was madly in love with Ysaure, a woman who professed to love him back but married the villainous Bluebeard anyway. Despite her marriage to another man, Arthur did his all to protect her.

Xenia had been cast in a small role as Anne, Ysaure's sister, whom Arthur danced with to cheer his unhappily wedded lover, and Luka had been thrilled to have the chance to dance with her onstage. Only once they had moved onto the black expanse, he got the feeling she was angry with him. Her face was lit with a confident smile, her movements light and lyrical as they danced in front of a full crowd, but instead of jumping up and holding herself in the way that made her lighter, she barely raised herself off the ground. She was a dead weight in his arms. Luka struggled to disguise it from the audience, his whole concentration focused on keeping her in the air whenever the choreography demanded it, his skin slick with sweat.

Finally, they were offstage and he was able to wipe his face on a rag, his hands trembling from exertion. Xenia stood in the wings, staring with pointed concentration at the mysterious figure of Curiosity, who was tempting Ysaure to follow him underground.

'Xenia?' Luka whispered, moving in close so he could speak right in her ear.

She didn't even blink.

'Are you angry with me?'

She glanced at him, then continued to watch the dancing couple.

'Please, if you're angry with me, tell me what I've done. I'll make it right as soon as I know what it is.'

He had every right to be angry at her too—her behaviour onstage was unprofessional and risked them both getting fines. But it was so out of character for her that any annoyance he might have felt was subdued by concern.

Xenia closed her eyes for a second in a gesture of exasperation, then took a step back so they were further from the stage.

'You didn't even think about it, did you?' she hissed, flicking her foot in an irritated battement frappé. A nearby dancer glared at her, holding a finger to her lips. Xenia glared back until the dancer looked away. 'You didn't keep your promise.'

'My promise?'

A group of dancers flitted off the stage and through the wings, and Luka grabbed Xenia's elbow to pull her further out of the way. The movement brought them closer, their heads bent towards each other so they were almost touching. He could see the tremble on Xenia's painted-red lips when she spoke again.

'Valentina Yershova,' she whispered, her voice so low Luka could barely hear it. Even so, he glanced around to check no one else could have heard.

'What is it you think you know?' he asked.

He hadn't spoken to Xenia about Valentina since they'd returned to the ballet. Whether it was because he had avoided the subject or she had, he couldn't be sure.

Xenia sighed and looked over her shoulder at a scene-shifter about to edge his way around them. He was dressed in costume so as to blend in with the ballet. Luka gently touched her cheek, urging her to look back at him. When she did, her eyes were shadowed, made larger by the darkness of the wings and her make-up.

'She came back to the ballet earlier than I've ever known her to. That alone was enough to make me wonder. But today, when you walked into the theatre, you were wearing a very fine pocket watch. A Buhré if I'm not mistaken. Those don't come at the kind of price a corps dancer can ordinarily afford.'

Luka let his hand drop and took a small step away. His knees, still trembling from carrying Xenia's full weight, felt even weaker. On the stage, Mathilde was making her way through a series of treasure-filled underground chambers, delighted as caryatids, gold and silver vessels, heavy silks and precious stones all came to life to dance with her.

'That's why you danced the way you did?' he questioned.

'That was unfair and unprofessional. I'm sorry. I shouldn't have behaved that way—especially on the stage where everyone could see. I was just so … Luka, I worry about you. I don't think you realise the risks you're taking. You have such a future ahead of you—'

'A future can be taken away at any moment by anything,' Luka snapped back, thinking of his brother. He realised he was being too loud and took a deep breath. 'I did keep my promise, Xenia. I did think it over. I just didn't come to the conclusion you wanted me to.'

'I see.' She took a long breath that echoed Luka's. 'I should never have brought it up like this, in the middle of a performance. I'll go and touch up my make-up, give us both a chance to calm ourselves. See you back on stage?'

'Yes.'

She turned to go, then paused, her gaze fixed on the stage. Frowning, Luka turned to look too. The music had softened and the delicate notes curling into the air weren't loud enough to cover the shout that had exploded from the audience. The words were unmistakable: 'Imperial slaves!'

With a glance at each other, Luka and Xenia moved closer to the stage, shoulder to shoulder with others who had done the same. Mathilde was still dancing, but her smile had a frozen quality. From where they stood in the wings they couldn't see the audience, but the next shout that came was clear.

'Are you content to dance while your countrymen die?'

Murmurs in the audience followed. Then the sounds of a scuffle, followed by another shout.

'How long will you continue to feed from the Romanov teat while the rest of us starve?'

Mathilde's face was stony now, no longer pretending she hadn't noticed. She continued to dance, and they heard the slam of a door as the man who'd interrupted was thrown out. The audience was unsettled, though, and their chatter competed with the orchestra, who played louder in an effort to bring their attention back to where it should be.

Xenia's face was white beneath her make-up. Instinctively Luka gave her shoulder a gentle squeeze, hoping she couldn't feel the tremble in his fingers. Never, in the entire history of the Imperial Russian Ballet, had an audience member dared to interrupt a performance. Remembering the scene at the private performance at the Hermitage Theatre, Luka was glad Rasputin was not present.

The dressing room was alive with chatter, everyone talking about the interruption that had marred what would otherwise have been a standard performance. Luka dodged between bags and hanging costumes to get to his place at the long bench that stretched around the mirrored walls. He wasn't interested in picking over the details; he just wanted to get his uncomfortable costume off.

But when he saw his spot, his feet froze. His belongings, which only that afternoon had sat in careful order, were all pushed to one side, some knocked over.

'Who did this?' he asked. 'Who moved my things?'

He turned to stare at the other men in the room, eyes burning as he waited for the guilty party to come forward. His chest was tight, and he tried to tell himself to calm down, not let anxiety get the better of him. He'd never been as superstitious as many others in the company, even getting on fine after losing his lucky pair of gloves. But an undisturbed ritual after a performance was essential.

He asked the question again; most of the men shrugged their shoulders and returned to what they'd been doing before.

'Excuse me.'

The arrogant lilting voice belonged to a young man who shouldered his way up to the chair next to Luka and sat down. He rattled through the belongings in front of him and his elbow knocked to the floor a little statuette Xenia had given Luka the Christmas they'd spent together. It was a flat wooden figure of the Ballets Russes dancer Adolph Bolm, striking a pose from Fokine's *Thamar,* and she'd ordered it especially from London.

Ignoring what he'd done, the man grabbed a comb and pulled it through his wavy hair.

'Excuse you indeed,' Luka snapped, snatching the figurine up and checking it for damage.

The young man glanced at him in the mirror. 'Did I do something?'

Luka gritted his teeth. Very deliberately he placed the figure down where it had been before. 'You knocked this. And my other stuff—did you move it?'

'Oh, yes. Sorry about that. I needed a little more room.'

'Well, you don't get any more room.'

Luka couldn't believe this man. It was true he was only new to the company, but even students knew a dancer's place in the dressing room was sacrosanct. He began slamming his belongings back into their original places. The young man pretended not to notice, but when Luka banged a greasepaint pot down particularly loudly, he flinched. Luka thought he knew what the boy was doing. For those newly accepted into the company, seeing their classmates overlooked and resorting to foreign companies could go to their head. A few years in the Imperial

Russian Ballet, only one of one hundred and eighty dancers, would bring him back in line. If he even lasted that long.

Luka continued to tidy his space, pointedly pushing the other man's belongings away. He carefully picked up a picture of Nijinsky that had fallen down and pinned it back on the edge of the mirror, smoothing it with his thumb to get rid of a small crease that had appeared in one corner. He'd heard the ugly rumours that Nijinsky was succumbing to madness and had pinned the picture up in defiance of them. Seeing it knocked down felt like a particularly cruel blow, not just against Luka, but against artistry itself.

Out of the corner of his eye, he saw his juvenile neighbour put down his comb and pick up a cloth. As he wiped away the greasepaint that decorated his face, he opened his mouth and spoke so quietly no one besides Luka could have heard him.

'Maxim Sergeivich sends his regards.'

Luka, who was lifting his own comb to his hair, froze.

The young man gave him a significant look in the mirror, and Luka's heart pounded in a way he usually didn't experience unless he was waiting in the wings, ready to step onto the stage.

'What are you … Are you saying—'

'Just his regards. That's all.'

The boy continued to groom himself and Luka knew with a sick feeling in the pit of his stomach that he would get no more from him.

CHAPTER EIGHTEEN

Autumn 1916

Valentina slipped out of the bed, careful not to wake Maxim. It was the very early hours of the morning. The air was balmy from the hidden stove, but when her bare feet touched the timber floor, goosebumps rippled up her arms. She reached for the manteau she'd left on the floor and wrapped it around herself, pulling the soft polar-fox collar high so it brushed her jawbone.

She hesitated, looking down at Maxim. One leg was thrown out from underneath the covers, the curve of his buttock exposed. She picked up the edge of the uppermost blanket and covered him, then tiptoed out of the room and made her way through the darkened house, one hand feeling the way. In her other hand was a glass perfume bottle filled with vinegar.

She had to bite her lip to stop from crying out when she tripped over a chair that didn't appear until she was right on top of it. She hated staying at Maxim's house; at least in her own, she knew where things were. Briefly she wondered if she were to become his wife, would he make her give up her house? She couldn't bear the idea. It would be bad enough having to give up Luka.

Instead of thinking about it, she stood on one foot and waved the other in the air, willing away the pounding in her stubbed toes. She was lucky she hadn't done herself an injury that would prevent her from dancing. She felt cold at the thought of it.

Gripping the manteau even more tightly around herself, she skirted the offending piece of furniture and entered Maxim's study. Once inside, Valentina pulled the door closed and opened the curtains to let the moon illuminate the room. Absent-mindedly, she drifted into a pas de bourrée, ending with a solemn arabesque. Her toe was still throbbing and she favoured her left leg so as not to hurt it more. Coming down out of the arabesque, she took another few steps then paused, staring at the perfume bottle in her hand. She'd left Maxim's presence in order to wash herself with the vinegar—another precaution against having a child.

She walked over to his desk and turned the velvet-lined chair around to face her. She placed one foot on it, ready to tip some of the vinegar into her cupped hand, when she noticed one of the desk drawers was open. What would she find if she looked in that drawer, she wondered. Would it give her some insight into the man she shared her life with? Perhaps a clue how to turn him from protector to husband?

She glanced at the doorway, folding her bottom lip between forefinger and thumb. If Maxim had wanted to keep the drawer safe from prying eyes, he would have made sure to close it fully, perhaps even lock it.

She placed the perfume bottle to one side, turned the chair back around and sat, then slid one hand into the open drawer.

Her fingers clasped what felt like a pile of thick papers, and she pulled them out. After checking the door one more time, she bent in close to look at what she'd found. A gasp slipped out of her mouth.

The papers were all about her. There were photographs of her, both in everyday dress and in ballet costumes. Ticket stubs from performances she'd been a part of—dating back to before she and Maxim had ever met—were caught up in programs whose corners were folded down to mark the pages her name appeared on. There was even part of a program from the disastrous Evening of Russian Fashion, torn so that only the little piece with her name was left. Her hands were overflowing with remnants of her own life. How many times had Maxim sat where she was, fondling the pictures, perhaps running a finger affectionately down her still face? Dreaming over a woman he'd set his sights on before even meeting her?

Trembling, Valentina let the papers fall into her lap. She sat completely still in the silent room, staring at nothing, trying to control her ragged breathing. A few moments later, she pushed the tangle of photos, programs and ticket stubs back in the desk drawer.

She mechanically washed herself down with the vinegar, not even its acrid smell jolting her out of her stupor. She stoppered the bottle, then tiptoed back to the bedroom and crawled into bed next to her protector.

Maxim's leg was twitching, and every time his skin brushed her own she felt her chest convulse. Somewhere in there, a cry was trying to get free. But she wouldn't let it. She closed her eyes and focused on quelling the feeling, squeezing it into a tight ball. She willed herself to sleep, but sleep never came.

When Maxim woke and turned to her, it was all she could do not to cringe away from him. She tried to be pleased, to welcome his embrace, but it was all an act. Once he was satiated, he left for his study, and Valentina dressed and escaped to the recessed balcony that adjoined his reception room, welcoming the weak morning sunlight that shone on her neck. Her head felt thick and heavy, like she'd drunk too many glasses of champagne.

She forced down some food that she didn't taste. Her lips were numb, her hands moving without thought. She couldn't stop picturing the bundle of programs, clippings and photographs she'd found. The secret collection was troubling. A certain amount of proprietorship was expected from a protector of course; and love had its usefulness when one knew how to keep control of it. Valentina had hoped to inspire in Maxim the kind of love that would lead to marriage. But that collection seemed to speak of something else, something she wasn't sure she liked. The fact that it had begun long before their relationship disturbed her.

She didn't want to hear the thoughts that began to surface, but they crammed her head, impossible to ignore. Perhaps it was time to find herself a new protector.

Valentina exhaled sharply, picking up a silver *podstakannik* and sipping the tea that had gone cold. She could practically hear Mamma's voice, icy with derision, asking how she thought she might go about getting a protector who could be of more value to her than Maxim.

She placed the *podstakannik* down with a rattle.

'Shouldn't you be going to the Mariinsky?'

Maxim's voice made her jump. She hadn't heard him step onto the balcony, and her face coloured at being caught at the exact moment she'd been contemplating leaving him. She tried to cover it by pouring a second glass of tea, slipping it into the ornate silver holder, and holding it out to him. He took it, but didn't drink.

'I'm not feeling well,' she said. 'I don't think I'll go.' It was rare for Valentina to miss a class once she'd returned for the season, but she didn't feel she could face it today.

'My poor Valechka.' Maxim caressed the side of her head, his cool lips landing a kiss on her cheek.

A pang of guilt hit Valentina. As he took the seat opposite her, she tried to smile, but her practised deference felt more hollow than usual. Maxim was looking at her with the superior expression that said he had something to tell her. She found herself dreading what it could be.

'Grigori Rasputin tells me the Imperial Russian Ballet is going to be rehearsing *Le Lac des Cygnes* in the coming months.'

Valentina's breath caught.

Maxim casually crossed his ankle over one knee and took a long, slow sip of his tea, placing the *podstakannik* back on the tablecloth with achingly slow movements. Valentina could stand it no longer.

'It's not been billed for the season.'

His lips twisted, almost a smile. 'No. It's being considered as a surprise performance. For the public, to raise their spirits. Much like your Hermitage performance was supposed to do for the soldiers, until they turned traitor. They'll be looking at casting soon. Mathilde will no doubt be given Odette/Odile, but there's some question as to who might understudy her.'

He raised his heavy eyebrows just a fraction. His dark eyes were grim, and Valentina felt a shiver go up her spine. She was almost too afraid to ask the question he was teasing her with.

'Do you ... do you think I might ...?'

'I already know you would make a perfect Odile, Valechka. But if I were to whisper a few well-timed words in Rasputin's ear, I could only do so if I knew you could be Odette too. After all, I would be putting my own reputation on the line.'

He leaned forward, his hands landing so heavily on the table between them that it shook. Valentina's stomach twisted. After so many years of dreaming, was Odette finally within her reach?

'If you want the role, you need to convince me you can be a good Odette.'

'How would I do that?' She licked lips that had suddenly gone dry.

'You know what the role calls for. A sweet nature, a woman dedicated to the man she loves. Faithful.'

The word hung in the air between them, and Valentina thought for a second she might actually stop breathing. Did Maxim know all she had been up to with Luka? Was he somehow aware that only a moment ago she'd been thinking of replacing him?

She worked a smile onto her face, forcing herself to ignore the ache in her head. 'I'm sorry if you don't already think me capable of all that, but I know I am. I can be Odette.'

A quick smirk flitted over Maxim's lips; the expression of a man who knew he had won.

'Good. I knew you would do anything to be Odette. It's the one weakness you don't seem able to overcome.' He stood and rested a hand on top of Valentina's head. The weight of it was oppressive. 'And, Valya? If you do get the role, you'll need to work harder than ever to prove that it was deserved. There won't be time for socialising with corps members. If you can't manage that, some dancers may have to be removed from the production, if not the company. Or I can arrange it so they find their body no longer capable of dancing. Remember, the eyes of Petrograd's elite will be on you. As will mine.'

With those words, he was gone.

Valentina spread her trembling hands on the table, needing to feel something solid under her palms. A tear slid down her face, and with cold fingers she brushed it away.

'I thought he'd never leave,' Luka said by way of greeting, stepping into the blue room where Valentina was waiting for him. He leaned down, and Valentina turned her head so that his kiss landed on her cheek instead of her lips. She wondered if he was able to smell Maxim's cologne on her. The part of herself that was ruling hoped he could; her heart felt differently.

'Is everything alright?' he asked.

'Of course.'

Valentina smoothed her dress in order to stop herself from picking at the skin around her nails. She had to do it now. It had already been three days; she couldn't put it off any longer.

But Luka cut her off before she had the chance to say anything. 'I have something for you.'

His sweet mouth was smiling, and Valentina longed to kiss it even as guilt convulsed her innards. She wanted to own that mouth forever. But it wasn't for her, not any more. No matter how much her aching heart protested.

Luka fished in his coat pocket and unearthed a small box. He held it out to her. 'Here. For you.'

She knew without opening it that it contained jewellery. She'd been gifted enough over her lifetime to be able to tell. Yet she accepted the box with fingers that felt as though they might get bitten by the gift.

'It's not from Cartier or the like,' Luka said, but Valentina wasn't listening. She was staring at the bracelet that sat on a white satin bed inside the box. Seven strands of fine silver chains were joined at either end by large clasps engraved with black vines. It was simple, yet delicate and beautiful.

'Why did you get me this?' Valentina breathed.

'Because I have something to remind me of you when we're not together, but you don't have something from me. Or you didn't until now.'

Luka didn't have the kind of money to throw away on jewellery—Valentina knew that. She wouldn't have bought something like this for herself when she was a corps dancer, and she'd had Dimitri funding the most lavish parts of her life-style. She snapped the lid shut and stood up, almost knocking over the chair she'd been sitting in. This gift made what she was about to do so much worse, so much harder. Despite her best efforts, this young man with his easy laughter and belief in what was right and what was wrong had managed to break through walls she'd thought impenetrable. The realisation was terrifying and exhilarating all at once, like standing on the edge of a precipice. But she couldn't pay it any mind. Not if she wanted to protect Luka as well as herself.

'I'm aware it isn't half as fine as what you already own,' he told her. 'But it's something. Put it away wherever you keep your stash of jewels.'

Valentina's lips were almost numb as she pushed out the words he'd unknowingly set up for her. 'My dresser. In my bedroom. Come.'

Luka smiled, thinking she meant them to spend time together there. How Valentina wished she could; one last moment of ecstasy before she returned to a life of only duty. She could have that moment, she knew, if she took him to another room—perhaps the blue reception room where they'd first made love. But she wouldn't. It would only make things more difficult.

Luka followed her to her bedroom. She pushed the door wide, then stepped inside, unable to look at him, hurrying instead to her dresser where she took her time putting the bracelet away. She heard Luka take a few steps into the room, then stop. His sharp intake of breath told her he'd noticed the bed.

It was usually tidy, its covers tucked in by the maid and a scattering of embroidered cushions resting on top—cushions Luka often made a game of kicking around, enjoying Valentina's exasperated laughter. Now it was a mess. The covers were a sweaty tangle, one of the pillows knocked to the floor and forgotten. The cushions were stacked on a chair in the corner, put there in preparation for the bed being used.

Valentina reminded herself that she had set this scene for Luka's benefit. It would lessen his pain to be reminded of what kind of woman she was. She turned to face him.

'This is my life, Luka. I belong to Maxim. I've forgotten that the last few months. But I can't any longer. There's too much at stake, too much to lose, if we continue. I'm sorry.'

She had never spoken harder words, but she was a good actress. Living with protectors had taught her how to be.

Luka's face had gone still and expressionless, and he swallowed.

'You shouldn't be,' he mumbled, turning away from her. 'We knew this couldn't last forever. You came to your senses first, I suppose. I should go.'

She had been afraid that he might fight for her. The realisation that he wouldn't was a sharp pain, like a muscle tearing in her chest.

'Luka, please … don't go just yet.'

She wanted to talk to him, to ensure that he was going to be alright. No, that wasn't it; her motives were selfish. She wanted to keep him with her a little longer, knowing this would be the last time they were alone.

'What else should I do? Wait while your maid puts fresh sheets on the bed so it's ready to use again? They've got to go all the way to London to be laundered, so it could be a while. Or should I just use the same ones?' The words, designed to hurt, found their mark. 'You said yourself we can't continue.'

'I did. Do you … do you want the bracelet back?'

'No. Keep it. Or throw it away, or sell it. Whatever you want. I bought it for you—it's yours. Whatever that's worth to you.'

Valentina was almost glad he didn't look at her before leaving. If his eyes had met hers, and she'd seen the pain and reproach in them, she didn't think she would have been able to keep the tears that so badly wanted to crawl down her cheeks in check.

Luka tossed his beer back in one go. The Wandering Dog, with its bohemian atmosphere and mismatched interior, was the ideal place to lose himself in his miserable thoughts.

It had been a stupid idea to give her the bracelet—she probably would never have worn it. He'd seen for himself the gold and diamond swan brooch Maxim had bought her; a handful of her jewels could probably buy Luka's entire apartment. Still, he'd thought she would be touched by the small gesture, would know that although the gift paled in comparison to her other riches, the cost to him had been great. But in the end Valentina had proved herself the person others decried her as. He was the one who'd been wrong.

A commotion began in the middle of the room, and Luka tried to ignore it. But then his table was being lifted right in front of him and he realised a space was being cleared.

'Who for?' he asked the nearest man, who shrugged and turned away.

Luka stood, allowing his stool to be taken away too. He moved back until he was against the piled-up furniture. A woman with a round face and severely parted dark hair stood in the clearing, her shoes kicked off, stockinged feet flat against the sticky floor. She began to move softly; it was ballet, but not as Luka recognised it. Her arms were curled in, hands almost making fists, and she flexed her feet as much as pointed them. There was something of the Egyptian hieroglyph to her movements, flat and side-on to the part of the room she was performing to, and he was transfixed.

When she finished with a roll of her shoulders, then gestured for the patrons to move the furniture back to its original state, Luka wove through the chairs, tables and crates to get to her.

'Excuse me,' he said, reaching out but not quite touching her dark sleeve.

She turned to him. Her face was a touch pink, her breathing a little fast, but she gave him a smile.

'Not as used to that as I once was,' she said, attempting to catch her breath.

She was handed a mineral water by a woman who'd evidently appreciated the dancing, and sipped it gratefully.

'But you are a ballet dancer, I can tell,' Luka said. 'Please, what is the piece you were dancing? I didn't recognise it.'

She surveyed him, her expression neutral. 'An imperialist, are you?' The word marked her as one who had danced with Diaghilev's Ballets Russes. Luka nodded. 'It was one of the tennis players from Nijinsky's *Jeux*. I was the first to dance the role. There's supposed to be another woman mirroring the movements next to me. But then there's supposed to be a white dress and pointe shoes, not silk petticoats and darned stockings.'

'You are with the Ballets Russes then?' Luka had never met anyone who had danced with the company, not face to face. Nor had he seen their unique take on ballet.

The woman was putting her shoes back on, one arm flung out to the side to steady herself. Luka pulled a spare crate over for her to sit on.

'Thank you. I was, but I came back to nurse for the Red Cross. Wanted to do my part for the war. You know how it is.'

Guilt, that old acquaintance, rose up to meet Luka. His brother had known; even Mathilde with her hospitals was doing her part. What had he, Luka, done to help the war?

The woman did up her buckles, then held out her hand to shake his. 'Ludmilla Schollar. So you're a Romanov dancer.'

'As were you.' Luka hadn't recognised her face, but he knew her name. Ludmilla Schollar had trained at the Imperial Ballet School and gone on to dance with the company for some years.

'Yes. I left when Diaghilev gave me an opportunity.'

'What's he like?'

Ludmilla sighed, glancing over her shoulder towards the stairs. She'd probably had to field such a question many times before—balletomanes were wild about the impresario. Still, she had the good grace to answer him.

'As one would expect mostly. Brilliant, temperamental, sometimes fatherly. But most of all, honest with his art. He once had the patronage of the Grand Duke Vladimir, you know, but lost it when he refused to be dictated to over repertoire and casting choices.'

Luka was impressed. How different would the Imperial Ballet be without the influence of protectors? That was never likely to happen, of course, but it made him think. Xenia had once said there were other options out there for a young man such as himself. Perhaps another company could be a way to escape Valentina and any lingering effects their cut-off affair might have—whether to his heart or to his career.

Ludmilla must have recognised his interest as more than just idolisation, for she softened towards him. 'Interested, are you? You'd be wise to consider it. I hope to go back myself someday, if this war ever ends. There's a freedom in the Ballets Russes you won't get in most other companies. They aren't afraid to break boundaries. Yet they also desire to drill into the very soul of what each ballet means. That is why Diaghilev attracts the best. Not just dancers, you understand. Alexandre Benois and Bakst have each painted scenery for him; Stravinsky was disregarded in Russia until Diaghilev made his name; and you'll find Jean Cocteau running around and making the dancers laugh during rehearsals. You work hard, though; perhaps harder than in the Imperial Russian Ballet. The Ballets Russes is not a job but a lifestyle.'

In that moment, a lifestyle sounded appealing to Luka. He could bury himself in dance, without time to remember his brother's death, or Valentina's touch, or his father's angry words. Such a decision was not something to make rashly, of course. But perhaps it was time he envisioned a life outside the Imperial Russian Ballet, even for a short while. Ludmilla had come back, after all. He could too if it turned out to be the wrong choice.

'I'll not take any more of your time,' he said gratefully, giving her a hand to help her up from the crate. 'But thank you. You've given me much to think about. And, perhaps, a little hope.'

Ludmilla took up the shawl she'd discarded and draped it over her shoulders. She smoothed back a few stray hairs that had emerged during her dancing, and gave him a soft smile.

'Hope is something we could all use more of these days.'

CHAPTER NINETEEN

Winter 1916

Luka began gently. As he moved forward, he felt the impulse resonating through his very bones. A tentative pirouette and joy shot through him, an electric pulse in his stomach. He barely realised when he'd taken the next step; everything felt as warm as the morning light that filtered through the opaque windows. Outside, others were gathering, but Luka ignored them, allowing himself to be lifted up on the air of his movements. This wasn't just warming up; it was a celebration of the life that was his—a life of dance. Suddenly he was racing around the studio, the ground flowing underneath him like it wasn't even there. He could no longer tell the difference between the air and the floor. He was in ecstasy, body screaming and reaching and embracing. He could no more stop than he could choose to stop breathing.

He wanted to push it further, to go to the very reaches of his limits. He was panting and grinning and flying and trying not to let out a shout. And then, just as his chest felt like it might burst from his rapid, hard breathing, he stopped. Sweat dripped down his face, tracing the back of his neck, and his muscles sang with life. The world of swirling colours he'd been in dissipated, and he was once again in the studio.

Men and women entered the room, some of them clapping, only a few sarcastically. Luka ignored them and wiped his sleeve over his face. He'd burst the toe of his right ballet shoe, and he turned to the door, meaning to go to the dressing room to fetch a new one. But he paused, noticing that Xenia stood there. Her lips were curved in a smile, and he was pleased to see it. He hadn't enjoyed the lingering awkwardness after their squabble, but since he'd told her the affair had ended, she'd gone back to her usual half-teasing self.

'Impressive,' she said when he reached her.

'I felt like coming in early to let out some frustrations. What are you doing here?'

Xenia wasn't in the class of perfection and should have been headed to a different rehearsal room.

'I've been called up to wardrobe. They asked for you too, and I said I'd fetch you.'

'Alright. Let me change my shoes and find something to wipe myself off with, and I'll be right with you.'

The rooms occupying the top floor of the Mariinsky were filled to bursting with wooden chests and hampers. Dull daylight filtered through the partially obstructed windows, muting the colours that would stand out brilliantly on the electrically lit stage.

Valentina stood in the middle of the room surrounded by a mess of tulle, linen, lace and feathers. The seamstress had just pricked her arm, and the resulting apology sounded insincere. As she shifted the costume her forceful movements almost caused Valentina to lose her footing.

Given her current mood, Valentina was tempted to have a word to someone about the seamstress's behaviour. But she decided against it. On some level she could empathise with the woman's frustration; it was one shared by the entire company. Until recently, they had always been given new costumes for each ballet. But the impact of the war on the imperial coffers meant such extravagances were no longer possible. Revivals of the classics were scheduled so the old scenery could be used; and the wardrobe department were forced to resize existing costumes to fit dancers they hadn't been made for.

'Turn around, please,' the seamstress said, breaking off the thread with her teeth.

Valentina obeyed, and the woman pulled in the corset of the knee-length tutu. The boning was poking through the aged silk and dug painfully into her side. The seamstress had said she would attend to it eventually.

Valentina recognised many of the costumes hanging up around the room. She found their musty smell unpleasant, but it was always impressive to stand in their midst. Some she had worn herself, including one of the tiny peasant dresses made for students. Not wanting to remember those days, she looked instead at the tutu she was wearing now. It was for a revival of *La Esmeralda*. Despite being second-hand it was still beautiful, with a bejewelled green and gold bodice, snow-white tulle skirts peeping from beneath a scarlet shawl tied around her waist, and tassels and pom poms that danced with her every movement. On her upper arms were cuffs of gold medallions, and when she was onstage there would be medallions in her hair to match. There would also be embroidered scarves and a tambourine dripping with yellow ribbons for her to dance with, but there was no sign of them now. Briefly she wondered if the coloured glass on her costume would shine as brightly onstage as the real gems on Mathilde's costume—paid for by the prima ballerina assoluta herself—then let the thought die. Of course they wouldn't.

'There we are—done for now,' the seamstress said. 'Take it off, and don't knock out any of those loose pins or we'll have to do the whole thing again.'

Valentina changed back into her white practice dress. It looked dull compared to the costumes, but at least it didn't have some other dancer's name from years ago on the inner tag. She wanted to get back to rehearsals and away from this room. It was too full of the ghosts of all the great dancers she would never live up to.

Out in the corridor, her polar-fox manteau draped around her shoulders to ward off the chill, she thought through her *La Esmeralda* part, marking out the steps with her hands as she walked. She'd been cast as Mathilde's understudy in the title role. It was the second time she had understudied Mathilde in a lead role, but the first time she'd danced the character the ballet was named after. When she'd told Maxim, he'd given her a satisfied look that was meant to let her know the casting was because of him. He'd acted as though she should be grateful; as though he was rewarding her for doing the right thing. But the role wasn't Odette.

Hearing voices, Valentina glanced up from the relevés and posé arabesques her hands were marking out. A few feet away, sitting on a chair with her feet balanced on the toes of her pointe shoes, was Xenia Nicholaievna. Next to her stood Luka, his arm leaning against the wall above her in a way that looked protective. Neither of them had noticed her as they spoke to each other in low voices.

Valentina's heart twisted. Since she had broken the affair off with Luka, she had returned to her pretence that nothing ever went wrong in her world. It was easier than admitting to being alone with no one to turn to for advice or support. But it was difficult to keep believing her lie. The aching maw within her was too big; her solitariness too acute. And having no one to confide in made her wonder if she had got this life all wrong. It was too late to change it now, though.

At that moment Valentina would have given anything to run back into the wardrobe room and hide behind the skirts of fictional characters. She couldn't return to rehearsals without passing Luka and Xenia.

Hearing her footsteps, Luka looked up. Valentina's breath caught in her throat as his eyes met hers; then his expectant smile disappeared, and it was as though cold water had been poured over her.

'Did they ask for one of us?' His voice was cool, his lack of greeting rude.

Ordinarily Valentina would have responded in a way that showed she was above petty displays of emotion, but all her energy seemed to have seeped from her. Her body felt weak, and her mind was too sluggish to think of anything smart to say.

Luka raised an impatient eyebrow at her. He hadn't looked that way at her for a long time, not since before the very first time they'd kissed.

Behind them, a voice called out—one of the dressmakers requesting Luka.

Finally mustering some energy, Valentina gave him a smile she hoped didn't appear forced and said, 'Be careful in there. They're wicked with the pins today.'

The voice called again, curt this time, but Luka was already walking down the hall towards the room. Valentina watched his retreating back, feeling as though she was saying goodbye to him all over again.

'See something you like?' Xenia asked archly.

Valentina kept her voice steady. 'What interest would I have in a corps boy?'

'I'd say he's more man than boy. But then, I would know.'

Valentina gritted her teeth; she'd known Luka and this Xenia had some kind of past. But she wouldn't rise to the bait. Being heartsick was a behaviour men indulged in over her, not vice versa.

'You see, not all of us require payment for everything,' Xenia went on, and Valentina was glad that her lack of response had evidently grated on the woman; she wouldn't be continuing to try to goad her if it hadn't. 'I get what I want without money ever changing hands. You can keep your protectors and your claques. I don't need them.'

The words were a slap in the face. A claque was a group paid by a dancer to sit in the audience and applaud every time he or she appeared on stage. One thing Valentina had never exchanged money for was applause.

She took a step forward, her voice rising. 'Why, you impudent little—'

'Oh, was I wrong?' Xenia asked innocently. 'About which part? The protector or the claque?'

'Xenia?' Luka's voice came from down the hall. 'They made a mistake. They want you first after all.'

'Coming.' Xenia hopped off the chair and brushed past Valentina.

Unable to help herself, Valentina grabbed the other woman's arm. Her fingernails curled into the soft skin and she felt Xenia's gasp shudder through her whole body. It was only a second, then she let go, staring at her own unfurling hand as though it belonged to a stranger.

'Xenia?' Luka's voice was concerned, his face twisted as he came towards them, one hand reaching out to Xenia.

Xenia stared at Valentina, rubbing the red marks on her arm. Valentina couldn't take her eyes off them. She'd seen so many similar marks on her own skin—remnants of Maxim's touch. But never before had she caused them. She wanted to say she was sorry, that she didn't know what had come over her, but her breath caught in her throat. Her eyes met Xenia's yet still she couldn't say the words. With a jerky movement she turned and began to walk away.

'What is the matter with her?' Xenia asked.

There was a note of bewildered sympathy in her voice that made tears sting the backs of Valentina's eyes. She took a sharp breath, not wanting to hear Luka's answer.

'Who can tell? I think she's just built for unhappiness.' The words were biting, but they weren't as cruel as what came next. 'Don't waste your time thinking about her. She's proved that she's not worth it.'

Valentina counted slowly in her head, forcing her feet to match the rhythm so she didn't run away as she wanted to. She kept her back straight, showing she didn't care, when inside she felt nothing but pain.

CHAPTER TWENTY

'You can't trust anyone.'

Maxim's voice in the otherwise silent room made Valentina jump. He hadn't spoken for the last hour, and she'd given up trying to coax any words out of him.

'Grigori Rasputin couldn't trust Felix Yusupov or Dmitri Pavlovich,' he continued. 'He couldn't trust the imperial family to keep him safe.'

He took a deep gulp from the crystal glass clutched in his hand. The decanter sat next to him on the sofa, tucked between its upholstered back and a matching embroidered cushion.

Valentina was standing near the window to avoid breathing in the alcohol fumes wafting from him. She'd been remembering the feel of the monk's arm in hers as they walked through the crowds at the Evening of Russian Fashion. It was impossible to believe he was dead—murdered.

'Nijinsky couldn't trust Diaghilev. And I can't trust you,' Maxim said.

Valentina's head snapped round to look at him. Had he really said what she thought she'd heard? He was staring at her, waiting for a response.

With a smile that didn't reach her eyes, she crossed to him and sat down on the overstuffed cushions. The alcohol smell was so strong that she had to breathe through her mouth, and the taste was one of despair. It was enough to make her feel sorry for him.

'Of course you can trust me.' The lie came easily. She tried to brush back the hair that had fallen over Maxim's eyes, but he jerked back and her fingers grazed only air.

'Let's neither of us pretend that's true.' He emptied his glass, grabbed the decanter and poured more vodka. 'You went through my desk.'

The urge to back away tugged at Valentina's limbs. Maxim wasn't looking at her, his gaze instead resting on his drink as he swirled it round the glass.

'Did you think I hadn't realised? That I'd forgotten I'd left the drawer open, not closed? I understand your curiosity, Valechka. But you need to know something.' He put the glass down on a side table and reached towards her. For a second Valentina thought he was going to kiss her. Instead he grabbed the back of her neck. The rough grip made her gasp. 'Odette would never behave so. Would she?'

Valentina's eyes watered from the pain. She struggled to shake her head, but his grasp made the motion difficult. She wanted to squirm free, but knew that would only make things worse. Instead she kept still, silently thanking her years in the corps for giving her the strength and patience to ignore an uncomfortable body.

It worked; Maxim's dilated eyes relaxed, and he let go. Her hands wanted to fly up to rub the raw skin of her neck, but Valentina folded them in her skirt, keeping her eyes lowered.

Maxim picked up his glass and took a couple of slow sips. Then, in a voice devoid of emotion, he said, 'Go now. I want to be alone.'

Valentina left the room without looking at him. Her hand drifted to her neck once she knew she was out of sight. The skin was tender, and when she drew her fingertips back they were decorated with tiny speckles of crimson blood.

She gained the sanctuary of her bedroom and let out a long, slow breath. She had to remind herself that Maxim had suffered a grave shock and must be feeling both grief and fear at the news of Rasputin's death. Still, doubt gnawed at her—the same kind of doubt that had made her wonder if she should leave Maxim for another protector.

Snatching up a pair of pointe shoes, Valentina left her bedroom for her studio. She needed to dance. Only she didn't feel like being Odette today; instead, she would dance Odile. As Odile, she would be the one in charge. Not someone whose fate was dictated by the men around her.

A whisper began in Petrograd. It spread from house to house, apartment to apartment; it went down the tram lines and through the areas where the poor were working at their chores. It gained life as it travelled, which was almost laughable given the topic: a life ending. The rumour was so ugly no one knew whether to believe it or not. An overwhelming number wanted to, though. They stepped out of their homes, glancing excitedly at their neighbours as they cried, 'Have you heard?'

In the centre of the city, Luka felt the whispers rippling through the air around him. Newspapers were being shaken open, groups of people gathering around them to scan the lines of type for confirmation. They wouldn't find anything, Luka knew, because he'd already done the same thing. None of the papers mentioned the great and terrible thing that gripped Petrograd.

Rasputin, murdered. It couldn't be true.

Valentina and a number of other high-ranking dancers didn't show up to the Mariinsky that day. It was left to the corps and coryphées to gossip and wonder without any confirmation. Eventually, sensing they would get nothing useful out of their dancers, the company sent them all home.

On arriving at his apartment, Luka once again found his father waiting for him, propped up in the hallway. If the last time had been a surprise, Luka was completely stunned this time. For a second, he felt vague curiosity. Then he remembered the last words his father had thrown at him, and he scowled.

Vladimir's face was thinner, but otherwise he looked the same. A touch of sadness making him sag around the eyes perhaps, but that was to be expected.

Luka walked up to his father, reaching around him to unlock his door. 'What are you doing here? We don't have any more family left to have lost.'

'No,' his father replied. 'We only have each other now.'

'Do we even have that, though?' Luka looked at his father, but the expression on his rough face didn't alter.

Luka sighed, pushed the door open and gestured for him to come inside.

Vladimir followed him in, keeping his arms tucked close to his body as though he didn't want to touch anything. Luka watched him scan the small space with its weathered floor and sparse, unimpressive furniture.

'I thought you were doing this dance business for the money.'

Luka could have laughed. Compared to his childhood home, the apartment was practically palatial.

'I'm still only a corps dancer. The money will increase with my ranking, or the number of years I spend with the company— whichever is of higher value. And there'll be a healthy pension on retirement if I stay long enough.'

He didn't bother to explain his other reasons for dancing. There was no way to explain art and passion. A person simply understood that, or they didn't.

Nor did he tell him that he'd begun dreaming of an alternative life with the Ballets Russes, where money would be even scarcer.

His father scratched his chin, gave one sharp cough. 'A pension, you say? A wise thing to set yourself up with.'

This time, Luka did laugh. After all these years, all the accusations that he was being selfish or cowardly, and now his father was expressing approval of his choices? He half expected Vladimir to take it back, or berate him for laughing; but when their eyes met he saw only regret. The old man's mouth twisted on one side; a strange expression that it took Luka a moment to recognise as an attempt at a smile.

'What are you doing here?' Luka asked abruptly.

His father fiddled with his sleeve cuffs, a gesture Luka had inherited from him. 'I've come to warn you.'

'Warn me? About what?'

'You heard the news about Rasputin?'

'Of course. It's not been confirmed, though. It could just be vicious rumour.'

'Doesn't matter. It's enough to galvanise people who are already unhappy. Have you heard what the men lucky enough to return from the front are saying? The things they've had to do out there, the decisions they've had to make? There's nothing noble about this war like we were told when it was first declared. I believed that lie; I was proud of one son for fighting in it, and ashamed of the other for not. But what those men have seen and done … what your brother must have experienced—no ruler who cares for his people could force men to go through that. I have a hard enough time reconciling how God could allow such a war; but God isn't answerable to mere men. The Tsar should be.'

'What are you saying?' Luka asked slowly. This line of thinking from his father was making him nervous. It wasn't the impassioned anger he was used to, but something deeper, almost resigned.

'I know nothing definite, except that the men and women of Russia may no longer be afraid to hold their supposed betters accountable. Not when the example has been set with Rasputin.'

Perhaps there was more his father could have said if Luka had pushed him. Or perhaps there might have been a proper reconciliation, with words of apology and regret spoken out loud. But Luka would never know, for his father's words sent him out into the streets again—to find out if there was truth to the rumour from the one person who would know, and to pass on the warning. He and Vladimir parted with a silent handshake—the only forgiveness they could muster after a lifetime of disagreement and resentment.

Luka didn't really want to see Valentina; it was hard enough being near her in the Mariinsky Theatre. But he was concerned by his father's intimation of what Rasputin's murder might mean for the country. The echo of his footsteps chased him all the way to the portico of Valentina's house, and he had to resist the urge to look over his shoulder for pursuers. To do so would only feed the fear.

He knocked on the elaborate wooden door with a sharp rap that hurt his knuckles. Madame Ivkina answered. Her face was pinched, and she showed no surprise at Luka's arrival.

'I need to see her. Please.'

Madame Ivkina stared at him for a moment, then nodded and opened the door wider. The scent of Valentina's house enfolded Luka like an embrace, but he tried to ignore it. He was there for one reason only, and it was not to reminisce on happier times.

'I think it's best you wait in the servants' quarters,' Madame Ivkina muttered.

A glance at her face told Luka all he needed to know: Maxim was there. Instead of angering him, the knowledge tightened the fear in his chest. Maxim could be there merely to spend time with Valentina, but Luka couldn't shake himself of the feeling that his presence was some kind of confirmation of the foul gossip washing through the city.

His heart flipped as he followed the *dvornik* through doorways he had never been through before. She led him to a small room that was sparsely furnished, gestured to a hard-backed chair, then left. Luka perched on the edge of the chair, willing his heart to slow down. His nerves were dancing a mad waltz that reminded him of the scene in *Giselle* where she gradually succumbed to insanity. He wished Valya would hurry.

'Luka?'

He smelled her perfume just before he heard her voice. It crept into his nostrils, invading his senses, and he closed his eyes against its onslaught.

When she spoke his name again, he looked at her. She was standing in the doorway wearing a practice dress, her ankles criss-crossed with the laces of her pointe shoes. He saw right away that her face, beneath the scarf which held her hair off her face for dancing, was pinched. Either he hadn't looked at her properly when they'd passed in the halls of the Mariinsky, or she had aged in a day.

He stood up, his breath catching in his throat. 'It's true, isn't it?'

She was so pale he could see the blue veins streaking her neck as she gave one sharp nod.

'My God.' He took an involuntary step towards her, raising his hand as if to comfort her.

She glanced behind her, then stepped further into the room, shutting the door quietly. His hand dropped.

'It's not in the newspapers,' he said. 'I had to come. To find out ...'

'It was Prince Felix Yusupov and the Grand Duke Dmitri Pavlovich.'

The names were like a physical blow. Luka wondered if she felt the same surreal sense of being caught in a dream.

'The Tsar's own relations murdered Grigori Rasputin?'

Valya's assent was a hiss of breath.

'*Bozhe moy* ...'

They were names familiar to everyone in Petrograd, if not everyone in Russia. Aristocrats, royalty, kin to the Tsar. And they had killed his most trusted friend and advisor, the most powerful man in all of Russia.

Luka couldn't help himself. He closed the distance between them and rested his hands on Valya's elbows. She looked down at the small space of wooden floor between them. Instead of the burning anger that her presence had caused over the last weeks, he ached to draw her closer. He stayed where he was, though, touching her with only his hands, trying to believe it was nothing more than fear and force of habit that motivated his desire.

'I wasn't fond of Rasputin,' Valentina said, her eyes still downcast, 'but he didn't deserve … They say he wouldn't die, Luka. He was poisoned and shot, and still he wouldn't die. So then they drowned him.'

Sabâkyé, sabâtchya smerte; a dog's death for a dog. That was what was being said on the streets. Luka felt the sour sting of bile in the back of his throat.

Valya pulled one arm away from him and pressed her fingers to her brow, as if trying to drum the truth into her head. 'What kind of men could do that? How could they …' Her voice broke.

Luka couldn't bear it any more. He pulled her into an embrace. She trembled in his arms and he squeezed her even tighter. He wanted her to feel safe, just for a minute, though it was a lie.

'The world is going mad around us,' she mumbled into his chest, the words muffled by his coat.

Luka cupped her chin to make her look up at him, then kissed away the tears that had appeared on her cheeks. She tensed for a moment, as if she would pull away, then her eyes fluttered closed. When he had kissed away the last tear, Luka rested his forehead against hers, his lips tasting of salt. This closeness, this intimacy with her … he didn't want to interrupt it with words for fear that his heart might break all over again. But Valya did it for him.

'The two of them are under house arrest now. What they'll do with them …' Valya pulled away from him, her long white fingers wiping at her face.

Luka suddenly remembered his father's warning, which had temporarily been driven out of his head by the sight and smell of Valentina. Fear crashed over him, an icy wave. Through Maxim and her relationship with the Romanovs, Valya had a very public connection to the monk.

'Valya, do you realise what this means for you?'

'Of course I do.'

'Then how will you … how will you stay safe?'

'I don't know. Rasputin's gone now. We knew the people were unhappy with his meddling, but perhaps we didn't realise how vehemently. Maybe this will be the end of it. Maybe they won't see the need for more violence.'

'No.' They were both startled at the abruptness of the word. Luka grabbed Valya's cool hands and held them to his lips, where he felt them tremble. 'No, that's not enough. I need to know you're safe. You've got money—use it to protect yourself. Do something, anything, my love. I can't—'

'What did you say?'

The air between them froze, and it took Luka a moment to realise why. That word, so powerful, had come without thought. For a second he wondered if he'd really meant it, or if he'd just been saying whatever was needed to impress on Valya the importance of keeping herself safe. But he didn't wonder for long. Slowly, as if he might break the moment by moving too suddenly, he made his mouth form the words again, this time with a deliberateness that he hoped she would see and understand.

'I said "my love".'

There was a pause, then Valya's hands were around the back of his neck and her mouth was against his. The warmth of her lips, the sweetness of her breath, was so familiar, and Luka tried to pull her closer even though they were already pressed together. The two of them stood entwined, silent and trembling, unable to tell any longer where one of them stopped and the other began.

Valya's breathing slowed, and eventually she pulled herself away from him.

'I thought you'd decided I wasn't worth wasting time or effort on? That I'm built for unhappiness?'

The echo of his own words, words that were designed to hurt, made Luka look away. 'Surely you see that moment for what it was ...?'

She was silent, and when Luka looked back at her, her face was unreadable.

'I should go back upstairs,' she said in a flat voice. 'Maxim will be wondering where I am.'

A sharp stab hit Luka's chest as she spoke her protector's name through lips that still bore the imprint of his own kiss. He ached to pull her back to him, to whisper into her hair, to kiss away any fresh tears, but he only nodded.

'Send for me when he's gone?'

Valya stared at him, her lips parted as if she might disagree.

But she did send for him; and instead of making love, they talked through the night. She wept in his arms, and he cradled her as gently as he could. They kissed a thousand times over, or perhaps more. But when he tried to talk of Maxim, and all the still-existing reasons she'd broken off their affair, Valentina refused to be drawn.

CHAPTER TWENTY-ONE

Winter 1917

Luka didn't think he'd ever participated in a worse class. He was holding on to a piece of scenery that served as a makeshift barre on the stage, kicking his leg in a grand battement. The ballet master shouted at the company, his words almost unintelligible. In the centre of the stage, where a couple of portable barres had been placed, a woman with a wig of dark ringlets already pinned to her head had tears streaming down her face. Luka watched the tears drop from her chin as she lifted her leg rapidly to shoulder height then back down to the floor. It wasn't the first time he'd seen someone cry during a class, and it wouldn't be the last. Tears were allowed as long as they didn't interfere with the dancing.

The exercise ended, and Luka turned around to do it again on the left side. He was looking at the painted backdrop now and was glad not to have to see the crying woman any longer.

The tension among the dancers had been palpable from the moment he'd stepped into the theatre. Among the singers and musicians too. They were preparing for the yearly benefit performance for the Mariinsky Opera chorus that night, an event that was usually looked forward to by those invited to participate in it. But not tonight. Tonight was different. It was because of the selected opera. *Fenella* was based on a Spanish uprising in seventeenth-century Italy, and there was one scene in particular that was making the cast edgy: a revolutionary mob burned down the palace in anger and hatred. That the revolution was put down, and divine displeasure shown by the eruption of a volcano at the close of the opera, didn't matter. They all felt that performing such a scene on the imperial stage would bring bad luck.

It wasn't their place to question, though. Their place was to bend to the will of the imperial family, no matter how ill-advised the instructions might seem. They were not Ballets Russes dancers with creative freedom and input.

The class came to a miserable end; not even the grand allegro—Luka's favourite part—able to lift him out of his mood. The dancers began to disperse, looking unhappy. Luka sat on the floor and stretched out his calf muscles by pulling on his toes, trying to find some focus before he entered the noisy confines of the dressing room. Nearby, Valya was holding a pair of pointe shoes, flexing their soles back and forth, her eyes distant as she stared into the auditorium where theatre workers were uncovering the chairs.

Luka got up and wandered casually over to her. 'Are you alright?' he asked softly.

She looked at him, a crease between her brows. 'No. It's all these nerves. I can feel them coming off the people around me, and it's making me nervous too.'

She fiddled with the brunette wig that sat on her head, then rested a shaking hand on Luka's forearm. He wanted to smile at the touch. Since Rasputin's death they had renewed their intimacy. Their meetings weren't as frequent as before—Maxim was spending far more time in Valya's company—but they both knew there was something more between them now. It was evident in the way their time together had changed; no longer was it about getting their clothes off as quickly as possible and tumbling into bed. They spent hours simply playing cards or taking turns reading to each other from books. Valya had even tried cooking for Luka once, much to his amusement and her cook's distress. One evening they'd lain on her loggia with no clothes on, a thick fur blanket spread over them, their shoulders, hips and feet touching as they stared up at the pinpricks of stars in the inky sky. Luka had felt as vulnerable and untouched by the world as a newborn baby in that moment, and neither of them had broken the silence until he'd noticed Valya's lips fading to lilac. Even then, he had the feeling she didn't want to go inside, back to her regular life. He longed to be outside with her again—to attend the theatre together, or even just stroll along the banks of the Neva. But theirs was a relationship for indoors, kept hidden behind walls.

'It's just a superstition, Valya. It doesn't mean anything.'

'I know.' She sighed. 'But I can't rid myself of the worry something bad will happen.'

She leaned down to slide her foot into her shoe. When she had tied the ribbons neatly around her ankle, she arched her foot, stretching the front of her ankle and making sure the shoe was on properly. Her eyes were distant.

'It will be alright. I know it will.' Luka touched the inside of her wrist gently, unsure which of them he was trying to convince.

'Excuse me, Valentina Fedorovna?'

Xenia's voice interrupted them, and Luka snatched his hand away. He was sure guilt must be etched on his face, but Valya looked at Xenia with such calmness that anyone might have thought they barely knew each other.

'I believe someone's here for you.' Xenia pointed to the wings of the stage, where Maxim was watching them, his eyes cold. He had a newspaper clutched in his hands.

Valya walked over to meet her protector. Luka turned away, rolling his feet in circles as if loosening his ankles. Out of the corner of his eye, he watched them.

Maxim held out a couple of small squares of paper that Luka recognised as telegrams. Valya flicked through them, then handed them back to Maxim, who spoke rapidly while looking onto the stage. Valya replied with one- or two-syllable words. She rested her hand on Maxim's arm, and he seemed to remember the newspaper he held. He shook it out, showing her a page. Valya scanned it, then her brows lowered into a deep frown. Maxim's mouth twisted in a grim, dissatisfied smile. He jabbed the newspaper once more, then crumpled it roughly underneath his arm and left.

Valya returned to the stage, her head low. She came to a halt near Luka, her feet tapping absent-minded piqués on the black surface of the stage. Luka felt a kind of pain he hadn't known before: of not being able to comfort the woman he loved, or even ask what was wrong for fear that Maxim was still watching from somewhere hidden. The stage wasn't fully set for the performance yet, but they were both playing a role: the dutiful Romanov dancers who had no personal desires beyond dancing to please the Tsar.

'Would someone get this viper off my heels?'

Mathilde's imperious voice burst onto the stage, making Luka jump. The prima ballerina assoluta was taking rapid steps, her eyes aflame. Behind her, equally agitated, came a soloist. Luka didn't recall seeing the woman, who was clad in her street clothes, in the class.

'Don't you turn your back on me,' she shouted.

They all froze, including Mathilde. She turned to face the lower-ranking dancer, her expression stony. The soloist's hand flew out, smacking Mathilde so hard it left a bright imprint on her cheek.

Luka's mouth fell open; he could see how the soloist trembled at what she'd done, even as she straightened her shoulders and looked defiantly at Mathilde.

'Do you think we don't see the newspapers? Your behaviour— it makes the rest of us appear beyond contempt.' She turned to face the crowd of dancers, scene-shifters, musicians and singers that had gathered. 'I can no longer be a part of this and face my own conscience. For the sake of your own souls, I suggest the rest of you follow my lead and leave this company. If you don't—may God have mercy on you.' She stormed off the stage.

There was a ringing silence, then Mathilde laughed. But as adept as she was at pretending, not even she could make the laugh sound genuine.

'It's disgusting,' Valentina snapped, flinging the newspaper onto Luka's bed. 'Absolutely vile, filthy stuff. I thought they'd get bored of this, but it's only getting worse. What kind of swine would print this in a newspaper?'

The cartoon took up almost a third of the page. It depicted Mathilde, wearing the necklace of walnut-sized diamonds the Tsar had famously gifted her over a decade ago. Seated at her feet were German soldiers. Her dress was open to the waist, and a few soldiers suckled at her breasts as she smiled benignly. Through the windows could be seen Russian people, skeletal in their starvation and knocking at the door to come in. Across the top were scrawled the words 'The Black-Eyed She-Devil of the Imperial Ballet'.

Rasputin's death had not had the effect the people had hoped for. The Tsar remained at the front, refusing to pull Russia out of the much-hated war. The Tsarina and Grand Duchesses were in virtual hiding. And the people, dissatisfied that their cries for attention had gone ignored, had looked for a new figure to hold responsible for all that was wrong. Mathilde, with her lavish lifestyle and relationship with the Grand Duke Sergei—who had resigned as Field Inspector General of the Artillery Department amid accusations of corruption and negligence—was an easy target. In her the newspapers had found the perfect example of everything the people hated.

'Why don't you ask Maxim to make it stop?' Luka suggested quietly. 'He works for a newspaper, doesn't he?'

Valentina glared at him as she paced up and down the small living room. She was making herself dizzy, but it would be worse to sit still. 'He's an art critic,' she snapped.

She didn't want to admit that she was avoiding speaking to Maxim as much as possible. She was afraid he would see through her lies, and know she had taken up with Luka again. Perhaps it was a blessing of sorts that Maxim had withdrawn from her since Rasputin's death, only caring about her physical presence, seeming as little interested in talk as she.

Flopping down on Luka's sofa, she pressed her numb fingertips against her eyelids. It was so cold in the apartment. Because of the shortages, Luka was unable to procure enough coal to warm the place for more than the coldest hours of the night. He'd refused her help in getting more. It made Valentina wish they were in her own warm house instead, but Maxim always seemed to be there, hovering.

'Besides, I did ask him,' she added. 'He says he's not in a position to say anything because my friendship with Mathilde is common knowledge.'

There was a pause while Luka no doubt took in the fact that her protector had failed to help her when she'd asked for it. He didn't say anything, but the very idea that he was thinking it made Valentina irritated, and she jumped back up and resumed her pacing. It was warmer when she moved, anyway.

'It's not that bad, is it?' Luka ventured. 'I know it's crude, but no worse than what they've printed before.'

Valentina saw that Luka was looking at the cartoon again. She swiped at the newspaper so the page tore. 'Stop looking at that thing. Or are you like the rest of them? Do you think it's funny and there might be some truth in it?'

She didn't know why she was making such accusations, but it felt good, and she continued to glare at him as if he was just as guilty as those who had drawn and printed it.

'No. Of course not.'

'Then why do you keep looking at it?'

Luka stared at his hands, taking a deep breath as though to remind himself she didn't mean her sharp words.

Valentina's heart was racing so fast it electrified her. She wanted to lash out at someone, to make someone answerable, and he was the only person here. The only person she could trust not to lash back.

'What is it *muzhiki* like your family don't understand?' she demanded. She saw Luka flinch and knew she was being dishonest, but she pushed on. 'If you want more in this life, you either get it, or don't complain about those that do. It's what I did. I was just as poor as any of them, and look at me now.'

'Not everyone can—'

'Sell themselves? Is that what you're going to say? That those pitiful peasants and factory workers out there are too good to sell their bodies like the rest of us do?' Her voice was rising in volume, threaded with venom. She couldn't stop herself. 'There is only one way to get ahead in this world. I didn't create the rules, and I won't be accused of indecency for following them. Neither will I allow it for my friends. And if you don't like it, perhaps you should go back to the way your life was before, *Malysh*.'

'Don't.' Luka's voice was as cold as the air around them, and Valentina came to a standstill. She'd never heard him speak like that to her before. 'Don't call me that. And don't make threats to separate us. Not again.'

Valentina felt her chest rising and falling rapidly. She didn't know what she was doing; why she was attempting to ruin the one good thing she had left.

Slowly, Luka raised himself off the bed. She tensed as he reached her, but all he did was put his arms around her. Her anger dissipated. Not wanting him to see her weakness, she buried her face in his chest, swallowing again and again in an effort to keep her emotions down.

'I'm sorry,' she whispered finally, her voice small and pathetic. She hated the way it sounded, but Luka only tightened his arms around her, giving her warmth that no stove could compete with.

'It's alright,' he said, and his voice was so gentle that she let a tear escape. He held her for a moment longer, then whispered in her ear, 'Leave him.'

At first, she thought she'd misheard. Then she started, as though the words were obscene. Luka tightened his arms around her, and she felt like a bird trembling within a soft grasp, looking to take flight. As he shifted his weight, the newspaper with the offensive cartoon crumpled underneath his foot.

'I know this is the one thing I'm not supposed to ask you,' he said. It was a silent agreement they'd both understood. 'But I am asking you. I can't help myself. I want you to leave Maxim and be only with me.'

'Luka, I—'

Perhaps he heard her instinct for refusal, for he stepped away to stop it. Her frozen hands were still in his, though, and she couldn't tell which of them was shaking.

'We don't know how you and I will end up,' he said. 'But I want to give it a chance. Valya, only months ago I could never have imagined kissing you, holding you in my arms. And if I had, I would have sworn that road led to nowhere. But think of all we'd have missed out on if we'd given in to that uncertainty.'

They were beautiful words, and they made Valentina's chest ache. But he was missing what seemed to her the most obvious thing.

'But what can I offer you, Luka?'

'I … I don't understand.'

She lived in a world where everything was for sale; and she had no value beyond what she could give away. Mamma had taught her that.

'You have no need of my connections, no desire for my money. You already have my body, but that will fade in time, as will my dancing. There's not much else I can give.'

Taking her face gently in both hands, Luka looked into her eyes for a long time. Valentina felt herself wavering under his intense gaze. She mustn't though; she must stay strong.

'How can you not see that to me you are the whole world?' he said. 'You offer me love.'

They stayed that way, looking into each other's eyes, Valentina searching for the hint of a lie. Her rage of a few moments ago had felt like a symbol of the control that was slipping through her fingers like watery silk. But this was something else altogether. Her heart lifted into her throat and it was as though she was no longer anchored to the ground.

'Luka, I … I don't know.'

She saw an infinitesimal shift in his features, a slight falling of disappointment. He was getting better at hiding his true feelings. For some reason, that made her unbearably sad. She didn't want Luka to become one of them; she wanted him to stay the outsider who said what he meant and could only lie clumsily. But if she wanted that, she had to offer him some truth in return. Not about Maxim's threats—that would only worry him. But about another, not quite as strong but still persuasive motivation.

'Maxim has offered me Odette.'

Understanding dawned, followed by confusion. 'But the company isn't scheduled to do *Le Lac*—'

'I know. But he says it's coming—a surprise performance. I know, Luka, don't look at me like that. I'm no fool.'

'Then why do you—'

'Because what if it's the truth?'

She could see that Luka understood, and loved him all the more for it.

'You can get Odette on your own merits, you know,' he said eventually. 'Without Maxim's help. I've danced with you, Valya, and I do believe that.'

Although she appreciated the assurance, Valentina knew it wasn't true.

'Grant me some time?' she asked.

Luka nodded his silent, reluctant agreement.

CHAPTER TWENTY-TWO

Luka sometimes felt he must be one of the last few young men left in Petrograd. He still saw many, the rich and aristocratic men who attended the ballet and dined in restaurants whose prices had become extortionate, but there were so many deaths reported in the newspapers that he wondered how they all continued to escape being sent to war. Perhaps that was why he accepted the invitation to dine at Mathilde's city mansion. With the worsening death toll, and the warning from his father, it seemed inevitable that his own time to fight must be coming, ballet contract or no ballet contract. Surely the country had run out of peasants, workers and farmers by now.

'Do you need help choosing, Malysh?'

Luka stared at the wine catalogue Mathilde had handed him, unable to tell the difference between the various vintages. She smiled at him from the head of the table, her Fabergé diadem glittering in the electric light. With her own power plant next door, her house gleamed with brightness and warmth; a stark contrast to the bitter cold outside. Luka couldn't help thinking of all the soldiers who had frozen to death at the front. Was that how Pyotr had met his end?

He gave his order, not knowing what he was asking for.

Tonight's party was clearly designed to flaunt; Mathilde's display that the ever-increasing public taunts hadn't hurt her. A lace cloth was spread over the long table, nearly obscured by the array of gold plates, silver sugar basins and antique *granyonyi stakan* that Luka was almost afraid to drink from. Scattered around the dinnerware were animals made from brightly-coloured polished enamel, and arrangements of hybrid tea roses from the imperial greenhouses that defied the fact it was winter. A large wreath made of solid gold hung on the wall behind Mathilde, with two smaller matching ones either side. They created a sort of hovering crown for their host, an image Luka was sure couldn't be accidental.

'Wait a moment!' Mathilde's cry caused the entire table to freeze. Djibi, seated at his mistress's feet, barked. 'There's thirteen of us. We can't have a dinner party with thirteen seated at the table. It'll bring bad luck. Where's Madame Roubtzova? She can join us.'

Madame Roubtzova entered the cellar at the same time a suckling pig with horseradish was brought in. Luka used the distraction to steal a glance at Valya, who was seated next to her sullen-looking protector. Apart from a cool-voiced greeting when he'd walked in, she'd carefully avoided speaking to him. Now, she seemed attentive towards Maxim, commenting on the food and slipping bits from her own plate to his. Luka wondered if he had ruined things between them by asking her to leave the man.

The guests dined with quiet but hearty enjoyment. Just as they were beginning to complain of being too full from the feast presented to them, Mathilde clapped her hands together in excitement.

'I have some entertainment for you all,' she cried, pointing towards the cellar door.

Her guests turned to look. Out came Pasha Alexandrovich, a first soloist in the company who had been sitting at the table not ten minutes ago. Piles of white feathers were tucked into his clothing, poking out from the cuffs of his sleeves, the neck of his shirt, even sticking up absurdly from his hair. His trousers were rolled to his knees, and on his feet were a pair of Mathilde's pointe shoes, bulging from toes that were too big for them. He strutted into the centre of the room, then struck a tragic pose.

Mathilde shrieked with laughter. '*Magnifique!*' she cried. 'It's just too delicious. Tell me who he is, my friends.'

Pasha stumbled around the room, his arms flapping futilely, his legs trembling with over-the-top weakness. Mathilde laughed so hard tears ran down her face. Her guests were laughing too, and Luka couldn't help but join in. It was an exaggerated imitation of Anna Pavlova in *The Dying Swan*, a solo created for her by Fokine. It was a popular piece, and the Imperial Russian Ballet had incorporated it into their productions of *Le Lac des Cygnes*. Mathilde, who was inadvertently responsible for the rival dancer's fame and thus harboured a hatred for her, refused to dance it. She insisted that when she was Odette/Odile, the ballet would end with her drowning in the lake, as it always had before.

Luka glanced at Valya again and saw that a stillness had come over her features. Only she, and Madame Roubtzova, hadn't joined in the laughter.

After Mathilde's joke, the diners became increasingly quiet, lulled by the fine wine and rich food. Maxim was the first to stand, making an excuse for himself and Valentina to leave. Luka didn't miss the way the man's eyes darted to him, then narrowed as he told Valya to wait by the front door. But Mathilde was oblivious to the tension. She took Maxim by the arm, demanding to know once again if he'd found Pasha's likeness of Anna Pavlova amusing, and if he thought it worth running a cartoon about her in the newspaper, like those that regularly skewered Mathilde herself.

Luka saw his opportunity and darted out to the front door where Valentina waited. She was wrapped in a thick fur coat, a flimsy piece of lace tied around her forehead in a poor approximation of their host's diadem.

'Luka,' she murmured in a pleased tone. She looked behind him to see if Maxim was coming.

'Mathilde has him by the arm,' Luka told her. 'We have perhaps a minute.'

'I'm glad. For there's something I want to tell you. I have decided. My answer is yes.'

Luka's heart skipped at least two beats. 'Do you mean …?'

'I don't want to give in to uncertainty. For once in my life I want to be bold and daring and, perhaps, foolish.'

A thrill ran through Luka and it was all he could do to keep his voice low. 'When?'

'I don't know yet. I'll need to figure out a way of leaving without Maxim retaliating against us, meddling with our careers. But know this: my mind is made up. It will happen.'

'I no longer care what Maxim does. The Imperial Russian Ballet isn't the only company in the world, and he has no influence in others. But … what of Odette?'

Luka saw the fear flicker across her face and immediately regretted asking lest she change her mind.

'Once again I catch you two in deep conversation.'

Luka jumped at Maxim's interruption. How had the man extracted himself from Mathilde so quickly?

Valentina, though, remained as cool as ever, even reaching an inviting hand out to her protector. 'He found an earring and thought it was mine. It wasn't.'

Maxim's jaw was tight as he directed his gaze at Luka's hands. Luka quickly closed one into a fist, as though it concealed a small piece of jewellery.

Maxim's upper lip lifted. 'No feather, Malysh?'

Valya gave a light laugh and answered for him. 'Of course not. That was a special thing, a sign from the world. You know that. Although not as special as this.'

She fingered the swan brooch she was wearing; the one Luka had carried for her the day they'd first made love. She'd pinned it at the lowest part of her neckline, and Luka had wondered during the dinner if she'd worn it to please Maxim, or as a sign for himself.

Valentina slid her arm through Maxim's. 'Come, I want to be at home with you. I'm sure Luka Vladimirovich is eager to get back to the party.'

Maxim's eyes were still narrowed with suspicion, but he straightened in triumph as he ushered Valya out the door ahead of him. Even though he knew she couldn't, Luka wished she would glance over her shoulder and give him one last smile.

Luka woke with a start. For a moment, he couldn't think where he was; his head was spinning, his mouth dry. Then he remembered. He had made his departure from Mathilde's party not long after Valya and Maxim, pretending he was headed home to sleep off drunkenness. In actuality, he'd made his way to Valya's house in the hope that Maxim's surly mood meant he would give Valya a rare night alone. His hope had proved correct. The carriage had taken off almost immediately after Valentina had stepped out, Maxim not even waiting to see if she got to the door safely.

Rolling over, Luka reached out to hold Valya close to him, to breathe in her smell and cherish this moment of intimacy. But his hand landed on an empty, cool space. He sat up, wondering what time it was, and squinted into the darkness. She wasn't sitting in a chair, covered by a fur blanket and gazing out the window, the way he sometimes woke to find her.

He rolled out of the warm bed. The trousers he'd been wearing to the party were on the floor, and he pulled them on. He couldn't see his shirt, so grabbed his thick broadcloth coat with silver fox fur lining to protect him from the cold night air, and walked out into the hall. Tiptoeing past crystal vases that held purple, yellow and white winter crocuses that stood out against the vaguely threatening dark shapes of the furniture, Luka thought he heard a noise. It came from the direction of the studio, and he realised with something like relief that Valya must be inside, perhaps going through some exercises to work off the effects of the champagne and rich food.

He walked softly to the studio doors, pulled one open and peered inside.

Valya was standing in the middle of the room, arms arched overhead, face downcast. She wore her nightgown, but had tied it in knots around her knees to make movement easier. On her feet were an old pair of pointe shoes, frayed threads sticking out around the toes. Her skin, glowing whitely in the darkness of the studio, was prickled with goosebumps, but she didn't appear to notice.

Luka opened the door a little wider, about to say something to her, when she moved. It was only slight, but enough to make him hesitate. He edged back, suddenly not wanting to interrupt, and watched.

She rose *en pointe* and began to move her feet in tiny waves, as if she was treading water. Her arms reached out to the sides, undulating and pushing at the air around her. Her head was tilted backward, her eyes closed, a sadness etched on her features that Luka had never seen before. It was the Dying Swan solo. Valya was dancing Odette at the moment when, heartbroken and defeated, the cursed woman slowly died.

There was no music, but it didn't matter. Valya sank to her knees, bent backward as far as her supple back would allow, and opened her arms wide in a silent plea. There was a softness to her movements Luka hadn't thought she was capable of. She was no Pavlova, but there was a beauty in the yearning extensions and resigned contractions that her typically vivacious roles didn't showcase. He held his breath, afraid that even that slight motion would be enough to disturb her.

Valya repeated the movements, and each time they became more damaged and broken. She kept her eyes closed, feeling her way around the small studio. When she curled her arms around herself protectively, one over her head and the other around her body, Luka shut his own eyes. He had wanted to hold her exactly like that when he'd woken. For some reason, it hurt to see her doing it for herself.

She turned on the spot a few times, reaching towards the sky, before falling to her knees again. Luka thought he saw tears streaming down her face, but didn't know if they were real or his imagination was placing them there. It was too dark for him to tell. Either way, he knew he couldn't watch any more. Silently, he pulled the door to. As he turned away, he could still hear her pointe shoes tapping softly at the floor of the studio.

He walked back to the bedroom, glad he hadn't stayed to watch the rest of the dance. He didn't want to see the moment when she sank to her knees, exhausted, an arm and leg stretched out in front in a last moment of yearning. The moment when Odette finally gave up her fight and succumbed to death, brought to it by the man who was supposed to love her most.

CHAPTER TWENTY-THREE

Luka jerked awake to the sound of his name, and saw Valya standing in the bedroom doorway. She was wearing an opera cloak trimmed in ostrich feathers that she used as a dressing gown, and her face was an unnatural shade of white. She ran to his side of the bed and as she grabbed his *shuba*, he saw that her hands were shaking.

'Valya, what—'

'Put this on.' She threw the coat at him.

'Is it—is Maxim here?'

'No. Put the coat on and come with me.'

At the tone of her voice, Luka didn't argue. His feet were cold against the floor, and he glanced at his boots standing nearby, but Valya's urgency propelled him forward. When he reached the door, he hesitated, still trying to lace his trousers.

'Valya, I don't even have a shirt on under this. Surely you don't want your staff to—'

'This isn't the time to worry about that.' She practically ran down the hall as she spoke, opera cloak flaring behind her.

Luka followed, concerned when she slipped her hand into his. It was icy, and he wanted to stop and chafe it between his own to bring some life back to it. But she kept him moving forward, leading him into the blue reception room. Once inside, she still didn't stop; she opened the tall doors that led onto the loggia and tugged him outside.

'Valya, it's freezing!' he gasped. His bare feet stung, and he shrank into the depths of his coat, wishing he'd put his shirt on underneath.

Valya raised a finger to her lips. She was staring over the loggia rail into the expanse of Petrograd beyond.

'Listen,' she whispered, putting both hands on the stone rail and leaning over it as far as she could. 'You can hear it.'

Lifting his feet off the ground one after the other to keep them from freezing, Luka tried to listen for whatever it was she wanted him to hear. At first, there was nothing. Just the usual everyday noises, muffled by the thick layer of snow that covered the ground. But then he began to make something out. His feet slowed their dance, and he shut his eyes as if that would help him discern it better.

'It … it sounds like chanting,' he said slowly. He opened his eyes again and saw that Valya had turned her back on the view and was leaning against the grey stone railing. Her shoulders were slumped forward. 'Valya, what is it? What's going on?'

'It's the people. The factory workers,' she whispered. Her lips had gone dry in the cold air and she licked them. 'I received a phone call telling me. They've gone on strike. They think we're hoarding bread from them.'

Luka didn't need to ask who 'we' were. He remembered the day he'd tried to take bread to his father and Vladimir's outraged response.

'They've stormed the bakeries and are helping themselves to whatever they find inside. But even then they're still demanding more.'

'Oh.' The word sounded pathetic in the face of all that had apparently changed overnight. 'How ... how many are there?'

'It's hard to say. Too many to count, I'm told. Tens of thousands at least, and continually growing. They're making their way into the centre of Petrograd—'

The telephone was ringing again. Valya glanced at Luka, then ran inside.

Luka stayed where he was, listening. The sound he had only just been able to discern before was louder now. It was still hard to make out, but he thought he detected a fierceness to it.

A sharp pain reminded him he was barefoot and he shuffled back inside. He sat down on the nearest chair, his floor-length coat wrapped around him, leaving the door open so he could continue listening to the protesting workers. He curled his hands around his frozen feet, waiting for Valya to come back with more news.

When she did, her face was even paler than before. Luka stood up to meet her, but he didn't need to ask; she was already talking.

'That was Mathilde. She almost couldn't get through—she had to ring several times. The telephone lines are overloaded. She said there's probably a hundred thousand protesters, maybe more.'

Luka sat down again, heavily. One hundred thousand. One hundred thousand angry, hungry workers marching through the streets and looting the bakeries. Even if they were right and bread really was being hoarded, there would never be enough to satisfy that many. What would they do when it ran out?

Food supplies had worsened all over Russia, and many had given up queuing outside the bakeries, resigned to the knowledge it wouldn't be worth it. This winter was a particularly brutal one too—if it hadn't been for his dancing and the hours spent in Valya's warm embrace, Luka thought he might have frozen solid. Beggars had become a common sight in the city; and Moscow was once again riddled with uprisings. And still men died. It seemed as though the Tsar was ignoring the cries of his country. And so the people had resorted to this to try to make him listen.

Luka wondered suddenly if his father was in the crowd, shouting out his own cries for food between each hacking cough, happier to steal it than to accept it from his son.

The hours that followed passed slowly and, for the most part, in silence. Occasionally the telephone would ring, and whoever had managed to get through would trade rumours with Valentina, who then shared them with Luka. Through these hurried conversations they learned that the marchers were holding signs that read 'Freedom or Death', and their shouts had changed from cries for bread to demands for the removal of the Tsar.

Maxim, who was closer to events, was able to give the most detail, but had been more concerned with ensuring Valentina remained safe inside and didn't go anywhere that day. It was an order that echoed Luka's own request, and one that Valya didn't hesitate to obey. They sat together in the blue room, loosely holding hands, ignoring the food Madame Ivkina brought them on a tray.

Eventually, the rumbling noise that had been building became too loud to ignore. The housekeeper and maid both appeared in the room, fear showing on their faces. Valya didn't pay them any attention; her gaze was directed towards the noise. Before Luka knew what she was doing, she'd darted back outside.

'Valya!' he cried, sprinting out to the loggia after her. He heard the maid gasp in fright. 'Valya, come back! It isn't—'

The words died in his mouth. At the far end of the road, a dark, pulsating mass slowly edged towards them. As the front of the crowd came closer, the back seemed to grow. The whole street would soon be filled up and still they didn't stop coming.

They were close enough now that Luka could begin to make out their faces. Some were grinning, enjoying the unruly display as if it were a holiday; others set their mouths in grim lines. He tried to scan for his father, but there were far too many people. Children laughed and ran among the legs of the adults, repeating whichever cries they happened to hear, oblivious to the real reason for the march. Hastily assembled banners waved above them. And the noise … Luka had never heard anything like it. It reminded him a little of the sudden thunderous applause that came at the end of a ballet, when the music had died away and the dancers finally stilled. The audience's clapping and shouts of delight always came as a shock to Luka and he felt as if he heard them twice as loud as they really were. But that noise was made by people expressing gratitude for an evening well spent. This noise was far more unsettling.

The rumbling became a roar. Face after face came into view, and Luka thought they would be burned in his mind forever. No one seemed to notice him, standing on the loggia of a fine house, food going cold on a tray inside. No one, that was, until a small boy looked up and caught his eye. The boy stopped, staring at him for a moment, then smiled. He turned to a woman and tugged at her skirt, one finger already pointing to where Luka stood.

Luka didn't wait to see what came next; he grabbed Valya by the elbow and pulled her back. 'We have to get inside, now.'

She didn't argue. They scrambled into the reception room and shut the door behind them, backing away so they couldn't be seen from the street. There was a pause, then a few dull thumps sounded on the door that had just been closed.

The maid screamed, sinking to the floor.

Valya waved a hand without turning to look at her. 'Stop that. It's just some snowballs.'

They listened as the snowballs pelted the outside of the house.

'Why are they doing that?' Valya asked softly.

'They know who this house belongs to.'

She said no more.

The noise of the crowd became so loud they could no longer hear the barrage of snowballs, only see the little white explosions as they hit the glass. The housekeeper and maid huddled in a corner, Madame Ivkina holding the quietly crying younger woman.

When Valya spoke, her words made no sound that Luka could hear. He gripped her tighter, as if she were drifting away from him on the sea of noise. She looked up at him, the concern in her eyes barely covering the fear that rippled underneath. She spoke again, only this time she shouted the words.

'It will be over by tomorrow. Won't it?'

Luka wished he had an answer.

It wasn't until the sky had darkened into a starless night that the last of the marching crowd passed through Valya's street.

Valentina wanted Luka to stay with her to be sure of his safety, but Maxim telephoned and, once he'd confirmed her surrounds to be clear, insisted on coming over.

'Let me pay for a taxi for you,' Valya whispered, as though Maxim might already be able to hear them.

Luka was going to refuse, but stopped himself. It was foolish to turn down the offer when he didn't know what awaited him in the surrounding streets. He twined her fingers through his own and kissed her knuckles.

The thousands of feet had cleared most of the snow from the road, so it didn't take long for the taxi carriage to arrive. The housekeeper alerted them to its presence, and Luka clambered in quickly, pulling back the furs at the window to look at Valya outlined in her doorway.

'I'll be in touch soon,' he called softly.

The carriage jostled to life and took him away.

CHAPTER TWENTY-FOUR

Luka hurried along the street, hat pulled low, eyes averted from what was going on around him. Petrograd was a nightmare come to life. He had no idea how many people were now on strike; the newspapers had stopped printing so it was impossible to get reliable news. Public transport had come to a standstill, and even taxis were no longer running. Looters did not bother to wait for the cover of darkness to commit their crimes, and many of the shops Luka passed had broken doors and windows. He wouldn't have dared to step outside if fear for Valya hadn't motivated him. He needed to find out how she was, even if it was only by whispering with Madame Ivkina at her front door.

It was the third day of strikes, and Luka had regretted going home ever since that first day at Valya's house. The disruption had escalated into violence and he'd been stranded inside his apartment, unable to make contact. He'd finally understood the appeal of telephones.

A policeman across the road from where Luka now walked was attempting to prevent a group of youths from breaking into a store. He was outnumbered by at least five. The youths picked up stones and blocks of ice and threw them at him until he turned and ran. Their laughter chased him down the snowy street. Luka kept moving. He had to remind himself not to run. Running would bring attention, and attention spelled trouble.

A gunshot cracked the chilly air. Luka had never heard a gun before, but the sound was unmistakable. It echoed through his bones, and sent a flock of birds soaring into the sky.

A second of pure silence followed. Luka watched the birds, desperate to cling to that moment, not wanting to know what had happened before it. But then the silence broke, disrupted by terrified screams and jubilant shouts. The sound of running feet seemed to come at him from every direction. He gasped for breath, too scared to keep walking. He couldn't tell which way to go; couldn't tell if he would be moving towards the gunshot or away from it.

And then he was surrounded.

'Down with the German woman!' a man shouted. He looked at Luka, grinned, and grabbed his hand to hold it up in the air with his own. Luka was suddenly glad he'd pulled out his oldest, most worn coat for the walk. 'Down with Niemka! Down with the war!'

'The gunshot,' Luka said, trying to get the man's attention, but he was too excited to notice. Luka pulled his hand free and grabbed the man's elbow. 'The gunshot! What was it? What happened?'

'You don't know?' The man crowed an ugly laugh. 'It was a Cossack.'

'They shot a Cossack?'

'No! The Cossack shot a policeman! They've turned; they're on our side.'

The man slapped Luka on the back enthusiastically, then marched on, crying out once more against the Tsarina.

Luka turned away from him. He forced his feet to move, stumbling in the direction of Valya's house. This couldn't be happening. The Cossacks had been brought in to aid the police in getting this protest under control. If one of them had shot a policeman … things had taken a far worse turn than any of them could have foreseen.

'You must be joking,' Luka said.

'No, I'm not.' Valentina pressed her lips together to still the tremble on them. She looked at her hands as she buttoned her sable-lined gloves; not seeing Luka's face made things easier.

'Valya, I just told you what I saw. A policeman, shot by a Cossack!'

'You didn't see it, you just heard it. Who knows if it's even true? That man might have just been trying to stir up trouble.'

'He doesn't need to stir up trouble. Do you know how scared I was coming here?'

Valentina closed her eyes. She could hear muffled cracks and knew it was too early for the ice in the Neva to be splitting. It could only be the sound of gunfire. The thought of Luka out there among that violence threatened to undo her. But she had to keep herself composed. She couldn't let him know how little she wanted to do what she had to do.

'I'm not a policeman, am I? Nor a Cossack or a protester. We can't let our lives come to a complete standstill.'

'Does Maxim care nothing for you?'

Valentina could still feel the purple bruises like fingerprints on her arm. She pulled the sleeve of her dress lower, glad Luka couldn't see beneath the fabric. He was right: this outing was Maxim's doing. He was determined to use long-ago purchased tickets for an anniversary performance by the actor Yuriev at the Alexandrinsky Theatre, despite her protests. She thought he was testing how far she would go to prove her loyalty to him, and tonight wasn't the night to push against those boundaries. She'd already chosen Luka; she could give Maxim this one thing before leaving him.

Luka wouldn't understand, though; and there was no use arguing, for Maxim would be there soon to collect her.

'I'm sorry. I have to go.'

Valentina clutched Maxim's arm, trying not to panic at the chaos around them. The closed carriage struggled to move, hands grasping at its exterior to slow it down, and angry shouts seemed to come from every direction. She could hear the driver swearing, and the snap of reins being flicked over and over in panic. Her ermine muff had fallen to her feet, forgotten in the terror of being rocked from side to side.

Across from them, Mathilde's white face was clenched with tension. 'No!' she screeched, leaning towards the window. The slip of fur that hung there to keep out the cold was being pulled away, dirty white fingers snaking their way inside.

One of the horses let out a loud neigh almost like a scream. It was followed by a human scream, and the carriage lurched forward. Valentina almost fell off the seat, while Maxim grabbed the edge of the window and pushed his face into the cold night air.

'What's happening?' Valentina gasped, clinging on to any surface she could.

Maxim sat back and grabbed her hand, squeezing it unbearably tightly. 'We knocked someone over.'

'What? Then tell the driver to stop.'

'No. They'll tear us apart. We've only been able to get away because the crowd went to help the person. Otherwise they might have tipped the carriage right over.'

Feeling like she might vomit, Valentina pulled her hand free. She leaned down to pick up her muff and pushed her gloved fingers inside it. The soft fur did nothing to warm her. She was shivering deep inside, a rattling unlike any chill or nerves she'd felt before.

It was the 1905 revolution all over again. She wasn't a child any more, and her life wasn't run by Mamma, yet here she was, stuck in a carriage as it careened wildly through violent streets, not knowing what to expect at the other end. Then, she'd been taken to safety at the ballet school, sheltered from the barbaric outside world until all returned to normal. It couldn't end the same today. She wished that Luka had been able to convince her to stay, that she was tucked up in her bed with his arms around her. She had the horrible feeling they might never lie together like that again.

When they pulled up at the Alexandrinsky Theatre, it was as if the carriage had passed through a veil into a different world. All was eerily quiet, the gas streetlamps flickering in a way that felt distinctly ominous as she followed Mathilde out of the carriage. She could smell the horses, their earthy scent intensified by their fear, and she wanted to press a perfume-covered handkerchief to her face. The smell echoed her own fear all too closely.

She pulled her fur turban lower around her face, still striving for warmth that wouldn't come. As they entered the theatre, she caught a glimpse of the silver cloth of Mathilde's dress beneath her *shuba,* and her diamond shoe buckles, and knew the prima ballerina assoluta had dressed her best for the occasion. Defiant in her extravagance, even now.

Inside was a small, quiet crowd. Valentina had the impression that all was a little faded, as if she were peering at the scene through misted glass. She wondered if those with true courage were the ones who had stayed away.

'Maxim Sergeivich, would you be so good as to fetch us some champagne? I'm sure our nerves would be the better for it after that ride.' Mathilde, as always, spoke with an authority that said she knew her request would be met.

Maxim bristled for a second, and Valentina was reminded of that long-ago evening when Rasputin had ordered him to bring her a glass of champagne. So much had changed since then. Thankfully, tonight Maxim only gave a curt nod before disappearing into the small crowd.

Valentina felt Mathilde's gloved hand slip into her own and tug her away a little. 'Valya, I need to speak with you.' The urgency in the older woman's voice made Valentina's heart beat a little more forcefully. 'In a few days I will no longer be on Russian soil.'

The madness outside had made Valentina feel she could never be easily shocked again, yet now it was as though the wind had been knocked out of her. She put a hand on the nearest wall to steady herself.

'Why? Where are you going? For how long?'

Mathilde gestured to stop her, her eyes as black as the newspapers had always declared them. 'Too many questions. I've had a telephone call, from a General Halle of the Russian army. He told me there have been threats against me and I should leave Russia. So I'm going tomorrow night.'

'Tomorrow night!' The words were barely more than an exhalation. 'Can it really be that bad?'

'These threats appear to be more than just idle. Should the crowds begin searching for new ways to escalate the trouble, the General thinks they'll look to me, thanks to the way those newspapers have tarnished my name and reputation. He says if I leave it any longer than a day or two, I might not escape in one piece.'

Valentina's vision began to swim, but she forced herself to remain composed and not think of what had been done to Rasputin.

'Valya, listen to me. I think you should leave too. If it's not safe for me, it can't be much safer for you. Or for anyone like us.'

Maxim returned just as Mathilde finished speaking, and Valentina could have sworn at him. She needed more time to ask questions. But she accepted the glass of champagne he held out to her in silence.

Mathilde took Maxim's arm with a demand to be escorted inside the auditorium, and glanced at Valentina one more time. It was a look so loaded with meaning that Valentina found she was unable to swallow the champagne that was already in her mouth.

The ride back home was mercifully uneventful. Nevertheless, Valentina clung to the leather seat with white-knuckled hands, terrified that at any moment they would again feel the crowd pushing at the sides of the carriage. Maxim kept his grim face determinedly forward, refusing to show any outward sign of nerves.

It was with relief that Valentina entered her home, familiar and welcoming in the navy night. The door closed behind them with a solid, satisfying thud, but it wasn't enough to block out the occasional gunfire.

Maxim walked away from her towards the second-floor library, which was kept well stocked with liquor. His normally straight shoulders were hunched as though a heavy weight lay between them. The sight almost made Valentina sorry for him; he must feel some guilt for putting her through this trying evening. She wondered why Mathilde had waited to deliver her message when Maxim was out of earshot. Perhaps to give her the choice to escape alone if she desired. Or perhaps she recognised Maxim's stubborn, authoritative streak and didn't want him to have the opportunity to dissuade Valentina.

'Mademoiselle Yershova?' Madame Ivkina stood nearby with a tentative look on her face. 'Please, I must tell you something.' The housekeeper glanced at the ceiling above them.

Valentina assured her they were alone for the moment.

'Luka Vladimirovich is here,' Madame Ivkina whispered. 'He never left.'

Relief so strong Valentina thought she might cry swept over her. 'I see. Please, tell him to sleep in your room tonight. It's … it's too dangerous out there to leave. You can share with the maid.'

Madame Ivkina nodded, showing no sign of annoyance at having to give up her bed. Valentina didn't need to say that any noises Luka made would be more easily explained if they came from a room that was always inhabited.

The housekeeper was about to leave, but Valentina grasped her arm, stopping her. For an instant she was reminded of the way she'd grabbed Xenia Nicholaievna's arm, the sudden violence she hadn't known she was capable of. Although her grip on Madame Ivkina was soft, she released it anyway.

'I need you to go upstairs to my bedroom—before Maxim retires there. Reach underneath the bed. In its base you'll find a candy box. Pack it in a suitcase with as many warm things as you can find. Get my thickest coat and some sturdy shoes, and put them all in the small room next to the bedroom. The one I don't usually allow you in.'

Madame Ivkina's face paled as she listened to these odd instructions, but she nodded without comment. Valentina could see that she was scared, and it made her think of something else.

'Tell me, do you have any family that don't live in Petrograd?'

'No, Mademoiselle.'

'I see. Then tomorrow afternoon, go back into the small room and there'll be money waiting on the table for you. Use it to leave Petrograd. Preferably to go somewhere outside Russia.'

Madame Ivkina gasped, already shaking her head. But Valentina silenced her.

'No arguments. Take the money, split it between yourself, the maid and the cook, then leave. All of you. I'll find you when this is over, when it's safe again.'

Her voice faltered at the stricken look on her housekeeper's face. The woman couldn't believe what was happening.

Well, join the rest of us, Valentina thought grimly as she followed Maxim upstairs to the library.

CHAPTER TWENTY-FIVE

Luka woke to red light filtering through the small window of the housekeeper's room. He wanted to lift the curtain to find the source of the otherworldly glow, but resisted the temptation. He couldn't risk being seen. His sleep had been punctuated with the sound of gunfire, both real and in his dreams, but waking was no relief. He didn't like being relegated here, while Maxim slept upstairs in the same bed as Valya. He understood, though, and told himself there were more important worries to fret over.

He moved to the only chair in the room and sat twisting his fingers, unsure if it was safe for him to leave. Eventually, Madame Ivkina brought him breakfast; then, an impossibly long time later, lunch. Luka's skin crawled with impatience, his nerves further jarred by the sporadic sound of the telephone. The room gradually darkened again, the yellow flicker of the single oil lamp doing little to interrupt the shadows.

Just as he thought he might scream from having to wait any longer, the door opened. Valya stood there, in one piece. She hurried to him, and Luka had to swallow multiple times to work back the emotion caught in his throat.

'He's asleep,' she whispered, glancing upward in the direction of her bedroom. 'Luka ...'

Luka didn't say a word. He embraced her, his lips finding hers; he would know his way to them even blindfolded. A moment later and she tried to pull away, but he wouldn't let her, not yet. She melted back into him, and he wanted to cry and yell at her at the same time. But all he did was silently thank God she was there with him, safe again.

'Luka ... things are getting worse,' she said when they finally broke apart.

He didn't want to hear it; not when he'd only just recovered her. But ignoring the situation wouldn't make it go away. If he'd learned anything from the Tsar's continued absence, it was that.

Valya explained in words that pierced Luka's skin what Mathilde had told her. 'She's leaving tonight,' she finished. 'And she said ... she said I should do the same.'

Everything came to a standstill—the noises outside cut off, the dust motes in the air stilled, even Luka's breathing stopped. It was almost impossible to believe. Unable to be a queen of Russia in name, Mathilde had spent a lifetime making herself one in every other way. It wasn't a position she would give up lightly.

Luka took three rapid steps to the door; there was no time to waste. 'Preparations, Valya—we need to think practically about what—'

But she was tugging at his hand, pulling him back. 'Luka, wait. That's not all. It's bad—outside, I mean. It was terrible last night, but from what I've heard today ... The crowds have gone from looting to burning buildings. Soldiers are arriving from the front; deserters riding around in lorries, waving red flags and shouting "*Grab nagrablennoye*".'

Take back the loot. Luka suddenly understood why the light outside had been red. Petrograd was burning, and it was the glow of the flames that had woken him.

He pinched the skin between his eyes. What had it all been for? His brother's sacrifice, so noble and patriotic, given for a country that was burning itself from the inside, because it was that or starve.

'Why doesn't the Tsar come back and fix this?' he asked, knowing Valya didn't have the answer.

Pyotr, and so many others, had died for the Tsar. Why wasn't he returning their loyalty? Perhaps it no longer mattered. The uprising had taken on such a force that even the man they were crying out for might not be able to stop it. For a second Luka wished Grigori Rasputin were still alive and truly did have divine powers that he could use to stop this mess.

But wishes would get them nowhere. He needed to start thinking which route out of his country, his home, would be least impeded by the heavy snow and ice of the harsh winter they were having. And which trains would be least likely to be mobbed by deserting soldiers looking for someone to blame for the years of starvation, fighting and death they'd suffered.

'We'll have to leave during the night,' he said, drawing the words out. 'It's too dangerous in daylight—you could be recognised.'

'We?'

Luka saw that Valya's chest was rising and falling rapidly.

'Valya, you don't think I'm about to let you leave Russia without me, do you? The Imperial Ballet isn't going to carry on amid all this. And even if it does, I don't care. We're going together.'

She took an unsteady breath, her eyes distant, and Luka felt something like fear tug at him.

'Valya, did you hear me?' His voice was insistent this time.

When her eyes focused back on his they almost held a note of laughter. 'They said it would last three months. Three months of war, then Russia would be victorious.'

'I know.' Luka swallowed, trying not to choke on the memory of the Russia they'd been part of; the Russia that was changing so dramatically.

Pulling her hands away, Valya ran trembling fingers through her hair. One of her rings caught and she gently undid it. The movement was so delicate that it reminded Luka of how she'd danced the Dying Swan. He was glad when her hand returned to his, its warmth assuring him that she was right there next to him.

'What about Maxim?' she said.

Luka closed his eyes for a second. He'd forgotten about Maxim. His mind raced to find a way to overcome this new roadblock, his thumbs tapping out impatient patterns on the backs of Valya's hands. He looked at her—her bobbed hair framing her face, her eyes shadowed and scared—and knew what he wanted her to do.

'Valya,' he began cautiously, 'I think perhaps now is the time for you to leave Maxim. You were planning to anyway. If you stay together, the danger—for both of you—is increased. You have strong ties to Mathilde; as does he to the imperial family and Rasputin. You'll each be less of a target if you separate.'

He paused, his heart drumming so loud he was sure it was drowning out the gunshots that echoed through the streets.

The strange light had turned Valya's dark eyes to garnets, making them hard to read.

'You don't understand the risks of leaving him,' she said. 'He's hinted before that he would take action against you. He would use his connections to push the company into demanding your resignation. Or if they refused, he would arrange to have you hurt.'

Luka decided against confirming her suspicions by telling her about the direct threats Maxim had made to him in the past. He needed to tread delicately lest he ruin everything.

'I've said before, I no longer care what he does. The Imperial Russian Ballet is no longer my whole world.' He gave her hands a gentle squeeze, smiling. 'He can end my relationship with them, but he can't end my career. There are other companies— in Moscow, or even around the world. No matter how many ties he cuts, I will still dance.'

'But what will I tell him?'

Luka's relief that she wasn't going to argue, that she'd meant it when she'd said she would leave Maxim to be with him, was intense. It was difficult for him not to smile, even though outside the world was still on fire and tearing itself apart.

'You don't have to tell him everything. Just that you need to leave, and it would be best if he didn't go with you.'

'Luka, I can't. I owe him more than that.'

'You don't. All he has paid you for, you've done. You've met his every demand, and if you want to make your life your own, you don't owe him any explanation.'

'Not every demand,' she murmured, one hand running up her arm as if she was soothing a pain there. Her expression was troubled. 'Perhaps I won't say anything at all. If I choose my time, I can slip out without him even realising … Yes, I believe that would be best for now. I can find him and explain later, when things aren't quite so … intense. Where should we meet?'

'Meet?'

'Tonight. When we leave.'

'We're not meeting anywhere. I'm staying here until you're ready to go, and we'll leave together.'

'Luka, as you said, we have to be practical. God only knows how long we'll be gone—you need to get your things together just the same as I do. If you wait for me, we won't have time to go to your apartment.'

'It won't take so long. Just gather the essentials, then we can leave for my apartment together.'

She hesitated, her head turning away from him a little. 'I want to sew some jewels into the hems and linings of my clothes. Don't look at me like that—it's not for greed or vanity's sake. Wherever we're going, we'll need food and shelter. I'm giving the money I have on hand to my staff, but there are plenty of jewels we can take to barter with.'

'Valya, we don't need them. We can get jobs in another ballet company.'

'We don't even know where we'll end up.'

'We don't need much. We'll survive somehow.'

She made an irritated noise. 'Why gamble on such a matter when I have the means to give us certainty?'

Luka opened his mouth to argue, but found himself short of words. What she was saying made sense, however little he liked it.

'I'll help then. I'm not much of a sewer, but if I can patch up ballet slippers I'm sure I can make a few pockets.'

Valya's face softened into a tender look, and she touched his cheek. 'You're a generous person, Luka Vladimirovich, but not a practical one. The point of sewing the jewels into my garments is so they'll be concealed from searching eyes, and anything other than fine needlework will alert a curious gaze to the presence of something hidden.'

Again she made sense, but Luka resisted. He didn't want to leave her here alone. 'Then I'll go to my apartment, pack what I need, and come back here to meet you.'

'And risk running into Maxim?'

Luka exhaled roughly. He knew now was the time for decisive action not lovers' sentimentality, yet still he loathed the idea of separating. He grappled with himself, common sense waging a war with fear.

'Why don't we meet at The Wandering Dog then?' he said slowly. At her quizzical look, he explained, 'It's a club, far enough away from the city's centre that we shouldn't come up against any trouble.'

Valya agreed, and Luka, still unsure if he was doing the right thing, wrote down the address for her. They arranged to meet just before midnight.

The time had come for him to leave, but Luka hesitated. A sick feeling churned in the pit of his stomach.

'Are you sure you'll be able to get there?' he asked her.

'A covered woman heading out alone in the middle of the night is hardly going to seem like the Valentina Yershova the crowds know. No one will look at me twice.'

'I can stay here until it's time.'

Valya took his face in her hands, then ran her fingers through the hair at his temples. 'No, you can't, my love. Go home, pack your warmest clothes for it's freezing out there, and be waiting for me at The Wandering Dog with a kiss on your lips.'

After a glance out of Madame Ivkina's bedroom door to make sure no one was in view, she led him quickly to the front door.

'Until tonight,' she whispered, holding it open just enough so he could squeeze out.

Luka looked back at her and he couldn't help it—he edged himself into the gap in the door and kissed her hard. All the passion he felt for her, all the frustrations of their past and his hopes for their future, went into the kiss, and when he finally pulled away her cheeks had turned pink.

Before he could change his mind, he turned and walked into the angry streets, headed for home. He thought he heard her whisper, 'I love you,' but he didn't look back for confirmation. If he did, he knew he'd never be able to leave her.

He would tell her he loved her when they met again; God willing, he would spend the rest of his life saying it over and over.

Midnight was only a few hours away, but he already knew they would be the longest hours of his life.

CHAPTER TWENTY-SIX

Valentina watched the red light darken Luka's silhouette until he became nothing more than a shadow. Gunfire continued to crack open the freezing air, and she could almost feel the bullets burying themselves deep in her flesh, working their way to her heart where they could do the most damage. She hoped that wherever the gunshots came from, Luka would stay far away.

As she closed the door, an unsettling sense of finality came over her. She slowly made her way back up the stairs and pushed open her bedroom door. Maxim was no longer there. She exhaled, relieved; it would be easier to pick out her best jewels without fear of waking him from his alcohol-induced slumber—a habit he'd acquired since Rasputin's death.

Moving to her dressing table, she rummaged through her belongings. Her hands felt thick and clumsy, her mind fogged by fear of what was to come. Soon she and Luka would be in the midst of that horror, with no carriage walls to separate them from the desperate hands and weapons of the revolting masses.

She swore softly as she knocked over a perfume bottle, spilling its contents. The room filled with the thick scent of musk. Checking over her shoulder that Maxim hadn't heard the crash—where was he?—she righted the bottle but didn't bother to clear up the spill. There wasn't time.

She flipped open an enamelled box and ran her fingers through the jewellery inside. Pulling out two pairs of diamond earrings, she tucked them into the sleeve of her dress. A few long strings of pearls were hooked over one arm. She was about to close the box and move on to others when she saw a smaller velvet box in one corner. She hesitated, then pulled it out and peeled open the mossy lid. Inside was the swan brooch Maxim had given her. It alone could pay for their travel, food, and a roof over their heads.

She wondered if Luka might take it as evidence of some indecision about what she was leaving behind. She didn't feel any. She was more scared of the choices she was making than she would ever admit to Luka, but it was a thrilling kind of fear. The only other time in her adult life when she hadn't known her future with any certainty was when Dimitri had blindsided her with the introduction to Maxim. This time, though, the uncertainty was her own doing, and the feeling was like taking a flying leap headfirst, not knowing if a partner would be there to catch her but blindly trusting he would.

It was hard to let the brooch go. Valentina took it out of the box, resting the heavy swan on the palm of her hand. With one fingertip she touched the pearl clutched in the swan's golden feet. This wasn't Odette; it was just a piece of twisted gold that showed her how lifeless she had become.

'Going somewhere?'

Valentina whirled around; the brooch flew out of her hand and hit the floor with a loud rap. She scrambled to pick it up, the strings of pearls on her arm clattering, and tucked it into her palm as she faced Maxim. Her heart was beating violently and her ears felt hot.

She tried to keep her voice calm. 'Of course not. Why would you say that?' She gave a breathy laugh.

'Those jewels are a little dressed up for staying inside.'

Maxim stood in the doorway, no shirt on, leaning heavily on the frame. His eyes were bloodshot, and his moustache stuck up on one side in an almost comical manner that yet had nothing funny about it. His breathing was heavy, and as he took a step into the room the stink of alcohol hit Valentina's nose—so strong, it was like poison.

'Oh. Yes.' She looked down at her arms hung with necklaces, and the retrieved brooch that sat in her hand. 'I was … I was just going through my things. Just admiring them.'

Maxim's unchanging expression told her he didn't believe her. 'When I woke you weren't there.'

She let the necklaces slide off her arm to the floor, and stepped over them as if they were nothing more than trinkets. She was about to walk to him, the way she usually would, but realised she needn't do that any more. Maxim might not know it, but she was free of him now. Still, the way his voice had dropped sent a chill over her skin. She wanted to lead him away from her room to rest and allow the drink to leave him. Anything to be alone again. In her head she could swear she heard the ticking of a clock, marking off the seconds she was wasting by not readying herself for her flight from Russia.

'You're all worked up, Maxim. Why don't you rest?'

Used to giving him comfort, Valentina found it difficult to prevent herself going to him. She tucked her hands nervously into the fabric of her skirt; they were beginning to go cold, although the bedroom was warm from the heat of the stove.

Maxim's red eyes finally focused on Valentina. She shrank back from his gaze. A mistake she instantly realised.

'A man demands obedience from his family,' he said, pulling the bedroom door shut behind him. 'And my family must be above ridicule.'

Valentina heard the lock fall heavily into place. Her heart was pounding. She was sure he would be able to hear it from across the room.

'Maxim, I … I'm not your family. Not really. I'm paid for. But even if I weren't, I would never expose you to ridicule.'

'That's strange, because your *dvornik* seems to be under the impression that you're running away in the middle of the night. Which is just the sort of thing that gets a man laughed at and pitied.'

Valentina froze; she hadn't told Madame Ivkina that her departure was to be a secret.

'Maxim, I—'

'No!'

The word was a shout, and she jumped. Her hands flew to her chest, pressing on the rapid beating of her heart as if she could still it with her cold palms. Maxim's own hands were gripping the hair at his temples. His face was red.

'You are taking what I gave you, a symbol of my—of *our* love—and using it to pay your way with another man.'

'That's not—it's not …' Her voice was breathy. The brooch in her hand suddenly felt like it was burning her. She wanted to fling it away. To pretend innocence when guilt was so clearly in her nature.

Maxim's eyes were shut, and he beat his fists on the door behind him. Valentina flinched.

When he opened his eyes, they were just a dark glint in his face. He crossed the room and grabbed her shoulders, pushing her back so she slammed into the dressing table. Something crashed off it to the floor. Valentina put her hands behind her, trying to grab the table for support, but they slipped in the slick puddle of her perfume. Maxim had pushed his face right into hers, and she could smell the alcohol strong on his breath.

'Maxim, please,' she gasped.

His hands stroked the sides of her neck, and she felt the sweat on his shaking palms.

'My Odile. My little, perfect Odile,' he whispered.

Through her fear came a flash of anger, hot and tinged with reckless panic.

'What about that?' she said, glaring into his feverish eyes. 'What about what *you* promised *me*? I did all you asked of me, yet Odette never came.'

Her hands still fumbled over the table behind her, looking for something to get Maxim away from her. She would have been grateful for the weight of the brooch now, or the sharp point of its clasp, but it had slipped out of her hand.

'All I asked of you?' His words were a roar, flecks of spit hitting her face. His fingernails dug into her skin, and his red eyes were so wild they looked like they might jump right out of his head. 'There was only one thing I required more than anything else. And you couldn't do it, could you? Couldn't keep your legs closed to that ... that *malysh*.'

Valentina couldn't move. Her senses were clouded by the spilled perfume, the musk becoming stronger and stronger until she thought she might choke on it.

Maxim's eyes met hers, and she saw something that terrified her. The man glaring at her was a complete stranger.

'You'll turn me into a laughing stock,' he said, and his fingers curled around behind her neck.

For a moment she thought he might be softening. Then his thumbs were pressing at the dip of her throat. She didn't realise at first what was happening. But the uncomfortable sensation turned to pain, and her breath wouldn't come properly. She panicked, grasped at his hands with her own. Her fingernails clawed him, leaving deep red lines in his skin. He didn't seem to notice.

The pressure increased, and dark spots swam in front of her. Valentina kicked her feet wildly, knocking over anything that was nearby. She wanted to scream, but didn't have enough breath left to do so. Why didn't anyone hear her struggles and come to her aid? But the house was empty; the staff gone on her own orders.

'Maxim,' she managed to choke out.

'Shhh,' he said, almost tenderly as he forced her to the ground. Valentina felt the floor meet her back like it had come up to catch her. She flung out a hand and grasped at a string of pearls. She tried to lift it, to hit him with it, but her body, usually so responsive to her orders, would not obey.

'If you fight, it will only get worse.'

Her hearing was fading, Maxim's voice and her own struggles drowned out by something else. What was that? A strange sound that didn't belong here, in her bedroom.

It was Tchaikovsky. The swelling score of *Le Lac des Cygnes* was filling the room, pulsating in time with the pressure in her ears. She still struggled, but it was becoming a distant feeling. As if she had stepped outside her body and was watching herself fight with one eye, and looking out for Odette with the other. Where was she? She should be here. Odette should be here.

The musky scent that Valentina had never liked filled her nostrils. Luka's name was on her lips, but she couldn't speak. And still Tchaikovsky's yearning melody continued to play.

Her hand caught on something. Lifting the object, she put all the strength she had left into thrusting it at Maxim. The delicate silk of the pillow gave way under her torn fingernails and white feathers burst into a billowing cloud around them.

The feathers danced mid-air, and in that moment all pain faded away. Valentina could barely see through her tears and the black spots that obliterated most of her vision. She didn't see the way the feathers hovered, nor how they descended in undulating waves. But she felt them.

Odette's feathers, landing on her face and neck in a gentle caress, resting beneath her dropping hands and shoulders so that they cupped her as she fell.

CHAPTER TWENTY-SEVEN

Luka tossed aside a pair of trousers that he'd only just placed in his suitcase, then picked them up and put them back in. He and Valya hadn't chosen a destination yet, but the enormity of the last few hours sat heavily on him and it was impossible to think with any clarity. By the time he'd finished packing he was no longer sure what was in the case beyond a few pairs of ballet slippers. He looked hopefully at his Buhré pocket watch: there were still three hours left until he could meet Valya. His heart sank. He put his case by the front door, underneath a heavy black *shuba*, then sat down to wait.

His nerves got the better of him, and he stood back up, grabbed the back of a chair and ran through a plié exercise. Pliés turned into battements tendus, then glissés, and soon he was working through a lengthy barre.

It was as he was unfolding his leg in a controlled développé that the urge to pray came over him. It was so strong that he kneeled down right where he was. Forehead damp with sweat, he moved his lips with a single-mindedness his prayers had never known before. He prayed for an end to the destruction in Russia. He prayed for the war to be over, for the Tsar to come back and somehow right all that had gone wrong. He prayed for his father, that he was safely inside his apartment with a bottle of vodka. He prayed for Xenia's safety, wherever she was.

But most of all, he prayed for himself and Valya, for the shared future he couldn't quite see.

When he'd finished, he got to his feet knowing he couldn't simply wait for Valya. He had to go back for her.

In the street, Luka had to elbow his way through the crowds. It was a struggle to take even one tiny step at a time, and he was horrified to think that he'd left Valya to face this by herself in the night-time.

Ahead, a cheering group stood around a fire; in its yellow edges Luka could make out imperial emblems that had been torn off buildings. Trash, stolen furniture and books served as kindling. As he pushed past the bonfire, a face caught his eye. It was withered and bearded, the eyes alight and feverish. Luka's breath caught. It was his father.

Vladimir had slid from view, but Luka saw a flash of sheepskin coat. He struggled to get to it, his cries drowned out by the cheers of those around him. Then he saw his father again—the back of his grizzled head on the other side of the bonfire, moving steadily away from him.

Luka tried to push some men out of his way, and in return was given a giant shove in the chest that sent him sprawling. He scrambled to retrieve his case, earning trodden fingers for his trouble, then clambered to his feet. Where had his father gone?

A sea of fabric, limbs and faces swam before him, and it was a long, terrifying moment before Luka's eyes found the sheepskin coat again, turning a corner. He hovered, undecided. Should he follow? He couldn't be sure, in this madness, if it really had been his father. So many of the men looked alike with their withered, underfed faces. And he needed to get to Valya.

But what if it was his father? He couldn't leave him to fend for himself on these streets. Vladimir was old and unwell. He might not believe he needed protection, but Luka had lost enough family already.

He sprinted forward, this time dodging men and women as best he could instead of getting tangled up with them. Glass crunched beneath his boots. He turned the corner and frantically scanned the street. It, too, was full of chaos. There were no fires, but windows had been shattered, and people were pulling anything they could off buildings with their bare hands, parading them above their heads as they walked back to join the bonfire.

Was that Vladimir slipping between two buildings half a block away?

'*Otets!*' Luka bellowed at the top of his voice, but he could barely be heard over the din of the rioting crowds.

He bent his head and barrelled forward. He'd made his decision, and he wouldn't give up until he found his father.

Luka spent so long following that elusive sheepskin coat that by the time he caught up to the man—not his father after all, but someone closer to Luka's own age who hadn't worn life well—there was no longer any point going to Valya's house. Instead, he went straight to their meeting spot.

His stomach dropped when he arrived to find no one waiting for him—he'd hoped she might already be there—but he told himself not to worry. There was plenty of time.

Even now, after loitering in front of The Wandering Dog for what felt like a lifetime, there was still time … He checked his pocket watch again: two minutes until midnight.

As the night ticked over to a new day, he thought he heard footsteps, and strained his eyes to see further into the darkness. The streetlamps had been damaged in the past few days and were mostly extinguished, so it was hard to make anything out.

The shape that came into view was that of a man, and Luka shrank back so he wouldn't be seen. A gunshot sounded close by, but by now the sound was so familiar to Luka that he didn't jump.

He looked at his watch again, holding it up to his nose to see the delicate hands properly. It was five minutes after midnight. When he put it back down, it was in the hope that he would see Valya standing in front of him, case in hand, shrouded in a heavy coat. But the street remained empty.

Back at his apartment, it had seemed impossible that time could ever move more slowly. But now, as midnight passed further behind him, it felt like it had come to a complete stop. Luka pulled his *shuba* tighter around him, trying to protect himself from the crisp air. When Valya arrived, they would hold each other, sharing their bodily warmth. Relief, too, would probably go a long way to warming him.

If only she would hurry up.

One o'clock came and went. A sick feeling gnawed at him. Had she changed her mind? Had she decided to stay with Maxim and take her chances here in Petrograd?

No. Luka had seen the expression on her face. She wanted to come with him, that he was sure of.

He reminded himself of this every quarter-hour that went by, using the refrain to try to quell his growing panic. There must be some other reason she was delayed. Something that would seem obvious once she arrived and explained it all.

'She will come,' he whispered to himself over and over as the hours passed. 'She will come; I know she will.'

She had to.

CHAPTER TWENTY-EIGHT

Dawn broke and still Valya didn't appear. Luka thought he might vomit with the tension of waiting for her, but gradually his panic turned into a dull ache that seemed to emanate from his very bones. Something had gone wrong.

The sky was turning from deep indigo to blazing orange, lit from beneath by hundreds of burning buildings. Luka picked up his case and began walking. His feet, encased in *valenki*, moved of their own accord. Every time he spotted a woman with bobbed hair his heart leaped a little. But every time he was disappointed.

As he neared the city's centre, the sound of gunfire competed with the roar of thousands of voices. Men and women ran past him, screaming that the troops had opened fire on them. Others cheered as they shared the news that the Grand Duke Cyril, a member of the hated aristocracy, had turned and was now marching on the side of the protesters. All was confusion, and Luka wished it would stop, just for a moment, just until he'd found Valya.

A pile of red-stained snow sent his heart leaping into his throat; but when he leaned closer, the smell of wine wafted up to him. On the pavement nearby were broken pieces of wood—the shattered remains of the barrel. The looters, unable to carry the heavy load away, had drunk their fill and then smashed it so nothing would be left for the original owners.

The closer he got to his destination, the faster Luka's feet went. His breathing sped up too, and he was almost sprinting as he turned into Valya's street. Her house was untouched. He couldn't understand how it had been passed over by the looters.

He walked up to the front door and knocked loudly. There was no answer, and he tried again, then again, this time pounding his open palm against the wood. Nothing.

He glanced up and down the street. It was almost deserted. He was partially hidden from view by the ridged columns of the portico, but still he waited for the street's sole other occupant to turn a corner and disappear from sight. Then he kicked at a window. Nothing happened. A second kick resulted in a few cracks splayed across the glass; a third and it finally broke.

Luka checked to make sure he was still unobserved— although anyone who saw him was more likely to join him than stop him—then crawled through the opening he'd made. The broken glass caught at his clothes as he tumbled into the house. His left palm was scratched, almost deep enough to draw blood, but he ignored it. Clambering to his feet, he ran up the stairs calling Valya's name, heedless if Maxim heard him.

He checked the blue reception room first, but she wasn't there. Nor was there any sign of her. The oil lamps weren't lit, and he noticed for the first time that the house was cold, meaning that neither was the stove.

He hurried to her bedroom. The door was closed. As he pushed it open, the smell of her perfume flooded him. It was as though the furniture had been drenched in it. Its familiarity almost knocked Luka backward. Instead, he stepped into the room ... and the world came crashing down around him.

Everything was a mess. Items from Valya's dressing table were scattered all around, many of them broken. Strings of pearls decorated the floor, and the swan brooch Maxim had given her lay at the toes of Luka's boots. And feathers. White feathers coated the room.

But it was Valya his eyes went to. Valya, lying in the middle of those feathers, eyes closed, impossibly still.

'Valya?' It was a whisper, childlike and scared.

He stepped over the mess and went to her, kneeling by her side. His hands touched her face, her shoulders; his fingers brushed her dark lashes. Still she didn't move.

Luka's mind tried to lock itself in a little compartment where the truth of what he was seeing wouldn't reach him. But it wasn't fast enough. An anguished cry broke from his chest and rushed up his throat. He bit his lips so hard he tasted blood. A satisfying sting accompanied the metallic taste, making him bite harder. The blood gave him something to focus on as he bent to lift her into his arms.

The physical pain kept at bay the greater agony that threatened to overwhelm him. But it couldn't stop him noticing how heavy she was now that her limbs had stiffened and cooled. This had to be some kind of nightmare. But as he lay her down on the bed, he knew it wasn't. The feel of the fabric of her dress on his arms was too real. The smell of her perfume filled his nostrils in a way no dream could. He saw the vibrant purple of the bruises that ringed her neck. Felt the iciness of her lips as he touched them with his fingertips. Luka kneeled next to the bed, picked up her cold hand. He began to chafe it in his own, then realised there was no point. He let his movement still, staring at her torn fingernails. They had never been like that before. Something was caught on the edge of one nail, and Luka carefully picked it off. It was a tiny piece of a feather, just a few downy white strands.

The memory of another white feather hit him, and he cried out, his control escaping him briefly. He desperately clawed it back. The pain was too much, too overwhelming; he wasn't ready for it.

He pressed his forehead against the bed, shutting his eyes so he could no longer see her, and concentrated on breathing. He couldn't let himself think; he just needed to hold on to her hand, squeeze it as tightly as he could, but not think of it. It was his lifeline. If he let go, if he opened his eyes, if he even breathed too deeply, it would all come crashing down.

He couldn't allow that. Not now. Not ever, please, God.

When he awoke some hours later, heart beating rapidly and sweat coating his forehead, he reached out for Valya. Those few seconds when he held her in his arms, thinking she would wake, were bliss. The moment he registered the stiffness of her form, the memory was a gunshot through his chest. He howled with rage, scrunching handfuls of her dress to his face to muffle his screams.

But he wouldn't sit here and cry; oh no. Not when the person who had done this to Valya was still out there.

He stood, knees protesting from the prolonged time he'd spent on them, and brought Valya's hand to his lips. He kissed her fingers, trying not to notice how cold and stiff they were, then folded her hand on her chest. He brushed the hair away from her bruised eyelids, as if it might bother her.

'I will not let this go unpunished. I promise you.'

He pushed the words through tight lips, then after one lingering look at the necklace of violence on her white skin, he was out the door, taking the stairs two at a time.

As he strode along the chaotic streets of Petrograd, he had no sense of time; only blurred impressions of broken building facades decorated with red revolutionary flags, and white snow, and grim faces shouting slogans he didn't hear. There was no point going to the police—those that were left had been newly instated from the ranks of former criminals. Maxim wouldn't go to jail for what he'd done. If anything, he'd likely be celebrated for destroying a woman who'd embodied all the revolution was against. Just as Rasputin's murder had been celebrated.

Luka reached Mathilde's house. A commotion made him pause outside, holding his anger tight in his heart like a closed fist. Marchers neared the house, and the front doors flew open. Luka's breathing stopped; for a second he thought it was Mathilde, facing up to the revolutionaries in a suicidal display of bravery. But it was her housekeeper, Madame Roubtzova. She was wearing one of Mathilde's fur coats, and spoke to the marchers in a triumphant voice.

'Come in, come in. The bird has flown!'

The crowd cheered and surged forward. They worked quickly, ransacking the mansion from top to bottom. Out of the front door came two revolutionaries dragging a man between them. His feet stumbled, unable to gain purchase on the ground. It was Mathilde's porter, Denisov.

'Who are you? Another of Her High-and-Mighty's lovers?' The man had to speak loudly to be heard over the screaming of the porter's wife from one of the upstairs rooms.

'No! I'm just her porter. That's all. Just a porter.'

'Well, porter, tell me. Where has your employer gone?' The man pressed a gun to Denisov's forehead.

'*Ya nye znayu*. I don't know!'

His answer was met with a round of laughter. Denisov began to cry, ugly sobs that stuck in his elderly chest. His breath came in little white clouds, obscuring his face.

'She's gone,' he said. 'She went in the night. I don't know where. No one told us.'

'What a shame,' another man jeered as he raised his own gun. 'We were going to kill her. But if she's not here, I suppose you'll have to do instead.'

Luka turned and ran. There was nothing he could do for the porter, except get himself killed in an attempt to defend him. And he couldn't die, not yet. He had to find Maxim first.

Valya had mentioned where Maxim lived that day they'd watched the protesters march down her street. Luka knew the street name but not the specific building. It wasn't hard to guess, though. There was a carriage waiting outside one mansion, its door flung open. The horses tossed their manes, eyes rolling wildly at the noise that surrounded them. The street wasn't under siege the way Luka's own had been, but the blazing roar of fires and the cracks of gunshots were inescapable all over Petrograd.

Luka moved towards the carriage, his feet slowing, his chest getting tighter and tighter.

Maxim was at its door, helping his valet fling into it items that clearly weren't his. Ruffled dresses, velvet bags that clinked with the sound of jewellery inside, silk petticoats and furs. And worst of all, dance shoes. All flung into the carriage as though they were something dirty Maxim wanted to get away from him.

'You,' Luka snarled.

Maxim turned. His eyes were wild, and underneath his fur-lined coat his shirt hung to his knees. Two red scratches flared across his cheek, and Luka couldn't take his eyes off them. Noticing, Maxim put his hand to his face; Luka saw that his fingers were trembling.

The man licked his lips once, twice, and when he tried to speak his words caught and he had to start again. 'What do you want, Malysh?'

'I think you know.'

Maxim glanced at his valet, who was watching them. 'Go inside. Make a pile of everything that is left, but don't bring it out. Come only if I call for you.'

The man nodded and went inside, leaving the door ajar.

'It's your fault for putting ideas in her head,' Maxim said, as soon as they were alone. He rubbed his face, and winced as his fingers ran over the scratches. 'You made her betray me and the safety I offered.'

Anger burned Luka's throat; he vibrated with it, only just holding himself back.

'A strange kind of safety! I've seen the bruises. The mess of feathers, her broken fingernails. That was no scene of safety!'

Maxim shrank back. There was a moment of silence, the unspoken accusation hanging in the air.

'You did this!' Luka screamed. He didn't know how, but suddenly he had Maxim pinned against the carriage, his hands making fists in the other man's clothing. Rage pulsated through him, hot and painful. It was almost comforting after the battle to keep those other feelings—a hopeless, overwhelming sense of loss and longing—at bay.

'You found out what she—what *we* were planning, and you couldn't stand the thought that another man could have for free what you paid for. *More* than what you paid for.' His voice hurt in his throat, a metallic taste filling his mouth.

He slammed Maxim against the carriage for emphasis, expecting him to fight back. He relished the thought. He needed to hit him, to make some of the pain he felt on the inside show itself on the outside. He knew he could cause some damage before Maxim's valet came to his rescue.

But instead of fighting back, or calling for help, Maxim choked out, 'You don't know how difficult it was to love someone the way I loved Valya.'

Luka's fist drew back and slammed into the other man's face. A satisfying crunch sounded as pain resonated through his knuckles. Then he had Maxim by the throat and was squeezing. He couldn't call for help now, even if he wanted to.

Maxim's eyes bulged, his toes only just touching the ground as Luka lifted him up. Luka's strength pulsated through him, fuelled by anger. The comparatively slight weight of Maxim assured him he could kill him. He tightened his grip, snarling in the other man's face. His eyes focused on his rigid hands around that neck, Maxim's smaller ones clawing ineffectually at them. And he remembered Valya's torn nails, the pattern of bruises on her white neck. His hands tightened even further, and then with a roar that sounded as though his very soul was ripping from him, Luka let go.

Maxim crumpled to the ground, making animal sounds as he gasped for air.

Luka was panting. White-hot rage still surged through him, the desire for blood almost impossible to suppress. He was shaking as he grabbed Maxim by the hair and pulled his head up. The sight of blood streaming from his broken nose gave Luka grim satisfaction, and it was hard not to go for more. But Pyotr hadn't died so good men could become beasts.

'I won't make myself like you,' he said. 'Not even to avenge Valya.'

Luka let get of Maxim's hair, and the man scrambled away towards the portico of his house, calling out for his valet. Luka spat after him, his rage dying into cold embers that left only emptiness in their place.

CHAPTER TWENTY-NINE

After Valya's death, Luka spent most of his time at The Wandering Dog. He hid from the world, and himself, in alcohol. He ignored anyone who tried to talk to him. He barely ate, unless food was pushed in front of him, and even then he didn't taste it. He didn't change his clothes. He hadn't cried, and he couldn't understand it. Perhaps his heart didn't believe she was gone, despite the emptiness inside him, despite returning to hold her cold body in his arms, stroking her lifeless cheek with knuckles that still bore the blood of the man who had killed her. Outside, the world continued to change. Former courtiers, gendarmes, generals and policemen were packed into trucks and locked up in the Peter and Paul Fortress, recently emptied of prisoners by soldiers who had changed sides during the revolution. The Tsar was no longer a Tsar. Lenin, the exile, was rumoured to be returning to Russia.

Propaganda against Mathilde was everywhere. Luka knew members of the Imperial Russian Ballet—now no longer imperial but some new and unfamiliar company—had been asked about her whereabouts. He probably would have been asked too, if he'd bothered to show up to classes. But he couldn't stand to be in the same place where Valya had danced.

The morning of the burials, however, he forced himself into action. He woke early and rose from bed immediately. He forced down some food, and put on the clean clothes he'd picked out the night before. He concentrated on these simple tasks, not allowing himself, even for a moment, to dwell on the significance of the day.

They were burying all the victims of the revolution in the Field of Mars, Valya included. Luka had decided it was best. Let her rest among all those who were wronged, her legacy fading into history as a tiny bit of a greater tragedy. At least she would have dignity in that.

He made his way to the large park, his numb feet keeping time with the crowd around him. The sound of ice cracking in the Neva was reminiscent of the gunfire that had filled the streets during the past weeks; and would no doubt begin again once this day of respect was over.

The mourners at the Field of Mars were numerous, solemnity resting over them in stark contrast to the revolution that had taken so many lives. The crowds made it difficult to see much, but the coffins—hundreds, thousands of them?—stood out brightly against the drab surroundings. Instead of the usual black, they were painted red, the colour of the revolution.

Members of the provisional government that had taken power after the Tsar had abdicated stood with their eyes downcast and the corners of their mouths tucked in as they shook hands and greeted people with slow, understanding nods. Watching their faces, Luka's stomach churned. They were pretending not to be gleeful in their victory; pretending that Russia was a better place now, where the people were safe, happy and, for once, equal; instead of the truth—that the country was still besieged with looting, arson and murder.

Luka shifted his gaze to the lines of red coffins. His Valya was laid out in one of them, never to dance or love or laugh again. Entombed in the colour of the people who would have killed her if they'd got to her before Maxim.

He turned his back and walked away.

He moved through a city now bare of the imperial eagles. He passed soldiers wandering aimlessly, their epaulettes torn, buttons missing from their tunics. They were shabby, dirty and hungry, yet still hoping for the freedom and land the revolutionaries had promised them. They should have known better by now.

Luka used the window he'd broken to enter Valya's house. Memories accosted him, and he held his breath against their sharp pain.

With heavy feet, he went upstairs, then flung open the door to Valya's dance studio. He almost expected to find her there, practising fouettés in front of the mirror. But of course there was only empty space in front of him.

He stepped inside and kicked his boots off. In one corner lay a pair of Valya's pointe shoes, their satin dulled with age. He tried not to look at them. Instead, he twisted his torso and arms, the movements familiar yet stiff.

But the pointe shoes kept drifting into his vision, and the fierceness he'd been fighting wouldn't be held at bay any more. He felt the walls within crack and then break, and suddenly he was a madman—flying jetés took him across the room, double tours en l'air spinning him like a child's top. He ran and he jumped, careless of how the movements tore at muscles that weren't yet warm. Sweat poured down his body and still the rage consumed him.

He moved into a series of grand jetés en tournant, the quick turns followed by a soaring leap taking him in a wild circle around the edges of the room. Faster and faster he went, the leaps becoming more out of control until it was their momentum that carried him forward.

And then he was on the floor. His chest ached from breathing so hard and the backs of his legs were alive with pain, but the rage was no longer there. There was only a gnawing hollowness.

Luka sat up and looked at himself in the mirror. He saw a man he didn't recognise.

He lifted one arm up in fifth position. Standing, he lifted the other arm to join it. The movements were slow, in time with the aching beat of the heart he'd often wished would just stop. As he carefully stepped into an arabesque a tear rolled down his face. His eyes rested once more on the pointe shoes in the corner, their pink laces curled around them like a frame; and this time he didn't look away.

Never again would they be filled with Valya's lyrical steps.

Luka's movements became softer as he continued to dance; there was no more wild leaping. His limbs stretched and contracted; his torso lengthened even as it curled. Soon, he was as fluid as the tears that ran, unchecked, down his cheeks.

Luka's thighs cried out in protest with each step he took down the hallway, and the sweat that soaked his clothes was turning cold. But the discomfort was worth it. He reached the blue reception room where he and Valya had first made love. It was cold and empty now, no more a part of Valya than the coffin she'd been buried in. He left without touching anything.

Unable to make himself exit the house just yet, he paused at the door to her bedroom. He'd pushed it closed behind him when he'd carried her out of there for the last time. He couldn't bear to reopen it now and be reminded of her last moments.

Instead, he opened the door next to her bedroom. Behind it was a small room containing an octagonal table coated with a thick layer of dust. On top of the table stood a candle in a silver holder, burned almost to a stub, and a plain photo frame.

Luka stepped forward, his heart pounding. He grabbed the photo, hoping it might be of Valya. Instead an angry, dark-eyed woman in a sombre hat stared back at him. Cracks marred the surface of the glass, and she looked annoyed by them. He ran his fingers over the cracks, wondering if Valya had done the same.

He replaced the photograph and turned to leave, when something caught his eye. On the floor next to the table stood a suitcase. Draped over one end was a full-length fur coat, a pair of gloves perched neatly on top. He sank down next to them, his legs screaming against the movement.

They'd come so close.

He picked up one of the gloves and pressed it to his cheek with a futile hope of feeling human warmth emanating from it. It was, of course, cool. He wondered if he'd ever noticed before just how small Valya's hands were; he couldn't remember.

The hollowness created by his dance was filling with pain again, and he gritted his teeth to keep it at bay. He put down the glove, and traced a finger over the corner of the suitcase and down its side. It left a clear trail through the dust. He stopped when he saw a small faded box next to the case, half hidden by the fur coat.

He pulled it out. It was a candy box. The exterior was faded with age, but Luka thought it was the kind the Tsar handed out to children on his naming day. With a sadness that surprised him, he realised there would be no more boxes like this. Russia had no Tsar any more.

He cradled the box in his lap. Careful not to damage it, he eased the lid off. On the top of its contents rested a small pair of tattered gloves. They were the gloves Luka had lost; the ones his mother had lovingly repaired for him again and again. He picked them up in disbelief. How had Valya come to have them?

Underneath was a white feather, plucked from a bush near the sea and announced as a symbol of things to come. A domino mask, taken off before the first of what would become many kisses. A silver bracelet of seven fine chains nestled inside a blue velvet box. The paper that had been wrapped around the Cartier brooch Luka had carried home for her. There was even a sock that he'd left behind when Maxim had almost caught them and he'd had to rush from the house half-dressed. All packed away in an old, crumbling candy box, ready to take with her.

Luka slowly stood, the box clutched in both hands. He no longer saw the room in front of him; his gaze was a long way away, looking to a future that would never happen. He saw himself and Valya walking in public, their arms linked, no fear of being caught. He saw them dancing together on the stage; Valya finally Odette, with Luka her Prince Siegfried. And the candy box, no longer kept secret, was overflowing with mementos, shared moments from a bright and happy life together.

The vision dimmed, and Luka was once more in the small room. There was no window, but even so he could tell the light outside was red again. The fires continued to burn, and the houses continued to be looted. He wondered—as Valya had, the day they'd watched snowballs explode against her windows—how long this could go on for. And whether he would continue to be a part of it.

EPILOGUE

Autumn 1920; Paris

Luka inserted the key into his rented apartment's door. He loved this time of the afternoon: rehearsals were over for the day, and he had a handful of hours to relax in the golden light that filtered through his tiny window, dappling the parquetry floors.

The apartment was smaller than the one he'd had in Russia, but it was neat and central to the theatre, which was all that mattered. He threw the bag containing his ballet slippers and practice clothing onto the settee, then pulled his shirt off as he crossed the room. As he watched the water slowly fill the enamelled cast-iron bathtub, his feet stroked out unconscious battements tendus on the yellow and red tiles.

Tonight, he would step onto the stage of the Théâtre National de l'Opéra in his first ever performance with the Ballets Russes. He would perform a whole season with them as a soloist; and afterwards Diaghilev had invited him to tour with the company. He'd warned Luka that the countries they

313

visited would pass by in a whirl of stages, both grand and in disrepair, and there would be no time to explore. This afternoon would be one of his last quiet moments for who knew how long.

Luka turned the taps off. He had to soak his muscles to prepare them for that night's performance, but he held off climbing into the warm water. There was something he needed to do first.

He went into his bedroom and reached under the bed to pull out an old, worn box. Only he would know it had once held candy; the image on its lid of the now-dead Romanovs was so faded, their faces could have belonged to any family. As always, Luka felt a dull pang as he remembered that bright family; the Tsar he hadn't loved, but who had made his life of dance and artistry possible. It was like an old injury that would never quite heal.

He carried the box into the living room and over to the window, collecting a pen and sheaf of paper on the way. He curled up on the windowsill, pen between his teeth, staring at the outside world through the mottled glass.

Luka's reluctance to leave Russia without Valya meant he'd stayed longer than he should have. A second revolution had broken out—and taken his father's life—and was followed by civil war. He knew then that he should have gathered the courage to leave sooner; and had found himself trekking through the mountains without food or hope, sure that the long bitter nights would kill him. He'd joined up with a group of other refugees: men, women and children who wanted to escape the violence Russia was inflicting on herself. Some had wagons, on which they carried the elderly or infirm until they died. Many times Luka had found himself facedown in the cold dirt, bullets whizzing over his head. When all he could see around him was trees, he wished for a village to come into sight; but when one did, he would become sick with nerves, not knowing if the village was held by friendly Whites, or Reds who would kill him if they recognised him as an imperial dancer.

At some stage—he could no longer remember when; those days were mostly a blur of misery and fear—Mathilde Kschessinska and her son, Vova, had joined their group. Mathilde had been unable to leave Russia after delivering her warning to Valya; instead, she and Vova had hidden in a friend's house, cowering from bullets that took the life of her dog, Djibi. Vladimir Lenin, the leading revolutionary, had requisitioned Mathilde's mansion as his headquarters; and the greatest dancer in Russia, and one of the richest women in Petrograd, had ended up trudging through the mountains in shoes worn down at the heel, wrapped in a coat that had lost all its fur and was cut off to the knee and elbows to disguise the many holes.

Finally, their dwindled numbers reached Tuapse; and from there they were able to take a boat to Anapa. Istanbul and Yugoslavia followed, then France, where the group had dispersed. Mathilde had taken Vova to the Alpes-Maritimes, and reunited there with the Grand Duke Andrei. The Grand Duke Sergei had been murdered just after the Romanov family were killed. Mathilde refused to dance again, despite many offers to do so.

Luka chose the safety of crowded Paris, where he learned that almost half of the Romanov dancers had been killed in the revolution or lost in the exodus of refugees. The few remaining dancers struggled to survive, sometimes performing in workers' clubs in exchange for bread. Ballet had become a pleasure most no longer admitted to because of its connection with the overthrown regime. There were rumours of attempts to begin a new company under the rule of the Soviets, but who knew where those would lead.

Luka sighed, shaking off the memories. With tonight's performance, he would leave behind that life and Luka Vladimirovich Zhirkov of the Imperial Russian Ballet. A new life was beginning, made possible by the great Diaghilev.

Ludmilla Schollar, whom Luka had met in The Wandering Dog so long ago, had heard of his arrival in Paris. Having returned to the Ballet Russes herself, she made mention to Diaghilev, who had sought Luka out and given him an audition. Tonight, he would debut in the role of Cloviello in *Pulcinella*. It was a light ballet, and Diaghilev had warned Luka that if he was to fully become the character, he needed to shrug off his past, which he said Luka wore around his shoulders like a heavy cloak.

That was why Luka needed to write this letter.

He had never been a good letter-writer. Not like Xenia, who loved to regale him with stories of her new life. She'd escaped to London, and there married a man who gave her a new passion—that of motherhood. Xenia said being a mother was better than trying to compete with Anna Pavlova, who dominated the stages there.

It was Xenia who had alerted Luka to Maxim's fate. She'd heard that he remained in Russia, and had taken to spending most of his time drunk. He slept wherever he happened to fall in the street; and if sober when woken, wouldn't settle until he found another bottle. His career had fallen apart with the loss of his contacts, and what money that hadn't been in the bank and thus stolen by the Soviets had disappeared quickly. He had so degraded himself that the Soviets weren't bothered by his existence and let him be, saying the drink would kill him before long. Luka never shared with Xenia that he knew what demons haunted Maxim.

Xenia had finished her most recent letter with the words: *Try not to be afraid to live your life. Although you might not think it now, you can be happy again. And anyone who has loved you wants nothing more than that—Valentina included, I'm sure.*

Luka took the pen from his mouth and looked down at the crisp white paper before him. Xenia was right; as was Diaghilev. It was time to do that which he'd shied away from for too long.

With only the slightest of sighs, he put the tip of the pen to the paper.

8 September 1920

My beloved Valya,

For years I have held off writing this letter, thinking if I didn't say my goodbyes it meant you weren't really gone. There were times I thought I would die too, so there was no need for it—we would be together again. But death didn't take me, no matter how many bullets came my way, nor how I longed for it. Life somehow kept moving forward.

Finally I have come to realise I can't keep trying to live with your hand still held in mine. So here is the goodbye I'll never be okay with having to say. I won't waste it with repeated regrets, for I am sure that even in the heavens you must feel the tremors that run through me every time I think of how I let you go to God alone.

I have a confession to make: I went through your candy box. I think you would be irritated with me for it, but then laugh—that was often your way. (I wish I could remember your laugh. Its sound seems to have faded from my mind.) If only you were here to tell me about the things within the box. It mystifies me how you ended up with my gloves from my years at the Imperial Ballet School. I wish—another futile, too-late wish—I had known you then. In my dreams, we would save each other from all the foolish mistakes waiting ahead of us.

I never wanted to leave Russia without you, Valya. Before then, I thought I knew the kind of man I wanted to be; what was right and what was wrong. But my journey out of Russia was something else. Surrounded by the worst that mankind could do to each other, I also saw the best. You'd be surprised to know I'm talking of your friend and mentor, Mathilde. We somehow ended up travelling together, and I assumed she would make things worse for the rest of us. But while we were scrounging around the villages for food, desperate and hungry, Mathilde was breaking up the little food she had herself and feeding it to the stray dogs.

Some ridiculed her for wasting something so precious on already starving animals, but for me it was like that moment when you are dancing, oblivious to everything around you. Then the music stops and the audience starts applauding, and you realise the world is so much bigger than the stage you were dancing on. I'd been on my own stage forever, and suddenly I saw the world for what it is—its potential for pain and loss, yes, but also for love that isn't defined by any parameters. A world where a woman who once had everything could lose it all, but still find something to give to those that were forgotten or ignored. I had always believed Mathilde to be the very worst example of what was wrong with Russia—I guess the revolutionaries and I had that in common. It took two revolutions, a civil war and countless deaths for me to realise: we can be so much more than our circumstances make us appear.

I wish I had learned that earlier. If I had, perhaps I would have come to know the Valya I loved—still love—sooner. But that is one of the many burdens I bear; and I'll not regret the time we did have, for it was so achingly sweet that sometimes I wonder if perhaps I didn't just dream it all.

Wherever you are now, my darling Valya, I hope you are free. That you are dancing the White Swan not alone at midnight, but with such exquisite truthfulness that the very angels cry.

I will never forget all that we almost had together. And one day, when I am old and frail in my bed, I hope to close my eyes and find you waiting for me.

My dear, my love, my Odette.

Yours always,

Luka

Luka folded the letter carefully in half, then half again. He looked at it for a moment, held between steady fingers. Outside, the streets danced with life. People ate, and laughed, and loved, and not a building was burning nor a gunshot firing. There was peace.

He would join them soon. In front of him, the candy box was open, its contents carefully repacked within. This was the last time he would ever see Valya's treasures, although he would carry the box with him always. It was only missing one thing now.

Luka raised the folded letter to his lips and pressed a soft kiss to it. Then he put it on top of the remains of Valya's life. With one long, lingering look, he closed the lid.

AUTHOR'S NOTE

It is often said that truth is stranger than fiction, and this never seems quite so apt as when writing a historical fiction novel. While Valentina and Luka and their story are entirely of my own making, many of the other people, locations and events are taken from real history.

It was a common practice in pre-revolutionary Russia for ballet dancers to take an aristocratic or influential protector to cement their position in both company and society. Given the Imperial Russian Ballet's requirements for a high level of health and cleanliness, their dancers were considered a safe and, perhaps more importantly, respectable alternative to prostitutes.

Mathilde Kschessinska is perhaps the most notorious example of a dancer's use of protectors. Her former relationship with the Tsar as well as her simultaneous relationships with two Grand Dukes amassed her the kind of wealth and influence that likely reads as unbelievable, but is true. She did have her own power plant next to her home, a private beach at her country house, and one of the first motor vehicles in Russia. She was truly a woman of extremes, and this ran to her behaviour

as well. Real life accounts from those who knew her, as well
as descriptions in her own memoir, tell of her attending the
theatre in the midst of the revolution, holding lavish celebrations at her homes (including a dinner party the night before
the revolution began), and refusing to dance the Dying Swan
when the Imperial Russian Ballet began including it in their
productions of *Swan Lake*, due to her personal hatred for Anna
Pavlova. It was these extravagances and wilful personality
traits that made her a target after Grigori Rasputin's death,
when newspapers were looking for a new symbol of the vast
divide between wealthy and poor; although propaganda was
not limited to print, with films denouncing her even after the
revolution was over.

Like so many historical figures, Mathilde was a person of
contradictions. To dancers she took a liking to she could be
generous, going out of her way to help their careers. She set
up a hospital for wounded soldiers during the war, and hired
the artist Nicholas Roubtzov's widow as her housekeeper so
she could support herself and her family – an act of generosity
which would lead to resentment and the housekeeper's even-
tual betrayal of Mathilde to the looting revolutionaries.
(For those wondering, the revolutionaries did attempt to kill
Mathilde's porter Denisov that day, but changed their minds
at the last moment when they saw he wore the military Cross
of St George.) One of the most striking anecdotes, that of
Mathilde feeding stray dogs in the midst of her escape as a
refugee, was taken from recordings of people who travelled in
the same group as her, and are a reminder of the great love she
must have held for her dog Djibi, who died from a heart attack
while she was in hiding during the revolution. After taking
on Lenin in an unsuccessful attempt to get back her mansion,

which he'd requisitioned as his headquarters, she fled to France, never performing again despite many offers to do so. There, she married the surviving Grand Duke Andrei. Having lost most of her wealth to the revolution, she eventually opened her own ballet school, which trained some of the leading dancers of the next generation.

The misguided Evening of Russian Fashion was a real event that failed as spectacularly as depicted. Similarly, the opera *Fenella* was performed only weeks before the revolution; records from the time note the nervousness of the cast in having to depict a revolution on an imperial stage. The use of the square outside the Mariinsky Theatre for training troops was somewhat more successful, with many dancers noting that they used the firing of the cannon to time their days to.

I have done my best to depict the lives of imperial ballet dancers as authentically as possible, including having all ballets mentioned within this story correct to the era (shifting exact dates of their performances here and there out of narrative necessity). Many of these ballets continue to be performed today, although some were lost in the destruction of the two revolutions and the civil war that followed.

Included in this novel are many small details on day-to-day life for both wealthy and poor in pre-revolutionary Russia. Their food and clothing, superstitions, Christmas rituals, the kinds of jobs available to them and the working conditions that went with them, hopefully give the reader some small idea of what life was like. While making a diaphragm out of a lemon, or washing oneself down with vinegar, might seem odd to a modern audience, they were just two of the many creative (and often ineffective) solutions to contraception women of the higher classes came up with. *Baudruches* had already been invented by the French, and were effective in preventing both pregnancy and disease, which was why they were in popular use by prostitutes throughout Europe; but women in Valentina's position needed to define themselves as being different to common prostitutes, and thus shied away from using them to lessen the connection.

Sadly, the Russian Revolution saw the end of the Imperial Russian Ballet. There have been other companies bearing the name in the decades since, but they are not a direct descendant of the original; it was disbanded, and ballet was shunned post-revolution as a reminder of the hated elite the country had overthrown. Many of the dancers who survived the revolution scattered across the globe, bringing with them the artistry and traditions of Russian ballet. This mass exodus resulted in a renewed interest in ballet, and helped shape it into the exquisite, demanding art form it is today.

For further discussion on the historical facts and figures of *The Last Days of the Romanov Dancers*, visit my website www.kerriturner.com.

ACKNOWLEDGEMENTS

In 2012 I opened a blank document and began the long process of creating this story. Since then, I have come across so many people who have shared their wisdom, given their support, and uplifted me with belief when I no longer had any, and I am so full of gratitude to them all. Specifically, and in no particular order:

Thank you to my wonderfully talented (and funny) agent Haylee Nash of The Nash Agency, for reading my book and instantly 'getting' it. I am so lucky to have your support, and I appreciate all the work you've done to get this story out into the world.

Thank you also to the amazing and dedicated team at Harlequin, for championing my book and showing such passion for a project by a debut author. In particular, thanks to Rachael Donovan and Julia Knapman for your hard work, kindness, support, and many encouraging words. You made this new and much-longed-for process so much less daunting, and I'm not sure I'll ever be able to express how much your enthusiastic feedback has meant after years of self-doubt.

I have been lucky enough to be gifted the extraordinary editorial skills of Nicola O'Shea on this book. Thank you Nicola for the most thorough, insightful, and understanding editing a person could be capable of. You saw what I was trying to do with this book, and helped me get it there. I am in awe of what you do.

To James Bradley, for teaching me so much about writing, and giving me that all-important thing without which many writers would never continue: belief. You don't know it, but at my most doubtful, it was your belief in my work which kept me going. Thank you also to everyone at Faber Academy, from the organisers to the tutors to the guest speakers, for providing an opportunity to learn about this marvellous, stressful, and rewarding process of writing a book. And to others whose teaching and/or feedback helped me over the years, with special mention of Kate Forsyth and Tara Wynne for invaluable feedback which helped shape the book.

To my husband Ross. Thank you for picking me up and wiping away the tears many, many times. Thank you for investing time, support, and money in this dream of mine. Thank you for proudly telling everyone that your wife was a writer long before I'd ever made it.

To Nelson, for sitting by my side during the long hours I write, when you'd rather be playing with tennis balls. You're a good boy.

A thank you to family of the Turner, Muller, Houston, or otherwise-named variety, for your support, commiseration, and excitement, and for being a book-loving bunch. Mum and Dad: you finally got to read it! I hope the wait was worth it.

To all the dance teachers I've had over the years, who have inspired such a love for this art form. And to everyone I have taught dance to over the years—you gave me back something I thought I had lost. Thank you.

Most of all, thank you to the readers. You make all this possible.

LET'S TALK ABOUT BOOKS!

JOIN THE CONVERSATION

HARLEQUIN
AUSTRALIA

@HARLEQUINAUS

@HARLEQUINAUS

HQSTORIES

@HQSTORIES